"Sometimes you ⬛⬛⬛
what happens to ⬛⬛⬛ **said.**

He was close enough she could feel his warmth.

"Sometimes," he continued, "you have to stand up and face what you're given and do your best."

She wanted him to kiss her again. For real... No, she really didn't. She honestly and truly did not want that complication.

She had been going to ask him if he wanted to sit down. To join her in the living room. But suddenly that seemed too comfortable. Too much like he was a closer friend than she could have him be.

They were opponents—both determined to win—and her son's future rested on the outcome.

And they were parents whose kids had wanted to see each other. He'd be leaving momentarily. It was almost time for Dawson's bath.

Dinner was what they'd arranged.

And dinner was over.

Dear Reader,

As I write to you to tell you about *For Love or Money*, I'm deeply into book two in this new miniseries! Family Secrets is turning out to be all I knew it could be.

Family Secrets is a reality-competition cooking show. Contestants compete with their secret family recipes. The show runs in segments with four regular competitions in different categories. And then the final round. Each book is one of those segments. Other than the host, you see all different people, with completely different stories, in each book.

This miniseries isn't only about secret recipes. In every novel, you'll find lives changed by a family secret. A secret that, though maybe kept with the best of intentions, is powerful enough, damaging enough, to affect the lives and hearts of all those who didn't know.

During this opening segment, you're going to meet a very special little boy. Dawson was inspired by a young man who captured my whole heart the first time I held him more than a decade ago, a close family member who brings a precious and unique joy into any space he occupies. He is wanted, adored and protected by all members of his family. Dawson and his experiences are completely fictional. The joy he brings is not.

I love to hear from my readers. Please find me at Facebook.com/tarataylorquinn and on Twitter, @tarataylorquinn. Or join my open Friendship board on Pinterest, Pinterest.com/tarataylorquinn/friendship!

All the best,

Tara

www.TaraTaylorQuinn.com

HEARTWARMING

For Love or Money

USA TODAY Bestselling Author

Tara Taylor Quinn

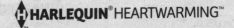
HARLEQUIN® HEARTWARMING™

Recycling programs
for this product may
not exist in your area.

ISBN-13: 978-0-373-36799-3

For Love or Money

Copyright © 2016 by Tara Taylor Quinn

Printed in U.S.A.

An author of seventy-five novels, **Tara Taylor Quinn** is a *USA TODAY* bestselling author with more than seven million copies sold. She is known for delivering emotional and psychologically astute novels of suspense and romance. Tara is a past president of Romance Writers of America. She has won a Readers' Choice Award and is a five-time finalist for an RWA RITA® Award, a finalist for a Reviewers' Choice Award and a Booksellers' Best Award. She has also appeared on TV across the country, including *CBS Sunday Morning*. She supports the National Domestic Violence Hotline. If you or someone you know might be a victim of domestic violence in the United States, please contact 1-800-799-7233.

Books by Tara Taylor Quinn

Visit the Author Profile page
at Harlequin.com for more titles.

For William Wright Gumser.
You are our miracle. Our gift.

And I hope you know the joy
you bring just by being alive.
Aunt Tara loves you!

CHAPTER ONE

"Forget it."

"Kels, I really want to make this right."

"Whatever."

Sometimes a guy had to know when he wasn't going to win. Sometimes even knowing, he couldn't quit trying. Most particularly when his adversary was his thirteen-year-old daughter.

And in this case, he couldn't quit even if he did win. Because he had something else he had to discuss with the woman-child sitting on the passenger side of his SUV. She'd flipped the button to activate the heated leather seats when she'd climbed in.

At which time he'd glanced at the outdoor temperature reading. A balmy 85 degrees. In the desert. California desert. And wisely kept his mouth shut.

"I'm sorry I was late. Dan Rhodes stopped in just as I was leaving. He's starting tonight and needed a cortisone shot."

Dan Rhodes, a Palm Desert high school

basketball star and one of her late mother's former students.

"Yeah, well, I told Melissa you'd look at her knee."

And he'd let Kelsey down by not being at the dance studio on time to pick her up. Never mind that half the time when he showed up as scheduled, she harrumphed because she liked to hang out and watch the older girls— the ones in "company"—take class and run through routines.

"I'll look at it tomorrow, before class," he said now, though technically, unless her parents consented to him treating Melissa, there was nothing he could do but advise her to get it looked at. Which he'd already done. Three times in the past month.

As an orthopedist specializing in sports medicine, he'd given the girl's dad his card. But he'd never heard from them.

"Whatever." She was staring out the side window, her expression…bland. He'd been told—by someone among all the well-meaning counselor types who'd flooded forth to advise him after Kelsey's mother had died—to watch out for belligerence. He'd be happy for it. For anything beyond…bland.

"Was Carlie at dance tonight?" Kelsey's best

friend had been having issues since Kelsey was chosen for junior company and she wasn't.

Her head swung around then, eyes almost piercing as she studied him in the falling dusk. "What's with your sudden interest in Carlie?"

Sudden? He gave his head a mental shake—ordering it to get in gear. "She's your best friend."

Kelsey's snort didn't bode well. "Not for like a year, Dad. Shows you how much you pay attention." That last was uttered under her breath, so he pretended not to hear.

"You just want to know about Barbara."

Carlie's mother. They'd gone out. Once. Shortly after her divorce. When the girls had both been on a Girl Scout trip.

"If I wanted to know about Barbara, I'd call her and ask how she's doing," he said now, firmness entering his voice. It didn't come often. But it was there when it needed to be. "Be angry with me for being late—that's valid. But don't disrespect me, Kels. I—"

"I know." Her tone completely docile now, she cut him off. "You don't deserve it, and I'm sorry, Daddy." He could hear the tremor in her voice and hated that even more than the cattiness. "You're the best and I love you."

"I love you, too, squirt." He cringed as the endearment slipped out before he remembered that he wasn't supposed to use it anymore. The mandate had come down that summer. She hated it when he called her that. Made her feel like a kid, she'd said.

"You haven't called me that in a while."

"You told me not to."

"Well, you weren't supposed to really stop."

He wasn't going to win. No matter how hard he tried. Because she was thirteen. And he just didn't get it.

"Look, Jane, I get it. You need to pretend that the kid's gonna be normal someday. As soon as his muscles develop. But he isn't gonna be. Ever. And I don't have the cash to fund your need to make him something he ain't. Do yourself a favor, and me and maybe him, too, and just accept what is."

If she hadn't been standing in the middle of a bay in Dillon's car repair business—his father's business before him—Janie might have clenched her fists. Or done something even worse, like start to cry.

In the olden days, back when she and Dillon had been so in love they'd been crazy with it, her tears had brought him to his knees. These days, they gave him strength.

"I'm not asking for a favor, Dillon," she told him, remaining calm by thinking of her son, sitting at a table in his preschool class, his tongue sticking out of his mouth, his face just inches from the table, while he put pencil to paper. If they were lucky, he'd make a mark that was distinguishable. "Per our decree, you are responsible for half of Dawson's medical bills."

"Speech therapy isn't medical."

"The state disagrees with you." She handed him the paperwork she'd brought, showing that medical insurance would pay for the therapy. They just had to come up with the copay. A measly 20 percent. And she had to have the time off work to see that he got there.

The extra hours, those in which she helped her son exercise muscles and do his therapy "homework," she was already handling. Like every single time Dawson ate and they played the blowing-bubbles-in-your-cup-through-your-straw game. Or every time she asked him for a kiss and he licked her cheek before turning to kiss her. They were games his speech pathologist had helped her design to strengthen his low muscle tone.

"If so, then why are you only just now bringing it to me? Who's been paying all along?" His tone, challenging as always, hurt. Still.

How could a man turn his back on his own son? Be embarrassed by him? How could

Janie still hope that someday Dillon would realize how phenomenal, how perfect, their son really was?

"The state paid, Dillon. Through age three. Dawson just turned four. Now insurance pays, but not the co-pay part."

Because Dillon provided the cheapest insurance he could get for his son.

"You're just doing this to get back at me, aren't you?" Wiping his greasy hands on a red towel he grabbed from his rolling toolbox, he walked toward his office. When they were both inside he shut his door.

The smell of grease and gas emanating from his overalls was one thing she did not miss. Dillon had been in college when they'd met—studying business. He'd had big plans. And then they'd gotten married and his father'd had a heart attack and he'd taken over the garage. She'd supported him on all of it. Had loved him even more for it. She just had never gotten used to the smell of grease that permeated him at the dinner table. Even after he'd showered...

You're just doing this to get back at me. His words were no less grinding even after taking a second to step away from them.

"What on earth are you talking about?" she asked, not ready for another one of their asinine confrontations. The kind where he hurled ludicrous accusations like they were truth and she walled herself against them.

But she'd known when she'd gotten up that morning that the moment was coming. She'd been happy the night before when she'd received confirmation in writing that Dillon had to help with the co-pay. She'd given herself the night to enjoy the small victory. The small feeling of relief.

And she'd arisen that day with the knowledge that if she did not hand deliver the paperwork to her ex-husband, in front of others, he'd spend months requesting it. Over and over again. Denying, each time, that he'd received it. And if she sent it certified post, he'd refuse to sign.

She could take him back to court.

If she had the money.

"You can't possibly think that I purposely had a child with Down syndrome so that I could somehow get back at you?"

"I'm not an idiot, Jane. Of course you wouldn't do that." He sat, pulling at his mustache as he looked up at her standing by the closed door.

Did he know she kept the handle within reach on purpose? Because it was the only way she could make herself confront him?

Knowing that she could choose to escape at any point.

"I need money, Dillon. I've covered the past two months of co-pays. I need you to give me this month's."

Until last night's letter had come, she'd been afraid she would have to borrow the money again.

At some point, her friends were going to run in the opposite direction when they saw her coming.

"And I think you're still doing this therapy thing because it's your way of making me pay. You're just trying to get more money out of me. You don't want me to move on, get ahead, because you can't. But I'm not the one who insisted on going through with a pregnancy with a known birth defect…"

Of course, having once been the love of her life, he knew best how to push her buttons.

"I am not trying to keep you from getting ahead." With extreme focus, and having had a lot of practice, she ignored the worst of his barbs.

"I didn't want to think so, but I'm not the only one saying it anymore."

"Who else is saying it?" She hated herself for asking. Heard the question come out of her mouth before she'd thought about it, enabling his ability to get her going...

"Wendy."

"Who's Wendy?"

"The woman who's been living with me for the past three months."

She hadn't known. He'd known she hadn't known.

"You're obligated to pay this money, Dillon. Please just give me a check and I'll leave you alone."

And Wendy. Leave him and Wendy alone.

She didn't want Dillon for herself. Hadn't wanted to be married to him since the second he'd denounced their son as not worthy of being born. The doctor had offered a medical abortion because they'd caught the Down syndrome diagnosis during her first trimester. Dillon had done everything he could to get Janie to agree to the procedure. He'd even made an appointment with the doctor's office, behind her back, to have it done.

And yet...for many years they'd been a couple she'd thought would be together forever. Hearing that he was with someone else, even though they'd been divorced since before Dawson was born...

A part of her died.

Another part needed a good cry.

"You think this therapy is so important, pay for it yourself." He looked smug. Arms crossed. His lips not smiling but his eyes looking like he was.

How could she ever have been in love with this man?

"I can't."

"Well, I can't, either."

"Yes, you can, Dillon." She waved around her at the four bays behind them, all full, the wall-size calendar at the side of his desk and the Dry Erase board, both also completely full. "You're doing well. Paying your obligation for your son won't even put a dent in your petty cash."

"And you resent that, don't you? That I'm doing so well? That Wendy and I can afford to take a Caribbean cruise over Christmas? That we went to Vegas for Thanksgiving..."

She hadn't known. Had never done either. But she and Dillon had always talked about doing both.

Focus.

She thought of her baby boy's face when he'd high-fived her that morning because he'd put his tennis shoes on all by himself, crossed the laces and considered them tied. He'd been happier than when she gave him ice cream. And she was happier, too. So much more than she'd ever have been without him. More than a cruise or any vacation would ever make her.

She was doing this for Dawson. Getting the money for Dawson.

"You're legally obligated to pay this." And he knew she had a friend who would see that he did. But not until he made her beg. "I need the money, Dillon."

"You're desperate." Eyes narrowing, he leaned forward. "You lost another job, didn't you?"

She could lie. But knew he'd find out soon enough. He always did.

So she didn't lie. She just stood there. As mute as Dawson would be without the therapies Dillon wanted to deny him. He had no way of knowing what Dawson sounded like. He'd never met the boy he'd fathered. Had no idea how Dawson sounded when he tried to communicate with her. No way of knowing that the therapy was helping Dawson learn to talk clearly enough to be understood.

"When are you going to admit that I was right all along? Look at you, Janie. What's this, three jobs in as many years? Admit that you made a mistake. That you should have taken the choice we were given back when you had that first ultrasound. You should have ended the pregnancy."

The words still hurt. Every single time. Because they deleted the happiest person she'd ever met from the face of the earth.

Gripping the door handle, she swung around. "Janie."

His tone had changed. For a second there, he could have been the man she'd married.

She looked over her shoulder. Maybe to remind herself that that man had never existed.

He was standing, pulled a few bills out of his wallet and walked over to hand them to her.

"Here," he said. "Never let it be said that I don't stand up to my obligations."

If it had been just her, she'd have spit on those bills. But they were hundreds. Would pay for far more than a few months' co-pays. She took them. Looked him in the eye as she said, "Thank you."

"You deserve better than this, Janie." He sounded sad.

And she figured he should be. She had the absolute best life had to offer waiting for her in a preschool across town.

While he'd lost the only thing of importance he'd ever had.

And didn't even know it.

CHAPTER TWO

"KELS?" BURKE TAPPED on his daughter's slightly ajar door just before ten that night. He'd let her have the evening her way. They'd stopped for the rice and salad bowl she'd wanted for dinner. He'd done some work on his laptop while sitting with her through the shows she'd chosen to watch on TV—if you could call her dead stare "watching."

He'd helped with the laundry—even though it was her night to do a load and she'd said she was fine doing it alone...

"I'm decent," she called through the door after a full thirty seconds had passed.

They'd had that talk last summer, too—with the help of her pediatric psychiatrist, Dr. Zimmers. He wasn't to walk in unannounced now that she was wearing a bra and having her period. Didn't matter that Burke was a doctor. He was a *bone* doctor. Kelsey's emphasis on "bone." And she was his daughter. And she had things to be modest about now.

"Can I come in?" he called.

"I guess."

Better than *whatever*. He missed the little girl who used to beg to sit on his lap. Or ride on his shoulders. *Ride high, Daddy!* He could hear that tiny little voice like it was yesterday.

But it wasn't. Not even the day before that. More like a lifetime ago.

She was on her bed, propped up with pillows, her tablet on her lap. Wearing the flannel, black-with-pink-heart pajama pants he'd bought her just before school started. With an old T-shirt left over from when her mother was a seventh-grade English teacher and insisted the three of them show team spirit, wear team colors and go to all of the athletic activities they could make.

Palm Desert's vibrant red clashed with the pink heart. The vibrant gold, not so much.

Her long brown hair, usually in a ponytail, hung around her face. At least she was leaving it long. She'd tried to insist on coloring it purple that summer. He'd held firm against that one.

Leaning over to glance at what she was doing on her tablet, Burke took a seat on the side of the double bed. Keeping a respectable distance.

She turned her tablet around. "It's just Friday's Fashion Boutique, Dad." She named an interactive fashion app that he'd seen her use many times before. Kind of like a modern-day Barbie doll, his mother had said when his folks had come from Florida the previous Christmas.

"A good parent checks, Kels," he reminded her. Another thing he was not going to budge on. All parental controls were in place when it came to her use of electronics and social media.

She had a phone. She could call and had limited text capability—enough to reach him when necessary. Period. And he could see the numbers she called and texted every day if he chose to check.

He didn't. But she knew he could.

"I don't care if you look." She shrugged, turning her tablet back around. She didn't fight him. Never had when it came to her limited use of social media. And from the horror stories he'd heard from his peers, nurses, even his patients, he had real reason to be thankful for that.

"Dr. Zimmers called me today," he said, getting right to the point.

She continued to move her finger along the ten-inch glass screen. Tapping and dragging.

"She wants to put you on medication." He

named a brand. Didn't figure it would mean anything to her.

"I'm not taking it. You can force it down my throat and then I'll stick my finger right behind it and throw it back up."

Thirteen-year-old drama queen had joined them.

"We need to talk about that."

Kelsey's gaze was resolute when she put her tablet facedown on the mattress and looked at him. In that instant, he could have been looking at himself in the mirror when he was getting ready to put his foot down with her.

"We've talked about it, Dad. I'm not going to start taking some upper pill because I'm sad that my mom died. Or because I get sad sometimes when I think about it."

"You're sleeping way too much."

"So get me up earlier. You're the parent. Help me out."

He could do that. "You're a grump in the morning."

"You can take it."

She had a point.

"You spend too much time alone."

"I'm dancing again. Be happy with that for now."

"It's not my happiness I'm worried about," he said. "You know how long it's been since

I've heard you laugh out loud, Kels? Or since I've heard a note of excitement in your voice?"

He could talk to her about an imbalance of neurotransmitters that could lead to serious depression if not counterbalanced.

"Then give me something to get excited about." Her quiet words, spoken to her tablet, stopped his thought process cold.

Rather than arguing with him, or giving him the rote "whatever," she'd actually given him a positive opening. In two years' time, it was a first.

Expecting a request for a smartphone, a trip to Disneyland or a week off school, he said, "I'm not talking about a momentary fix, Kelsey. You know that." Though he was tempted to give her any of those things, all of them, to reward the open, non-defensive approach. "Maybe you need to try the medication…"

If Lil, Kelsey's mom, had been able to take something for her paranoia, would she still be alive? Not that the paranoia had been the actual cause of death. No, the onset of labor at the beginning of the third trimester had done that.

"Dad, you promised me…"

A promise he might have made a mistake in making. Lil had, by example, made her daughter petrified of "drugging herself up." She'd been almost fanatical about medication—to the point of toughing it out through headaches so she didn't have to take an over-the-counter painkiller. She'd had Kelsey on the same pain management regime.

It had taken Burke getting really angry, raising-his-voice angry, before Kelsey had taken the antibiotics she'd needed for strep throat the previous year.

The girl seemed to think putting drugs in her body was disloyal to her mother. But there was so much she didn't know. Some things Burke hoped to God she never knew.

Still, antidepressant medication was not going to be as easy a win.

Maybe because he didn't want to medicate her, long term, either. Not unless she truly needed the help.

"It's been two years since Mom died."

"So give me something to get excited about."

There it was again. That opening.

In all of the advice he'd received over the past two years, most of it well-meaning, and some of it professionally sought, no one had told him that raising a thirteen-year-old was going to make him dizzy. He'd never have believed, even a year before, that his sweet, rational, logical-beyond-her-years little girl was going to morph into a confusing mass of humanity that he could no more predict than the weather.

"What, Kels? What can I give you that you'd be excited about?" Knowing as he asked the question that he'd walk through fire to get it for her. As long as he didn't think it would do more long-term harm than good.

She grabbed her tablet. Swiped and tapped so fast he didn't know how she could possibly even read what she was choosing. She stopped. Seemed to be skimming the page. And turned the tablet around to him.

"This," she said. "I wanted to enter but I can't because I'm just a kid, and besides, you're the master chef left among us."

Lil had been a certified chef. Official ranking. In addition to teaching, she'd put in the hours necessary in professional food service. Because her dream was to open her own catering business. She'd talked him into taking classes, too, while he'd still been in med school. As something they could do to spend a little stress-free time together. And to his surprise, cooking had been right up his alley. Engaging him scientifically and yet offering him a relaxation he'd been unable to find elsewhere.

"I'm not a master chef," he told her. He'd

obtained a culinary art certification. That was all.

He looked at her tablet.

Made a cursory visual pass. Then read every word in the headline.

She was handing him the tablet, so he took it. Heart sinking.

She wanted him to be on a reality cooking show. As in, television. Like he could just pick up a phone and volunteer.

Like he had a chance in…any chance at all of making it on the show.

"It's that one filmed here." Kelsey was up on her knees, beside him now. He swore he could still smell that sweet baby-powder scent that had entered their home with her thirteen years before. "In Palm Desert. *Family Secrets*. Remember, they had that Thanksgiving special where they chose the first one of this year's contestants…"

He remembered.

He'd wanted to go to Disneyland over the holiday. Thanksgiving—a food day by all counts—was one of the hardest without Lil. Kelsey wasn't bouncing back from her mother's death at all. If anything, with the onset of puberty, her moroseness was getting worse. He'd thought to distract her by heading to the coast for the holiday.

Instead she'd been adamant, to the point of tears, which always suckered him, that they cook dinner together, with all the trappings, and spend the day watching cooking shows. To honor Lil.

"So now it's open auditions for the other seven contestants. It's right here in town, Dad. You want me to be excited about something? Audition for this show." She'd scooted closer, was resting her chin on his shoulder as she looked at the tablet with him.

"You have to use your own family recipes," she said as he sat there, feeling more lost, more alone, than ever before. "It's the recipes that are the real competition," she went on, her voice gaining an energy that seemed to encompass their entire world.

"There's an audition, and then four weeks of competition between eight candidates. Then whoever wins at least one of the four competitions goes to the final round. Each week you're given a category and you have to make your family recipe with a secret ingredient. It says here that the candidates have to appear for one day of extraneous taping, too, before the competition starts."

She was setting him up to let her down. He could see it so clearly even if she couldn't.

There was no way he was good enough to compete against real chefs.

"You can use Mom's recipes, Dad! It's a way for her to get what she wanted—to have her cooking recognized and appreciated. It's a way to keep her alive. Like make her immortal or something. You have to do this…"

It was best to be honest with her. To face the tough stuff head-on. He'd been told. And he also just knew…

"I can't."

She slouched back. "I knew you'd say that." There was no accusation in her tone. Just resignation. "That's why I didn't say anything before. It's probably too late anyway. The auditions are this weekend and they were only taking walk-ons, without preregistering, if they had space."

She hadn't been going to ask him. Until he'd told her they had to find something to be excited about.

Lil, if you can hear me, now's the time to jump in. What happens if I try and fail? Do I send our baby girl further into the dark hole she can't seem to climb out of?

Will your recipes sustain me? Us?

"I was going to say I can't force them to take me on." He improvised while he waited for some kind of sign from above.

He'd take one from below or beside if it was clear enough.

Kelsey stared at him. And he could have sworn there was a glimmer of light in her blue eyes. His eyes.

"I took some classes, Kels. I do well enough here at home. I'm nowhere near the cook your mom was. TV? That's for people like your mom. Real chefs. With real experience. And the auditions will be judged by people who are used to eating from the best of the best. All of which is completely out of my control." He couldn't make this happen for her.

"Like Mom always said, cooking is a lot about artistic talent, about knowing what foods go good together and stuff. She always said you had that talent, too." Her tone wasn't pushy. Or even persuasive. She sounded like a lost little girl. "Besides, this show is about the recipes. And Mom's are the best."

"And I might not be able to do them justice." It wouldn't be the first time he'd let Lil down. Or Kelsey, either, though he hoped she never knew just how badly he'd let them both down.

"You tell me that the important thing is to try."

"I have no problem with trying, Kels. I'll go to the audition." He would?

Her mouth dropped open.

"But you have to understand that I might not win. And if I don't, you have to be willing to find something else to get excited about."

What was he doing, here?

"You're going to do it?" She didn't move. Just sat there. Staring at him. But the glisten in her eyes told him that he had to grant her request.

"And you're going to help me," he said, speaking the words that came to him as they presented themselves. "We have three days…" He'd have to cancel his appearance at a fund-raiser for the clinic Wednesday night. And dinner with the Montgomerys, friends of his and Lil's who still continued to invite him and Kelsey over on a regular Friday-night basis. "You are in charge of choosing the recipe for the audition. I'll make it each night this week, under your supervision, and you taste the finished results and give me feedback."

"I'll do all the dishes," Kelsey said, still just watching him.

"Okay."

"Okay? As in you're really going to audition?"

"I'll call tomorrow and get myself on the schedule." There was a special slot for locals, he'd just read. And according to the website, which had been updated that day, there was still an opportunity to sign up. Which Kelsey must have known, too. Since she'd also read the website's advertisement.

She was staring at him. "For real."

"I said I would." And he always did what he'd told her he'd do. Even if he was a few minutes late on rare occasions.

"Woooooo-hoooo!" Her scream hurt his ears. And warmed him up so much he laughed out loud as he caught her flying toward him. Her hug was heaven.

And Burke warned fate that it better not let him let her down.

Not this time.

Not again.

CHAPTER THREE

THE *FAMILY SECRETS* cooking show had been on for five years yet still received the highest ratings of any cooking show on television. But it wasn't the program's ratings that had prompted Janie to choose the best of the best in her attempt to give her son every shot at living a full and productive life. No, it had been desperation. And proximity. The show was local. And had run a contest before the Thanksgiving holiday that allowed people to just send in a recipe to compete.

She hadn't had to audition to get a chance at being a contestant. She'd just had to print out her grandmother's recipe for turkey dressing.

Even after she'd been notified she was a finalist, invited to be in the audience on Thanksgiving Day for the taping of the show, she hadn't believed, that day in the studio, that she'd actually heard her name called.

It had been Dawson, sitting in her lap in the small, darkened studio, who'd recognized her name. His hoarse "Ma!" might have sounded like a very excitable grunt to everyone else there that day, but she'd heard her name. And his, too. "Me! Ma! Me!" Over and over again. As his butt bones dug into her thighs and his heels kicked new bruises into her shins.

Then she'd looked at the monitor, panning the audience for the day's winner, and seen what Dawson had seen. His gargantuan grin, and her grimace of pain, splashed on national television.

Even now, six weeks later, she couldn't believe she'd won. That in less than two hours she'd be in the studio, being filmed with the other candidates as they received a tour of their kitchens and instructions for the next four or five weeks of the competition. Four if none of her recipes won. Five if at least one did. Snippets of today's pre-competition taping would be dubbed into shows in the weeks that followed.

So much had happened since she'd won the Thanksgiving competition.

She'd lost her job, but found another one making deliveries for a flower shop. She could work while Dawson was in preschool, and if there was an emergency, she could run by and pick him up. And she'd taken a second job with a political campaign, making cold calls to constituents from home. Neither paid very well. But both paid. And allowed her to attend every one of her son's therapies.

A must if she was going to be able to repeat exercises at home.

Which was essential if any of it was going to be of benefit to her four-year-old son.

Pulling up in front of the house she'd felt more at home in than any other her entire life, Janie glanced at the car seat behind her. She hated to wake Dawson. He'd been fighting an ear infection and hadn't been sleeping well.

But he loved Corrine and Joe Armstrong. And, by some miracle, they adored him back just as much. How she'd ever been blessed with such good friends, she had no idea, but...

The door to the ranch-style stucco home opened and Corrine came flying down the walk. "Hello, big boy," she said, a huge grin on her face as she opened the back door. And then stopped when she saw Dawson asleep.

"You're going to be late!" she said softly, but lacking none of the urgency, as she glanced at Janie.

"We had a rough night," Janie told her friend quietly. "I hate to do this to you, Cor. You know if I had any other..."

"Shut your mouth right now," Corrine said in a fierce whisper. "Before you say something I'll regret. I'd have this boy, happily, every hour of every day, if it worked out that way. You know that. Is it just the ear infection?"

Because of Dawson's narrow ear canals, he not only had tubes in his ears, but was prone to infection. Had had his share of them.

And then some.

"Yes," Janie said, feeling her stomach relax for the first time that morning.

Joe appeared behind his wife. "I had to come out and wish you luck."

Corrine picked up Dawson's bag. "His medicine's in there, right?" she said to Jane, who nodded.

Of course it was. This wasn't the first time her friend, an attorney, had covered for her. It wasn't even the tenth or twentieth.

And not just with Dawson. Though Corrine was a prosecutor, not a divorce attorney, she'd still done a lot of advising and behind-the-scenes work in Janie's dealings with Dillon.

Joe glanced into the backseat, a grin on his face. And then, seeing the sleeping boy, exchanged places with Corrine. With expertise born from a lot of practice, he had Dawson's restraints unfastened and had the boy on his shoulder without Dawson even so much as emitting a heavy breath.

These days, Corrine's stockbroker husband was the only one who could get the boy out of his car seat without waking him. Of the three of them, he was the only one strong enough to lift Dawson's bulky weight easily enough not to disturb him.

He wished her luck again and headed up to the house, where, Janie knew, he'd put the boy to bed in the room they kept for him.

His room, they all called it.

For a split second Janie longed to grab him back and hold on. Because life always felt better with Dawson by her side. Because she was nervous as heck and didn't want to fail him.

Corrine ran around to Janie's side of the car, pulling the door open. Janie tried not to hold on too tight when Corrine gave her the hug she'd been needing so badly.

"You're going to do fine," she assured her.

"I'm up against master chefs, Cor. With certifications and professional experience."

"Your recipes are the best."

"Dawson's going to need a tutor over the summer if he has any hope at all of being integrated into a mainstream kindergarten class next year."

She didn't have any illusions where her son's abilities were concerned—contrary to what his father thought. Dawson had challenges. But he'd been tested. Many times. He was high-functioning. Which meant that, with the right help, he could possibly grow up to be anything he wanted. Except maybe a professional athlete. Or a father.

"And Joe and I will help with that if it comes down to it…"

Janie shook her head. "I can't keep taking from you guys. I'm—"

"Shh." Cor's finger was soft as it touched Janie's lips. Reminding her, oddly, of her mother. A woman who'd turned to methamphetamine when her husband left her for another woman and her own job pressure and single motherhood had grown to be too much.

Janie hadn't heard from her in years. Wasn't even sure she was still alive.

"We'll cross the summer's bridge when we come to it," Corrine said. "For now, let's just think about today's bridge. Today you go from a woman breaking her back to make ends meet to a TV star!"

"I'm not going to be a TV star."

"That camera's going to love you!" Corrine said.

"I'm too bony." She had to go. And needed these few minutes. More than Corrine, her best friend since forever, probably knew.

"Good—you curled your hair," Corrine was saying as she gave the long blond curls a fluff. "And that color looks good on your eyes. We chose well."

They'd had a mani-pedi makeover session the day before.

"My clothes have no shape anymore."

"You're leggy and thin and there's no hiding your shape up top. You're star material."

Janie laughed. Right. A girl who'd married, at nineteen, a guy she'd known for only six months, because she'd been so certain she'd found what would sustain her happiness for the rest of her life.

She had no formal training. No post–high school education.

And she couldn't quite swallow the lump in her throat as she looked up at Corrine, who'd never forgotten her, or made her feel less, as she'd gone on to grad school and then passed the bar exam. "I need this so badly," she said, blinking back tears. "If I win this, the money and prestige combined…added to a commercial packaging of my winning recipe… I could open my own catering business. It's the answer to all of my prayers."

"I know." Corrine's smile was…calm. Comforting. "Just be yourself, Janie. Life has a plan for you—you know that. Trust it to take care of you."

Corrine was right. And speaking from experience. Even when it looked like Corrine and Joe—truly a couple meant to be together forever—had been on the verge of divorce, Corrine had trusted that all would be as it was meant to be. And now that they had found their way to a deeper, healthier marriage, with communication and utter honesty between them instead of walls, Corrine was even more of a pro in the trust department.

Janie, not so much.

"Be you," Corrine said, giving her hand a squeeze as she stepped back from the car.

Be you. That was what Cor had said to her just before she'd walked down the aisle to marry Dillon. *Be you.* She'd said it to Corrine just a few short weeks later when her friend had moved from the apartment they'd shared into a dorm room because she'd no longer been able to afford the apartment on scholarship money.

"Be you," Corrine had said when Janie had decided to have Dawson at the expense of her marriage. "Be you," she'd whispered to her friend on Thanksgiving night when Corrine had called to tell her that she and Joe were getting back together.

Be you, she told herself as she pulled into the back lot of the small Palm Desert studio and parked her old station wagon next to all of the newer, fancier cars.

Be you. It was the only thing she knew how to do.

But wasn't at all sure it would be even close to good enough.

"OKAY, YOU'VE GOT THIS. Just don't forget to smile at the camera. Women get all gaga when you smile and *Family Secrets* has a lot of women judges."

Backstage, in a private alcove she'd found for them, Kelsey was straightening the tie she'd insisted Burke wear for this pre-competition taping session.

As a sports medicine specialist, he favored collared polo shirts. But this was Kelsey's deal and, so far, it had been a miracle worker.

In the two weeks since he'd won a spot as one of eight contestants on the show, Kelsey had been a different child.

He was lucky if she slept more than six hours a night. She'd brought home two major tests—both As. Was full of ideas every night when they got home, pulling out more and more of her mother's recipes and making plans for packaging as he prepared one dish after another.

The grand prize included one of the winner's recipes being commercially packaged and nationally distributed.

She'd held parties, inviting various friends over to taste his results. Making spreadsheets filled with opinions. Assessing. Analyzing.

Best of all, he'd seen her dancing in the kitchen again. Running through a routine.

And this morning he'd heard her singing in the shower.

"You're going to win this, Daddy," she reached up on tiptoe to whisper in his ear. "I just know you are. We're a family again, you and me and Mom. Just one more time. This is how we live without her. Keeping a piece of her alive."

Claws squeezed his throat until drawing breath was painful. "Kels…" She was wise beyond her years. And…so fragile, too.

"Trust, Daddy," she said, tears in her eyes as she lowered her heels to the floor and looked up at him. "Mom's going to help you."

"It doesn't always work that way."

"That's what you said before the audition and look what happened." Her expression dead serious, she waited with an expectant look on her sweet, tortured features.

He had to tell her that he might not win.

To make certain she understood that some things were out of their control. That maybe someone else had angels watching down on them, too.

And that sometimes, no matter how many angels you had, things didn't happen as it seemed they should.

That he could let her down. Again.

Lil, the "entity" she wanted him to trust, was a case in point.

If everything had gone as it should, Lil would be standing there in the wings, getting ready to go on the show. Lil would be alive. In her daughter's life.

Helping him raise her.

And neither of them would be worrying about a thirteen-year-old on the verge of clinical depression.

But...

"Okay." He nodded. Gave her a big grin. "I'll trust."

She grinned then, too. Relief flooding into her expression. "Then everything will be fine. Just like at the audition. We'll win."

"Yes, ma'am, I believe we will," he said as he heard all contestants being called to the green room.

"You promise," Kelsey said as she turned

to head out to her seat in the small, nearly empty studio auditorium.

"I promise."

"You'll trust."

"Yes."

As he turned to join the others whose dreams were going on the line that cool January Saturday, all Burke could see was those big blue eyes that compelled him to make promises he wasn't sure he could keep.

CHAPTER FOUR

JANIE ALREADY FELT like she didn't belong. The eight contestants had gathered in a green room—nothing elegant: four walls, used couches, a tray with water and tea, a side bar with snacks, a refrigerator, lockers and television monitors so they could see the stage—for a few moments before being called on stage.

The introductions and instructions were going to be done in front of the camera. On-air instructions and official rules, that was. They'd all been sent an entire packet full of information, instruction, on-air makeup and dress tips, dress code and what had seemed like a million forms to sign.

Throughout the five weeks, any of the footage filmed during this initial non-cooking session could be tapped for airing. A facial expression, a line someone said during separate interview sessions, could be dubbed into a particular show at any time. Not really sure how that worked, realistically speaking, Janie didn't really care, either. Other than it meant she had to be "on" every single second she was there.

Had to stay focused.

Couldn't be worrying about Dawson. Not that she had to worry today. He was with Cor and Joe. But what about next Saturday when the first show was being taped? And the competition was on?

She'd focus then, too. And pray there were no Dawson emergencies his therapist couldn't handle on her own. Everyone at therapy and at preschool knew about *Family Secrets*—a video of the Thanksgiving show with Dawson had been sent around—and everyone was rooting for her.

Cor and Joe would have him the following week, as well. If there was a problem during his session, they'd handle it.

Her job was to focus.

To let go of Dawson a little bit. Trust him to the world in which he had to live...

Trust that his "gang" would have his back.

She didn't feel like one of *her* current gang. Each of the other seven contestants had already cooked for the host of *Family Secrets*, Natasha Stevens—albeit not on air. They'd all had to audition live for their place on the show.

She'd never cooked for anyone other than family and friends.

Her mailed-in Thanksgiving recipe had won her a spot on the famous cooking show.

She had no idea if she could even pull this off.

At the end of the line, waiting to walk on stage and take a seat—eight bar stools were lined up for this first segment—she pulled her phone out of the waistband of her black skinny jeans. Checked to make sure there were no calls. Sent a quick text off to Cor, asking if Dawson's ear was okay. Deleted same. Pushed and held the power button. Tucked the phone away and straightened the black silk jacket over her hip bones. All cells had to be turned off.

The line was moving.

It was time for her to go on.

FROM HIS STOOL at the beginning of the line on the stage, Burke took in the cameras—on rolling stands—that moved around them. He counted three but figured there might be more behind or above them. The guys and one woman working them were straight-faced. Moving, as if on cue, they stared at attached screens. The woman, in jeans and a T-shirt, seemed to be the one in charge. Both men, in black pants and shirts, looked to her more than at each other.

His stomach tightened a bit. So much was at stake. He was a bit…curious, too. He'd never been in a television studio before. And while, in some ways—the intense lighting, for one—it reminded him a bit of an operating room, it was also very…different. As the other contestants came in one by one, each taking a solo walk across the stage for the camera just as he had, he got a little caught up in their excitement, too.

Competition aside, winners or losers, they were all going to be on national television.

Directions rang out. Something clanged in the distance. A door closed someplace. This few minutes of filming was without sound. They were just after clips.

Glancing out toward the theater-style seating holding the hundred or so people that would be their "live" audience during the final round, he tried to find Kelsey. Stage lighting blinded him to anything beyond the edge of the platform.

Number seven was on his way across the twenty-five-foot expanse between the curtain and his stool. In jeans, a black leather jacket and biker boots, he strutted, turned toward the cameras, smiled and strutted some more. The guy was probably going to win. Viewers would eat him up. They'd tune in just to see him, which would boost ratings, and in television everything was always about the money in the end. Everyone knew that.

I'm going to lose. He was on a road that would end with him letting Kelsey down and he had no idea how to change his course. Without letting her down.

Adrenaline pumped through him anyway. Probably feeding off the other contestants. If any of them doubted their ability to win, they sure weren't showing any signs of it.

He watched for contestant number eight to appear, impatient for their instructions to be given and the tour of the kitchens to take place so he could get home. He had a patient file to peruse a second time. A delicate surgery on Monday that could determine if an athlete ever played again. A surgery that could change the entire course of a young man's life.

But it wasn't going to. When it came to orthopedics, Burke had all of the confidence in the world. Confidence his patients depended on.

Eight was on stage. He'd have to lean forward to see her, though, as the other contestants were blocking his view. Conscious of the camera, he didn't move. Didn't want to appear as stupid as he felt when the show aired...

Burke leaned forward.

And froze. He knew her. Ripples ran through him.

She took another step. Moving more quickly than any of the rest of them had. He'd never met her before.

But he knew her in the most private way.

He'd been dreaming about her. Had thought she was just a figment of his imagination. And other than the fact he found it a bit odd that his partner-less brain was cooking up the same image night after night, he'd barely given her a conscious thought.

Men dreamed.

It was normal. He was normal.

Except for the part where he'd been dreaming about a real woman without knowing it. And now he knew why. He'd seen her on TV. She'd been the angel who'd infiltrated his thoughts on Thanksgiving—giving him a touch of good feeling in an otherwise dreadful day.

That was...unsettling.

She caught his eye as she neared her stool. Didn't seem to know him from Adam. He smiled at her—to hide his supreme discomfort. Hoped he pulled it off. Looked away.

And wished to God he was anywhere but on stage with a camera on him.

Was this it, then? The part where he lost his mind? How could he have been dreaming about a woman he'd seen on TV and not realized it? Was it because of Lil? Was she messing with him? Making him pay for the fact he'd ignored her last plea for help?

His hands resting lightly on his thighs, the look Kelsey had decided was good for him, Burke had to resist the urge to get up and leave. He had a couple of patients in the hospital, rounds he could do.

"Okay, great." Natasha Stevens, the show's host, and the only person Burke had expected to recognize, walked out on stage. "Welcome to *Family Secrets*, everyone!"

Secrets. He had a secret. Was she in on it, then? This host? Did she know how he'd failed his wife?

Get a grip, man.

He was acting like an idiot.

Because he was nervous. There. He'd admitted it. Being on television, even if only for panned camera shots with no sound, had him on edge.

He'd get used to it.

Television was the least of his worries. He had an at-risk thirteen-year-old counting on him. And a fellow contestant sitting at the other end of the line with whom he'd shared very passionate kisses, in his dreams...

The Stevens woman was giving them a rundown of things he already knew. Procedures and timelines that Kelsey had read to him from the packet sent to his address by show administrators.

Was his sweat visible through the T-shirt and shirt he'd put on this morning? Stage lights were hot. Maybe he should have forgone the more formal attire as he'd first thought.

Stevens was talking about ingredients. The contestants had submitted their recipes and would find all necessary ingredients in their kitchens each week.

"In a few minutes we'll be taking a walk back to the kitchens so that you can familiarize yourselves with the area..." She caught his eye as she mentioned the kitchens and nodded. She knew he'd already seen the setup during his audition.

But he smiled at her. Trying to live up to expectation. She was a beautiful woman. With long auburn curls, a figure that could easily grace a fashion magazine, a confidence that reeked hard-earned, and success written all over her.

Why in the heck didn't he dream about her? She'd been on television that day, too.

And why not develop some hots for her now, with her parading back and forth in front of them? She was the one he needed to please. The one who could ultimately determine whether or not he disappointed his daughter.

She had his fate in her hands. At least, one very important part of it.

"So, now, let's get to the introductions. You'll have some time to get to know each other over the next weeks. You'll find that your kitchen quarters are compact, necessary so that we can get shots of all of you at once, and you'll all do much better if you go into this with an attitude of healthy competition. In other words, get along with your neighbors, ladies and gentlemen."

She'd already gone over the part where any contestant who purposely interfered with or in any way sabotaged a fellow competitor would be immediately disqualified from the show and fined an amount commensurate with all costs *Family Secrets* incurred on his or her behalf.

"This is a show about families, for families," she said—not for the first time, either. "As such, my introduction of each one of you will include pieces of the family history you submitted in the packets you returned. For this next portion of today's business, we are going to have sound as well as video. Quiet on the set, please!"

Burke's stomach knotted at the sudden silence. It was like they'd been transported into a world all their own.

There was no big call of "roll 'em" or a board being clapped loudly in front of a camera. All eyes were on Natasha Stevens. She glanced at the female camera operator. Nodded. Paused while cameras moved, whirring like a spring breeze and...

"Burke Carter!" With the overabundance of instruction and buildup, there'd been absolutely no warning that he was going to be called upon. He was pretty sure he was smiling, though, when several cameras pointed at him. He hoped so. And figured out, too late, that Ms. Stevens had purposely called on him without warning. Getting reaction.

For ratings.

"Burke is a single father of thirteen-year-old Kelsey. He's an orthopedic surgeon and is from right here in the Palm Desert/Palm Springs area! He learned to cook while in medical school. Cooking class was date night with his schoolteacher wife, who went on to become a master chef. Unfortunately, Dr. Carter's wife passed away. He is going to be competing with her recipes."

He kept smiling in spite of the fact that he sure as hades hadn't put "date night" or "deceased" in his very brief, hastily written, responses to the show's questionnaire.

He nodded at Natasha, thinking about the talk he was going to have with his daughter. It was one thing to do his best to win this competition, but he would not exploit his wife's death to do so.

The woman next to him was from Las Vegas. When he was sure the cameras were off him and he could move, Burke noticed that television monitors had come on and he could see a close-up of Showgirl. Somehow she'd gone from showgirl to restaurant owner. Natasha didn't explain that one. What was very clear was that she ran a very successful romantic diner in one of the upscale resorts on the strip. Reservations required. A sure win.

And…a showgirl. Taking his gaze from the monitor, Burke studied the beautiful though modestly dressed brunette seated next to him. Figuring he should feel some kind of attraction.

Nothing.

Next to Showgirl was a grandmotherly type, with two kids and six grandkids, whose husband was a retired farmer. Burke figured her for some fabulous family recipes. Another good possibility for the win.

The guy with slicked-back hair was single. He had an Italian restaurant in Manhattan, above which he lived. Listening to his cooking credits, Burke figured him for the win.

The short, pleasantly grinning woman was the mother of seven children. She was also a home-economics teacher. And an artist. Burke figured if she could manage to be accomplished in all three areas she was definitely their winner.

The woman with bountiful black hair had four children, and a slew of younger siblings, too. She was the head chef in a prominent Phoenix restaurant and was commuting the three and a half hours back and forth for every taping.

Then there was Biker Dude. A stay-at-home dad of three elementary-aged boys. His wife was mayor in their southern Kentucky town. He did all of the cooking for a church kitchen and a homeless shelter, in his home, while his boys were in school. Cooking under pressure was obviously not going to be a challenge for him. Burke knew karma was going to make sure he won.

"Janie Young."

He stared at the monitor. Felt...too much.

"Janie is a single mother of a little guy most of you will remember from our Thanksgiving—"

Burke didn't hear the rest due to the ringing in his ears. The wave of embarrassment that sloshed over him. He felt exposed, like everyone could read his mind...

Her recipe for turkey dressing had won the Thanksgiving Day competition. But as he sat there, the rest of it came back to him. She'd been in the audience for that special live show, one of several contestants whose recipes had been chosen for Natasha to prepare that day. The judges had voted on their favorite recipe. In the audience, her son had been bouncing around on her leg, gesturing and hollering out, having seen himself and his mother on the television monitor. What Burke remembered was the look on her face as she'd sat there, containing an overly excited little boy and still managing to have nothing but love in her eyes as she'd watched him.

Not the screen.

She hadn't even known she'd won.

She'd clearly cared more that her son was having a good time.

His literal dream woman was going to win.

And he was the show's biggest loser.

CHAPTER FIVE

THERE WAS A benefit to being a local contestant. Janie would have known, if she'd read all of the fine print in her contract.

She'd read the requirements. Memorized all time commitments. Filled out every line of every necessary form. And signed her name a lot.

She'd ignored the parts about traveling from out of state. If "it" didn't pertain to her, she usually did ignore "it" these days. Her non-Dawson time was spread that thin.

"Janie Young, right?" Turning as she collected her Coach bag—an extravagant gift with Janie's name on it under Corrine and Joe's Christmas tree the previous month—from the locker she'd been assigned at the far end of the green room, Janie saw Dr. Burke Carter standing there.

The only other local contestant. With a cooking certificate from a highly respected culinary institute. And a deceased wife who'd been a master chef, whose recipes Janie had to compete with.

"Yes?" Her tone was kind. Because it was the only way she knew how to be. In spite of Dillon's constant attempts to "toughen her up."

Out of the kitchen, there was no battle here. No reason to be "tough."

"I noticed that you didn't go to collect your per diem," he said.

"Actually, I noticed." A slender, dark-haired waif in boots, leggings and a matching sweater stepped gracefully up to them. "I'm Kelsey, and I told Dad that you hadn't gone to get your per diem. I'm just sitting out in the audience, and all, so I noticed when you didn't join the line."

"She noticed because she wanted to meet you," Dr. Carter said, at which Kelsey's face turned abruptly toward him, her ponytail swinging so hard it brushed Janie's shoulder.

"Daaadd," the girl said under her breath.

Janie tried to remember what she'd heard about the doctor's daughter in his introduction. And couldn't. Except that it was just the two of them.

"She's in love with your son."

"I am not!" The girl's wide-eyed, stricken look focused on Janie for a long second before she turned on her handsome father. "Dad." The one word was uttered in a clearly disciplinary drawl.

"From what I've gathered, you'd be in the minority if you'd seen the show and hadn't noticed Dawson," Janie said with a smile, hoping to put the obviously embarrassed girl at ease. "If I'd had any idea we'd make such a spectacle, I wouldn't have been there. Not in a million years."

"Spectacle? He was great!" the teenager said. "He's just so cute!"

People often said that Dawson's joy was contagious.

"Thank you," she said, moved in a way that didn't happen often. Not anymore. Not since life had become as much about pain as about joy. Since she'd been left to cope, largely on her own, with burdens she wasn't positive she could handle.

Not Dawson. He wasn't a burden. At all. But money? The ability to give her son every chance to live an independent, productive life?

"So… I just wanted to… Well, I'd like to—" Kelsey broke off, looked at her father, her brows raised. With a curiously vulnerable expression this time.

"My daughter is going to be present for all

of the tapings and would really like a chance to spend some time with your son. So, if ever there's a time when he's free, when you can bring him, she'll be here and would be happy to take charge of him for you."

She couldn't, of course. Janie knew that right off. Dawson wasn't easily understood. But could be quite easily upset.

A sudden loud noise could...

The girl's expectant look caught at her. "I'll keep that in mind," she said, adding, "Thank you."

Then when a shadow of something...stronger than disappointment—sorrow, maybe?—crossed Kelsey's face, she added, "If your dad is willing, I'll make sure you get to spend some time with him. Even if it's not during taping."

And had another expression to deal with. The dad's. Which was when she realized she'd kind of proposed a personal get-together between her and Dawson and Kelsey and her father. Off set. As though she was hitting on him.

Or something...

"He's... Dawson wouldn't... He doesn't take to new people unless I'm right there with him," she tried to explain and felt like she was blubbering. Making the distressing situation worse. "If I brought him here, he wouldn't spend time with you. Not unless he already knew you. Or I was right there with you."

There were so many other reasons she couldn't bring her son to the tapings. She'd never get any cooking done. Not with all the unfamiliar sights and sounds that would distract her son. Not with tiny kitchen space being shared by other contestants. Dawson wouldn't be able to amuse himself at her feet as he did at home.

"And it wouldn't be fair to you to leave you alone with him until you understood a little bit about being around him…"

"But if I spent time with him first, then I could? I mean, like, I could help you out maybe during the tapings or something?"

For some reason it was important to the girl. Whose father was an opponent.

"I don't plan to have him on the set, except for the promo family times…"

"But for those…"

"Let's do this…" Dr. Burke Carter took a step forward and placed a protective arm around his daughter's shoulders. "Why don't we make a plan to introduce Dawson to Kelsey this next week and then go from there?"

He was agreeable? What was with these two? They seemed so nice. But Dillon had told her she was too gullible. Too trusting. That it was her fault she was all alone and struggling financially. Because she was too nice. She let people use her.

Kelsey's gaze was turned on her again. Expectant. Alight.

"I'm so busy..." she said. Dillon was not right. Her situation was not her fault. At least, not because of any wrongdoing. Other than... she'd married too young. Chosen the wrong man.

She noticed several things at once. The drop of Kelsey's gaze. The droop of her shoulders. The concerned glance from her father. And the resolution in Dr. Carter's gaze as he looked at Janie.

"We don't want to intrude," he said, and she breathed easier, knowing that he was going to let her off the hook. "But if there's any time we could meet up, maybe if you ever take him to the park or something, or we could somehow join in an activity that wouldn't require you to give up any time..."

He was a doctor. He must know at least some of the challenges she faced on a daily basis.

She needed to ask him why he was doing this. Why he was pushing.

He glanced at Kelsey, who was watching her again.

It had to do with the girl. Obviously. If she was going to get any information, it would have to be parent to parent.

"I…" Technically what they were asking wasn't necessarily onerous.

"He's, like, famous now and I just want to meet him…"

The girl seemed curiously vulnerable. She was at that age…

And Janie had to beat Kelsey's father in the competition of her life. An opponent far better qualified for the task before them.

"We're at home all day tomorrow." Even as she said the words, she regretted them. And didn't, at the same time. Kelsey's reaching out to her seemed like…something. Surely not just to find a way to sabotage her so her father could have one less opponent in the competition.

A thirteen-year-old girl with a doctor father could hardly need the money and prestige that came from winning. Besides, the money would go to her father, not to her.

Janie had campaign calls to make. Hundreds of them. Because she hadn't squeezed them in during the week that had just passed.

"If you'd like to stop by around three…?"

Dawson would be just up from his nap. At his best.

"We don't need to intrude on your home," Burke Carter said, frowning. "We could meet for burgers or something."

A vision of her son with pieces of hamburger smeared all over his face, of the drool that would be on his chin from a tongue with low muscle tone that didn't always stay in his mouth, brought about another vision. The disgust on the face of a fellow diner at a local restaurant.

"Dawson would do much better if you visited him at home," she said. Adamant on this detail.

"Can we, Dad?" Kelsey turned to look up at him.

And before Dr. Burke Carter said a word, Janie knew, just by the expression on his face as he looked at his daughter, that she and Dawson were going to be entertaining them. When she didn't have enough minutes in the day to get her calls done.

Dillon's voice, telling her that she'd been a sap again, blared through her brain.

BURKE COULDN'T BELIEVE his good luck. Kelsey was showing interest in something besides his cooking. The show she'd set her sights—and emotional health—on him winning wasn't her sole focus.

At least for the moment.

She'd always had a thing for kids. And he had to admit the Thanksgiving episode of *Family Secrets* had stayed in his memory bank because of the Young woman's kid. As, purportedly, it had with much of America.

But who'd have thought Kelsey would take initiative to actually meet the boy? These days, anyway.

Maybe when Lil had still been alive, he could have seen it happening. Kelsey had always been one to champion the underdog. To try to fix the broken. Like her friend at dance whose parents wouldn't take her to the doctor for her sore knee.

"Oh, and don't forget your per diem." His daughter turned back to the woman who'd just given them directions to her home.

Right. The reason they'd approached her to begin with.

"We're given an average of the travel allotment offered to out-of-town contestants as well as meal per diem," Burke added.

"We are?" The consternation on Janie Young's face gave him a sudden desire to kiss her. Just…he had no idea why. And was uncomfortable with having even had the thought.

"We are," he said, naming the weekly figure. "Payable at the beginning of each week that we're on the show."

"Which is today," Kelsey added.

"Thank you." The smile that spread across her face struck him. Not in any particular way. For any particular reason.

It just struck him.

And he knew he'd been hit.

A complication he most definitely did not need.

CHAPTER SIX

JANIE WASN'T EVEN out of bed on Sunday before Dawson put a DVD cover on her face.

"Eee, eee, eee," he grunted in his husky voice.

"You know you have to brush your teeth and get dressed and have breakfast before you're allowed to see," she said, pulling him up beside her on the bed as she struggled to get her eyes fully opened.

"Eee, eee," he said, resisting her hug to hold the plastic cover an inch from her face.

It wasn't unusual for the boy to ask to watch his favorite movie the second he got out of bed. The highly unusual part came when, that morning, Janie let him.

DAWSON'S POTTY-TRAINING UNDERWEAR had leaked during the night. Not only were his sheets soaked but his blanket was, too. Stripping the bed down to the plastic cover that protected the mattress, Janie thought about the shower she'd intended to take while Dawson's movie kept him occupied.

She'd hoped to wash her hair. Maybe put on a little makeup. Not as much as she'd had on the day before. She wasn't going on television.

But neither did she want to treat her afternoon guests to the shock of her bare, dull, worried-looking face.

She'd hoped to find something halfway cute to wear.

Instead she'd climbed into the first handy thing—a pair of old jeans and a sweatshirt she'd had on the night before to ward off the chill—and used the limited hot water to wash her son's bedding. Made some of her campaign calls. And felt guilty for bothering people on Sunday morning.

AT NOON, HAVING watched his movie twice, Dawson left his seat on the carpeted floor, came over to the linoleum, opened the pantry door and pulled peanut butter off the shelf. Bending down, he flipped the latch on the shelf below and took bread out of the box. On tiptoe, he slid both up onto the kitchen counter. Right next to where Janie was sitting at the Formica-topped table.

"Eee," he said, looking at the ingredients of his sandwich, not at her.

She grinned. Wanting to call Cor and Joe. She'd been certain he was making choices when, the week before, he'd opened the pantry door and brought her a can of tuna. Every day since, whenever they were home, she'd waited as mealtime approached to see if he'd know he was hungry and tell her what he wanted to eat. Dinner the previous night had been SpaghettiOs. Breakfast that morning, frozen waffles he'd pulled from the side-by-side refrigerator that had come with their small rental home.

Just as she was about to get up from the lists of numbers and pre-scripted phone messages she'd been hired to deliver, the four-year-old turned and headed back for the pantry door on his short legs. Inside, he pulled out a can of peaches. Tiptoed up to shove them on the counter. And then crossed his arms and looked at her.

Janie laughed.

He laughed, too. A full-bodied, husky sound that filled her heart to its brim.

"Eee!" he screamed, jumping from foot to foot as quickly as he could and then dropping down to his butt to stare up at her.

"Let's get you to the potty first," she told

him. And had to hurry to keep up as he ran to the bathroom, yanked a new pair of potty-training underwear from the cupboard and proceeded to take off his sweatpants. He knew what it was all about. Knew the point. Was even, according to his doctor, feeling the sensations.

His muscles just weren't developed enough yet to give him the control necessary to be able to "hold it" for any length of time.

They'd get there eventually. And until then, potty-training underwear were an easy fix. Easy...and expensive. Insurance didn't cover them. And neither did Dillon.

KELSEY WANTED HIM to make her mother's bourbon pork twice on Sunday. It had turned out great the first time. She'd just wanted him to work a little faster. And to make certain he could prepare it perfectly twice in a row. The first official competition was being taped the following Saturday and his schedule was completely full this coming week.

His first entry was the pork dish. The ingredients would be in his kitchen on set. He couldn't take in any notes, let alone a written recipe.

Kelsey had her counter filled with notes. Gave him a critique after each session. And never mentioned the little boy they were going to see that afternoon.

The unease that had settled upon him sometime during the night came back to haunt him. He knew his daughter. Knew her heart and soul. Even if he didn't always understand her thoughts. Even if her emotions weren't always clear to him these days. He knew her.

Yet...

"Kels?" They were on their way to Janie Young's house. Her neighborhood was across town from theirs. The houses were smaller. No gated communities with private pools and other amenities.

"Yeah?"

She'd changed from the flannel pants and tank top she'd had on at the house into jeans and a T-shirt with her favorite pony character on it. Her hair was in a ponytail. And her sweetness nearly choked him up.

"Why did you push so hard to spend time with Dawson Young?"

He didn't want to doubt her. Hated that he was doing so. Felt like total crap. And yet... there was so much he wasn't getting about her these days. Like, what he could and could not call her. Was this a "squirt" day or a no-"squirt" day?

"I didn't."

When he glanced over, hoping her expression would tell him something, all he had was a glimpse of her ponytail. Her face was turned toward her window.

"Yes, you did." He pulled out the firm tone. If there was any chance she was... Well, he would not be a party to it. Or enable her to be a party to it, either.

He'd drop out of the competition immediately.

There were worse things than watching your child suffer from clinical depression. Like watching her sell her soul, for instance.

She shrugged. "I just wanted to meet him. That's all."

"Kelsey..."

"What?"

"Are you...?" He couldn't even get the words out. His heart told him he was wrong. Emphatically.

But it made sense.

"Am I what?"

She was staring at him now. All wide-eyed. Stopped at a light, he studied her.

"Are you hoping that by becoming friendly with Dawson you can somehow find out the secrets to his mother's—"

"What!" Her shriek filled the car. And then

some. "I can't believe you'd even think such a thing! Oh, my gosh!"

She sounded like he'd just accused her of murder. He felt as though he had.

They rode in silence for a few blocks. The rift between them deepening, becoming a chasm, a sinkhole he could lose her in…

Reparation was up to him and he panicked as he scrambled for answers.

"For the record, I never felt like you'd do such a thing."

"Then why ask?" Her accusatory tone reminded him of her mother. Not that he'd tell her that. Ever.

Lil had had her issues, sure, but she'd been a great mother. And a good wife, too. He'd loved her. Truly loved her. He'd never missed her more than he did in that minute.

"Because I don't understand why, after months of not caring about anything, you suddenly care so much about this kid." That didn't come out right. "I get that he's cute," he added. Even he'd felt something when the mother and son duo had lit up the television screen on a rather dreary Thanksgiving day. "But he's not the only cute child we've run across in the past year."

"She's a single mom trying really hard."

"She's not the only single mother we've come across, either."

"He's special, Daddy. You can tell that just by looking at him…"

He understood that. Somewhat. And liked it a whole lot better than his sabotage theory.

"And the way she looks at him. The way he seems to matter more than even winning a spot on the show…"

He remembered that Thanksgiving Day show—the way the boy had been the one to notice that Janie Young had won…

"He's lucky that he has her," Kelsey was saying, her voice soft. "That she loves him so much. And I just…"

He was really starting to get it now. The boy had his mother's love. Totally. Completely. Something that Kelsey was drawn to be a part of. If she could.

"I feel guilty," she continued. Blowing his newest theory.

"Guilty?"

"Yeah, because, like, when we win, that means she's going to lose." She shrugged again. "We can't do anything about that, because, you know, there can't be two winners. So, I was just thinking that where we can help out, we should. You know, with her being the only other local contestant, we're going to be living in the same town even after the show and might run into her and I just…feel like we should make this as easy on her as we can."

And maybe, without knowing it, she was drawn to the mother/child closeness? The bonding she was missing?

Burke had no way of knowing. Of predicting what might happen next. Or, apparently, of preventing the disappointment he was convinced he was bringing upon his daughter. One step at a time. He just knew, as he pulled into the small, garage-less drive, that he loved his daughter more than life. And that he was ill-equipped to guarantee her happiness.

WHAT ON EARTH had she been thinking? Inviting a doctor and his daughter to her tiny house situated in a neighborhood without the community landscape standards that governed most of the neighborhoods in Palm Desert. Her place was clean—well, picked up, at least. But other than the two bedrooms and one bathroom, it had only the L-shaped living and kitchen area. Plenty big enough for just her and Dawson.

She was starting to feel slightly claustrophobic as the time neared for their guests to arrive. Funny—she never felt that way when Cor and Joe were over.

Standing in the opened closet doors at the far end of her kitchen, pulling Dawson's twin sheets out of the dryer, she watched as her son sat, knees apart and legs crossed at the ankles, on the floor in front of the television, playing the video game Joe had bought him for Christmas. A nonviolent game with a cute little character who had to run and jump and face a lot of challenges on his way to wherever the next level would lead him.

And she wondered how he'd appear to the strangers coming to their home that afternoon. Would they see Dawson for who he was?

"Gah!" Dawson's rounded shoulders jerked downward, his little neck having to tilt back even farther than normal for him to see the television.

"Gah!" The passion in his voice as he urged his man on made her smile. Just that quickly she was awash with the warmth of love she felt for her little guy. And then assailed with guilt for the thoughts she'd been having. Thoughts of him appearing less than perfect to others. And her caring at all what they thought.

He'd played all of his exercise "games"

with her in great humor. Had worked hard to hold on to the large pencil and draw straight lines and then circles on plain paper. And she wanted him relaxed and in a good mood when their guests arrived.

Guests he didn't yet know about.

Dawson tended to take life as it came. A lesson she tried hard to learn from him.

"Hey, bud, you want to help Mommy make your bed?" It was a long shot with the video-game controller in his hand, but she always asked for his help when doing anything she knew he could attempt.

Washing floors. Dusting.

A lot of the time he joined in happily. Most particularly when she was cleaning bathrooms. He loved swirling the brush around the toilet water.

While his game ran on without him, he looked at her, his mouth hanging open as it so often did.

He grinned at her. She stared at his drool. And wished she'd never invited the Carters over. Had been wondering, since the moment she'd issued the invitation, what on earth she'd been thinking.

Or, more accurately, why she hadn't been thinking.

Yeah, Dr. Burke Carter was a handsome

guy. Maybe the most compelling man she'd ever met.

But she was a mother now. Full time. First and last.

As Dillon had been quick to point out every time he wanted her complete attention and didn't get it. Which had been at least once a day…

Jumping as the doorbell rang, Janie shook her head.

"Gah!" Dawson, apparently unconcerned by her lack of response to his smile, was back at his game.

Arms still filled with sheets, she stood there. And the bell rang a second time.

"Dooo," Dawson said, throwing down the control and rolling onto his knees to stand.

Dropping her sheets onto the only armchair in the room, Janie went after him. He'd just learned how to unlock the front door and she didn't want him running outside in his bare feet.

Nor did she want him facing their inquisitors alone.

She hadn't even had a chance to wipe his face.

He was her angel.

Perfect in his imperfection.

She would die before she'd have anyone look down on him in his own home.

CHAPTER SEVEN

As a PHYSICIAN Burke came into contact with people from all walks of life. While he didn't make house calls, or visit any of his patients at home, he was fully aware that not everyone lived in a neighborhood like his own.

Heck, even as plebeian as it was, Janie Young's street was nicer than the one he'd grown up on. At least during the two weeks out of a month he'd been with his dad.

He just hadn't expected the beautiful cook to reside in such a *plain* place. Weed-spattered hard dirt for a front yard. A porch that could have looked cute with a chair or plant on it.

And…

The door pulled open and she was there… or at least, someone was. It took him a second to realize that the frowning woman opening the door to them was the same perfectly turned-out beauty they'd seen on set the day before.

"Doo!"

Burke glanced down at the husky utterance in time to see Dawson's backside as he raced away.

Typical toddlers could create havoc without warning. He could just imagine the kinds of things that could crop up with a special-needs child.

"We can come back another time if you'd rather."

In sweats, a ponytail that was half falling out, and completely bare-faced, the woman didn't look like she'd been expecting company.

Which was when it hit him that she'd forgotten their appointment.

"Come on, Kels. We can do this another time." He turned to head back to the car.

"No!" Janie's voice called out to him, "Really, you've come all this way and it's fine."

"It wasn't that far. And we were going to have dinner on this side of town anyway." He named a family-owned Italian place known around the entire valley for its authentically delicious cuisine.

"Dad!" Kelsey frowned at him. "We were not! We've got p—" She stopped. Glanced at Janie. "Well, dinner's already made," she finished. And then added, "Besides, this is my only chance to meet Dawson before next

Saturday, and if he's at the studio, I won't be able to help out if I don't meet him…"

"She's right," Janie said. "I was expecting you. I'm just running behind today. Come on in." Her smile came out.

And hit Burke in the gut. Those lips softened in an upward curve, the light in her vivid blue eyes held his gaze—even more than the figure her sweats didn't disguise.

"Please come in."

Embarrassed that she'd had to ask another time, Burke followed his daughter inside.

JANIE DIDN'T KNOW for sure what she'd been expecting. Probably nothing good, which was why she'd been in a tizzy all day long. But it certainly hadn't been the way Kelsey's blue-eyed gaze sought out Dawson and stayed with him. Almost to the point of rudeness. Except that the girl's expression seemed to be filled with a compassion beyond her years.

"Dawson?"

The boy grunted when he heard Janie's voice—his attention seemingly on the little figure racing around the screen. The music coming from the set gave a downward spiral, signaling a lost life, but Dawson pushed buttons and had the critter up and running within seconds.

"Dawson," she said again, more firmly.

What, if anything, the boy paid attention to when he was enrapt with whatever was in front of him, no one knew at this point. But she knew he'd heard her.

And understood her, too.

He continued to play. Janie felt the heat creeping up into her cheeks and hated herself for it. Dawson was being Dawson.

And she'd be darned if she was going to start wanting him to be someone different. She, of all people. What was the matter with her?

What was it about this family that she felt the need to impress them?

Because she had to be good enough to best them on television?

Taking a deep breath, she felt calm come over her. And walked over to stand between Dawson and the television set. "Time to turn it off," she told him, aware of the two people standing just a few feet away, still behind the couch that separated the foyer from the living room, and yet focused now on what mattered.

She could turn off the television herself. Dawson might just smile up at her and move. He might not. No matter, they had their ways of doing things and she was not going to do him the disservice of changing them.

Not for anyone.

"Gah!" Dawson blurted loudly, continuing to press the buttons on his controller.

She couldn't see behind her, but recognized the sound when another life was lost.

"Time to turn it off," she said again, her voice as patient as usual. The air in the room was cool and comfortable, light, as she stood there, remembering who she was. Who they were. Until it was just her and Dawson, alone in their own world.

"Dawson, time to turn it off," she said again. As she would until he minded her. What part of his stubbornness came from lack of putting two and two together, and what part was typical rebellion, she didn't know.

What she knew was that her son had to learn his boundaries and the only way he was going to learn was if she taught him.

She couldn't do it for him. He had to do it for himself. Whether he wanted to or not.

"Dawson..."

"Kaaaayyy." Dawson dropped the game console. Picked up the TV remote. Pushed the off button. And then sat, facing her knees, his arms folded across his chest.

She wanted to hug him. And looked at her guests instead.

"Come on in," she said. "Have a seat." She

motioned toward the couch. And sat on the edge of the sheet-filled chair.

"Dawson, you want to show Kelsey and Burke your cars?" Realizing how familiar she sounded, she looked at the orthopedist. "He's seen so many d-o-c-t-o-r-s in his lifetime that the word upsets him," she said.

"You have cars?" Kelsey asked, sliding down to the floor and then, on her butt, scooting over to Dawson. "I used to have some cars," she told him. "Until my mom took them away because she didn't think they were good for little girls to play with. Can I see your cars?"

Dawson didn't even look her way. But he got up, went to the hall closet and pulled open the door to reveal the shelves of neatly stacked toys and games. Taking out his case of cars, he brought it over and dropped it on the floor in front of Kelsey. He then went back and grabbed the plastic track that Joe had bought him—a one-piece circle that stood on end beneath the bottom shelf—and carried that back, too.

He half dropped, half tossed it at Kelsey. It hit her knee and, with a startled look at Janie, the girl backed up.

Dawson picked up the track again, brought

it close to Kelsey and dropped it a second time, this time falling down in front of her.

"Gah!"

Janie waited. Holding her breath, mostly.

Dawson sat, cross-legged, hands in his lap.

Kelsey reached for the case of cars, looking between Dawson and Janie. "Can I see them?" she asked when no one reacted.

Dawson's nod was short. Succinct. And Janie had to restrain herself from laughing out loud.

Her boy was a sucker for a pretty girl. Who'd have thought?

WHERE BURKE MIGHT have found himself eager to be finished with Sunday afternoon's appointment and have dinner—preferably at the Italian place and not at home eating a pork recipe he'd prepared twice that day—instead, he sat in Janie Young's living room, chatting up the beautiful woman like he was on a date.

The turning point had come when Dawson had suddenly stood from his cars, grabbed Kelsey's hand and dragged her down the hall—off of which he counted three doors. Assuming one was a bathroom, that left two for bedrooms.

"Most of his toys are in his room," Janie had said as she'd watched the pair depart.

Her smile was full-on now. And he wondered if he'd ever seen a woman who looked so attractive while doing absolutely nothing to help herself appear that way.

He scooted down to the end of her dark brown leather couch. "You don't have to sit on the edge of your seat," he told her. "I don't bite."

Her legs looked longer than he'd remembered as she got up and walked toward him—folding them under her as she settled on the other end of the couch.

"I won't let him monopolize her for long," she assured him. "But this couldn't have gone better if she wanted to get to know him."

"She's a sensitive kid," Burke said, lowering his voice, though he didn't think Kelsey could hear him while talking at the same time. She'd been conversing with Dawson nonstop since they'd left the room, though he didn't see how she could understand any of the boy's grunts.

"She seems very sweet." Janie's gaze was direct. Not shy at all. Unusual for someone so soft-spoken.

He was curious about her. In so many ways.

He nodded. "In some ways she's old beyond her years."

"I just don't understand why she's so taken with my son. I mean, my world revolves around him, but other people usually have to get to know him before they appreciate him—"

When her voice broke off, Burke wanted to know where the words had led her—someplace she'd chosen to travel to alone. He wanted to know badly. Not just with the curious interest of a stranger.

The idea—him wanting access to the inner workings of her mind—bothered him. As did whatever compelled him to be honest with her.

"She's convinced I'm going to win the show," he told her. They were competitors. Contestants going after the same prize. He wasn't going to pretend otherwise. Or lure her into thinking he was forgetting that. "And so she wants to help you out in any way she can to soften the blow."

"So she's got plans to aid the other six contestants, as well?" She sounded mildly curious. Nothing more. And didn't seem the least offended—or surprised—by his comment.

That kind of bothered him, too.

Which bothered him.

"No. Just you."

"Just me? Why just me?"

"Because you're local."

She nodded. As though he'd answered all her questions. As though, if he didn't keep talking, he'd lose what interest of hers he had.

"My wife was a chef." He blurted what had already been revealed during his introduction the day before. And added, "Kelsey's mom," as if that wasn't self-explanatory.

She nodded again. Seeming interested. But adding nothing.

"She died suddenly, unexpectedly, and Kelsey's taken it really hard."

Those gorgeous brows drew together and he could have sworn he saw an actual shadow cross Janie Young's face. "I'm so sorry," she said, the softness in her voice seeming to convey more emotion than yelling would have done. "I knew…the introductions yesterday and all…that you were a widower, but I had no idea it was recent. Or sudden."

Sudden seemed to make it worse for some. His jury was still out on that one. During his residency he'd seen too many families whose lives were forever changed by debilitating long-term and ultimately fatal illness.

"It's been almost two years," he said. Needing her to know that he wasn't so recently widowed made no sense to him.

Guilt surged. Just because he was familiar with its company didn't mean he was at peace with it. Welcomed it. Or even handled it well.

A song started to play in the other room.

Something about learning to brush your teeth. It was vaguely familiar.

Burke could hear Kelsey singing along.

"Because she's been struggling, I wanted to take Kelsey on vacation over Thanksgiving. She insisted we stay home. That we cook a full dinner, using all of her mother's recipes. And that we watch cooking shows all day."

Janie nodded, a sad smile spreading across her face. "That's when she saw *Family Secrets*."

"She talked about Dawson all during dinner that day. Normally she focuses on the cooking, trying to take after her mother, I suppose. Anyway, she smiled when she talked about him. She doesn't smile all that much these days."

Shocked when Janie's bottom lip began to tremble, Burke started to rise. "I'm sorry. I'll…"

"No." She motioned him back down. "Sit." Wiping at her eye, she chuckled. "I just get emotional where my boy is concerned. I'm so glad he made her smile. He really is a source of true joy. It's not that often that people who don't know him, or spend time with him, see that."

She'd said "a source," like one of *the* sources. Like the boy had special powers or something.

Burke knew better than to believe in any of that woo-woo stuff.

But it was great to know that Kelsey had picked up on something rather remarkable about this mother and son. Puffed up with pride in his constantly amazing daughter, Burke relaxed back against the couch.

For the first time in a long time, he was smiling, too. For real. Completely.

While telling himself it wasn't actually possible for this little boy to be *the* source of true joy.

Still...the thought was nice.

CHAPTER EIGHT

JANIE BREEZED THROUGH her week. The Carters' visit on Sunday seemed to have been the precursor for a week when everything went according to plan. Dawson didn't just do his therapies with her at home; he seemed to actually be benefiting from them.

One exercise that she'd been doing since he'd started on solid foods, pushing down on his tongue with his spoon when he ate, was designed to help not only with swallowing but with keeping his tongue from hanging out of his mouth, and it seemed to be finally paying off. She'd been doing it since the first time he'd had a spoon in his mouth. And had taught him to feed himself that way. Four years of continuous exercise. And worth every day of it. They'd gone an entire twenty-four hours without her having to tap at his tongue to remind him to put it back in his mouth.

That night she called Cor and Joe, had them get on speakerphone and started to cry when Cor did as she told them the good news.

Dawson's life was a series of challenges, but not impossible ones.

As long as she kept up with the seemingly tedious and sometimes seemingly useless games they played.

"I read about this councilwoman today," Joe said as they talked Friday night over dinner at the Armstrongs' artfully designed home. They'd fed Dawson earlier, all three of them sitting at the table with the boy. They'd played with him until bedtime. And then, once he was down, Joe had left Cor and Janie to enjoy a glass of wine while he'd grilled steaks for the three of them.

"She interned for a senator. She's worked in social welfare…"

Glancing at Cor, still a little nervous that her friend's reconciliation could be fractured, Janie wondered why Joe thought singing another woman's praises at dinner was a good thing.

"Here in Santa Raquel?" Janie blurted, hoping not, and hoping that knowing that would settle any uneasiness Corrine might have at Joe's interest.

"No, in Spain, actually," Cor said, smiling at her husband and then at Janie. "She has Down syndrome, sweetie. And in 2013 she was elected councilwoman."

Trusted by her fellow citizens to make critical decisions for the welfare of all of them.

An hour later, as Janie drove her sleeping son home in the quiet darkness of Palm Desert, she was still smiling.

Definitely a good week.

DAWSON WOKE WHEN Janie pulled into their drive. But he was in bed and back to sleep ten minutes later. He'd had his bath at Cor's. Was already in his pajamas. A quick potty trip for a Pull-Up change and he climbed happily into bed.

When he was tired, Dawson wanted bed. Period. He didn't fight sleep. Didn't fight stopping whatever he was doing. When he was tired, he went to sleep.

Another good lesson that   uld be learned from her remarkable son. In her kitchen, she pulled out the recipe she'd be using for the competition the next day. She'd hoped to practice sometime during the week, but there'd been double the flower deliveries—it wasn't even Valentine's Day yet, who'd have figured—which meant more money, so she'd gratefully taken every job offered. And she'd finished all of her political calls, as well—afraid that if she left them to Sunday again, someone would find out and fire her.

The first week's dish had to involve meat. She was making a simple meatball recipe that she'd created years ago. Cor and Joe loved it. As did anyone else who'd ever tried it. It was her weakest entry. If it didn't work, she had three other chances to make it to the finals.

Still, locking in the finals the first week would be nice. A godsend. Being able to relax for the next three weeks, to prepare, mentally if nothing else, was all she asked. Though if she won the next day, and then again, she'd have an advantage in the final round. That would be good, too.

Raw ground beef—pulled out of the freezer and left in the refrigerator all day—in a bowl, Janie hardly noticed her fatigue as she added grape jelly, chili sauce and a few other ingredients without measuring. And then, for her last, secret ingredient, the red cooking wine she used so sparingly because of its cost.

There was something elementally pleasurable about being a grown woman and inserting her hand into a bowl full of mush. Squeezing it between her fingers. Feeling it slide and gush across her palm. Something…good about getting her hand dirty.

She'd be seeing Burke Carter the next day. That was good, too. In the same kind of way. A slight, pretend, hint of naughty. Because the successful, good-looking, eligible-bachelor doctor had been in her home?

Maybe.

Didn't hurt anything. As long as she kept her daydreaming in check. And no one else knew about it...

The ring of her cell phone blasted the peace right out of the room, leaving her heart thudding. Who would be calling so late?

It wasn't like she had family who'd call in case of emergency. Except Joe and Cor, and she'd just left them...

With her messy hand suspended in air to prevent dirtying anything, she shuffled in her purse to reach her phone. Set it on the counter and pushed to answer.

"Hello?" she said, her mouth almost down by the counter as she picked up the phone and straightened.

"Your first episode is tomorrow." Her stomach dropped as she recognized Dillon's voice.

"I know." She'd told him about winning a spot on the show. She'd had to. The way people in Palm Desert had been talking, he was sure to have heard from someplace. But the last thing she needed now, tonight, was more of his put-downs.

She should have cared more about looking at

the caller ID than about answering her phone one-handedly so she didn't miss the call.

Anyone who mattered would have called back anyway.

"What do you want, Dillon?"

"I thought…maybe…you know, I should take the kid tomorrow. So's you can be on the show and all."

"What!" Was he kidding? He'd never even met the boy! Not once.

"Since it's Saturday. What with no day care and all…"

Pulling back the phone, she stared at it, as though someone else was impersonating her ex-husband's voice and the screen would tell her so.

"You don't know him. Have no idea how to take care of him," she reminded him.

"I want to learn. And to get to know him."

Ground-beef mixture sitting in the bowl, Janie slid to the floor, resting the elbow attached to her messy hand on her knee.

"I don't get it," she said.

"I've been thinking about you, Janie. About us. About how we were…you know…before. I was wrong to be so hard on you. And I'm sorry, is all."

Dillon apologizing? That hadn't happened since…ever? Had he ever apologized? Or had she always just been willing to assume he was sorry as he joked with her over any wrong-doing, sweeping it all under the rug to disappear into the ether.

The ether of her mind, that was.

Or was she being unfair? Had Dillon been different before she'd found out she was pregnant with a Down syndrome child and insisted on going through with the pregnancy?

Joe and Cor had thought so at first. Until she'd talked a bit about what went on when she and Dillon were on their own. The way he'd always been certain he was right because she had only a high school education, no experience at anything and a druggie for an only known parent. Then they'd been horrified.

But they'd been reacting to her perception of her ex-husband's words. Which had been, admittedly, biased.

"Come on, Janie. Let me start over. Just give me a chance."

"What about what's-her-name?" The words were beneath her. Wendy. The woman's name was Wendy. And deserved the respect of Janie saying so.

"She's in agreeance."

Agreement. Janie bit her tongue on the correction, knowing from experience that Dillon wouldn't take it in the manner offered.

Or maybe he would, since the manner offered had drastically changed over the years. There'd been a day when she'd thought her husband respected, admired and looked up to her as much as she'd respected, admired and looked up to him. Back when she'd thought they each had their strengths and were open to benefiting from the other's.

"Okay?" He prodded her.

She didn't get it. Why would Dillon and *Wendy* suddenly want her son's company? And could she rightfully deny Dawson's father the right to see him if he wanted to?

Legally, she could, for now. She had full custody. But only because Dillon hadn't wanted shared. Still, technically, he had visitation rights. Not without more than a few hours of prior notice, though. Since they'd never set up a schedule.

At least she hoped that was the case.

Heart pounding again, Janie got scared. What if Dillon pushed this? What if he took her to court?

She couldn't afford a lawyer.

And couldn't imagine dropping her son off at his father's garage one night a week and every other weekend.

Dawson would be petrified, sleeping somewhere unfamiliar.

And all of the missed exercises…

"He has therapy in the morning," she said. Dillon had a schedule of Dawson's therapies. And an insurance accounting, too, if he ever looked at it. "Cor and Joe are taking him."

"It's not going to kill him to miss a day," Dillon was saying as whatever little piece of Janie's heart was opening up slammed shut again. "I'm sure seeing his father would help more than a bunch of time spent tapping his tongue to the roof of his mouth."

Had he known the morning's session was speech therapy? A tiny spurt of hope trickled out. Did he read the reports he was sent on a regular basis?

And care more than he'd let on?

Dillon had always been such a tough guy on the surface. Determined that no one would ever think him weak.

She'd thought it was because his father had been so hard on him all his life. Mocking him when, as a kid, he'd cry after his dad hurt his feelings. And his body, too, when the occasional blow had come his way.

Not that the elder Young had beat his son. Or even come close. But he'd pulled his belt on Dillon on more than one occasion. And had hated that his son hadn't been able to take his punishment with a stiff upper lip. Hadn't held back tears and just broken out into a sweat instead.

"So what do you say?" Dillon asked.

"You got rights, Dil."

Janie heard the words in the distance. From Dillon's end. *Wendy.*

"I appreciate your apology, Dillon," she said without any further thought. "And I'm thrilled that you want to spend some time with our son. He needs a daddy. But tomorrow isn't going to work. I've already made plans for him. And it's too late to cancel therapy without having to pay for it—not unless we have a medical emergency, which we don't. Tomorrow is the last Saturday therapy until after the show is done."

Dillon had rights. But so did she. And Dawson. And saying no to a visitation without any prior notice was one of theirs.

Squeezing her eyes shut, she waited for his response. And hoped she wasn't making a huge mistake.

"Next week, then?"

Dillon's words made her jaw drop. And her eyes shoot wide open.

"O-okay," she said, drawing the word out.

Okay? What was she doing? "As long as you can keep him until I'm done with the show."

She couldn't just turn over Dawson to the father who'd never cared for him.

But she had to know her rights.

And know them before she went head-to-head with Dillon Young. Her ex-husband liked to get his way. And could get pretty ugly when he didn't.

"I'm sure that can be arranged." He sounded genuine. Kind.

Reminiscent of the man she'd fallen in love with after her senior year in high school. The man she'd thought was the love of her life.

"I'll call you on Monday, then," she said, standing at the sink as she held the phone with her clean hand and rinsed her food-caked one.

She was just going to get it dirty again. When she rolled the meat mixture into balls. Didn't much matter. At the moment, she needed to be clean.

And to cry.

But she didn't. She'd expected to. As soon as she got off the phone.

Instead she stood at her bowl of ground beef. Rolled meatballs. And wondered what Burke Carter would say if she told him about her life with her ex-husband.

CHAPTER NINE

KELSEY LET HIM go without the suit coat for Saturday's show. She'd seen an apron online and had begged him to order it and wear it instead. It wasn't long, tied at the waist, and looked like a tool belt.

The part she liked best was that she could have whatever she'd wanted printed on it. She'd wanted Lil's Kitchen—in purple because that had been her mother's favorite color.

Burke could have done without the apron, in general. But when he saw how such a relatively small thing could seemingly give his daughter so much pleasure, he'd placed the order. And paid extra for expedited shipping so he could have it for Saturday.

Kelsey aced another test and talked about Dawson Young almost as much as she talked about *Family Secrets* and cooking. On the other hand, she also refused to audition for a solo number at the studio, even after the senior company director told her she'd choreographed the piece specifically for her. And because they weren't cooking during the evenings that week, she'd been in bed before nine each night.

Burke had been up much later. And had taken a knot in his stomach to bed with him each night.

A knot that had grown to almost concerning proportions by showtime on Saturday. They were taping the show. But if he made a mistake, his mistake would be seen nationwide. Because reality still meant reality to Natasha Stevens, the producer and host of *Family Secrets*.

Now, there was a beautiful woman. One so much in control of her world she wouldn't need to rely on her man for anything.

She was the woman Burke's thoughts should be homing in on.

Not an amateur cook with more weight on her shoulders than any one person should have to carry.

Just before taping began, they were assigned kitchens. He cared that his was within easy sight of Kelsey. Because he didn't like her out in the darkened studio without someone keeping an eye on her. And because he wanted her to be able to see him, to see that he was really trying, that even when he didn't ultimately win, he wouldn't have disappointed her in the moment. She'd know he'd tried his best.

So she'd know it wasn't his fault?

But it would be, wouldn't it? If he wasn't good enough.

Or maybe she'd see how much he loved her and understand that all anyone could ask of her, or of anyone else, was that they tried their best.

Had he tried his best with Lil?

He wanted to think so. Lord knew she'd been a challenge at times.

Maybe he would have been able to successfully convince himself that he'd done all he could—if it hadn't been for one phone call.

One hauntingly, hideous, ignored phone call.

Pleasantly Grinning Home-Economics Teacher with seven kids was the first of the contestants called and was assigned to kitchen one, stage left. Burke's kitchen was stage left, as well. Number two. Which was fine. Kelsey could sit twenty feet away. The way the stage was configured with kitchens for optimal camera angles, stage right wasn't as clearly visible to the small studio audience seating— which for the show's purpose didn't matter as they weren't live.

They couldn't really be, as many of the foods they'd been asked to include would need cooking time beyond the show's hour-long time slot. They had a portion of the hour to prepare their dishes. And then a cut in taping while things cooked. That was their lunch break—from a catered food cart. The last bit of taping would include taking their dishes out of the oven—if necessary—describing what they did without giving up their secret ingredient and tasting by a group of guest judges.

Biker Dude, stay-at-home father of three sons, who cooked for a church kitchen, was stage right. Burke tensed as Natasha looked at her list to see who she'd placed next to Biker. He was certain it was going to be Janie.

Good vibes for the viewers if handsome and beautiful were sharing airtime.

Handsome was married. Janie wasn't the type to get involved with a married man. Funny how it didn't occur to him that maybe Biker wouldn't be the type to go for Janie.

What heterosexual guy wouldn't at least think about it?

Grandmotherly with two kids, six grandkids and a retired farmer husband was called next.

Not that he'd remembered personal information from the week before. Kelsey had been testing him all morning. Wanting him prepared. As though knowing details about his opponents could somehow change how he made his pork. Or how they made their dishes.

Or how much the judges liked any of them.

Manhattan Italian Restaurant Owner was assigned to stage right and walked with confidence to claim his kitchen next to Grandmotherly.

Las Vegas Showgirl with a successful romantic restaurant on the strip was assigned to kitchen four on stage right. She grinned at Italian Guy as she took her place. He nodded back.

Burke let out a breath he hadn't meant to be holding. And glanced out to see a grinning Kelsey. Janie was going to be joining him, stage left.

Along with Bountiful Black Haired, who was a prominent chef in Phoenix.

Kitchens three and four. In that order.

Had their hostess placed her two local contestants in adjoining kitchens for a reason? He turned to Pleasantly Grinning Teacher and tried to remember what kind of art she made in her spare time. Certain that it had been on Kelsey's list.

Certain he could strike up a conversation with her if he could only remember…

"Kelsey's trying to get your attention."

Janie's voice was just off to his left, softer than usual, like she was whispering in class or something.

Since he'd been hearing it in his head all week—with her all the way across town—he wasn't surprised how easily he picked up her words.

While Natasha dealt with some technical issue with the cameras and a light bar, he glanced out to Kelsey, nodding his permission for her to move so that she was in the middle between his and Janie's kitchens. Her call to switch seats was a good one. He could see her more easily.

And Janie was standing there watching the whole thing transpire.

"I told her she couldn't move out of her seat without permission," he said, also under his breath.

Who knew which mikes were live?

"At least until we see how this all works. I don't like the idea of her out in the dark studio alone."

"She could wait in the green room." Other contestants were rummaging around their kitchens. Opening drawers. Re-familiarizing themselves with the layouts they'd seen the week before. "I saw a couple of other family members back there when I went in to get my sweater," she added.

He liked her sweater. Hanging down almost to her knees, with a fashionable gather at the waist, it made her legs look even longer.

"They've got the television monitors on in there now," she added. "And bottled water and tea."

He wished he could get Kelsey to lighten up enough to join other family members in the green room. But was thankful that he'd at least gotten her to acknowledge that if he didn't win today, it wasn't the end of the world. They had three more tries.

Today wasn't the day he'd be failing his little girl again.

"Unless Dawson is here to occupy her, Kelsey's going to be staring at me the entire time we're on the air," he said with a hint of self-pity in his tone. For humor. Mostly. "The monitors, she tells me, will cut back and forth between all of us. Which makes sense."

"She's done this before, then?"

"No!" He shook his head. And grinned, unable to keep a hint of parental pride out of his voice as he said, "Kelsey just likes to know everything about what she's getting into. If she can't find it on the internet, she finds some-one to ask…"

It was nice. Knowing someone on stage. Natasha Stevens called them to silence. To position. And Burke wasn't sweating bullets yet.

JANIE COULD HAVE made her meatballs blind-folded. Literally. She'd made them so many times. Had even helped Cor make them once by simply staying on the phone and guid-ing her friend through every single heartbeat until Cor's perfectly rounded balls were sim-mering in her Crock-Pot.

It wasn't the preparation that worried her.

It was the ending that did that. The part where she was judged. Against all of the other great chefs sharing the stage with her. They had professional experience. Professional cooking education.

She had what she'd learned from Corrine's mother, who'd despaired when her own daugh-ter had been far more interested in debating with her than in learning to cook. Cor had ana-lyzed every word her mother said, growing up. A sign of a great lawyer to be, as it turned out.

This first cooking day was turning out to be as stressful as Janie had feared it would be. Some people cooked by precise measurement.

By instructions on paper. By carefully sifting certain things, separating, mixing slowly or rapidly, adding ingredients slowly or rapidly. Others relied on taste. Janie cooked by her nose. She could tell how good, or off, something was going to be by smelling it.

And her nose was telling her, just moments into that first taping, that some superb, winning dishes were being prepared around her.

Burke left the stage as soon as his dish was in the oven. He'd been completely focused. Hadn't even looked her way as he'd worked. Nor did he as he left.

A crew had been hired to come in and clean up their kitchens while they were on break. Guidelines stated that all entries had to be within a two-hour cooking or setting limit and the crew had that much time to get the set cleaned and ready for the judges.

Depending on her time constraints, Janie had been known to let her meatballs simmer for twice that two-hour span. But two hours would be enough for their flavor to come fully out.

She just wasn't sure any amount of time would be enough for them to win out over other dishes prepared that day.

Burke's in particular. Whatever he'd done

with that pork had been sheer bliss to her olfactory glands.

"I wonder if we'll get to taste each other's dishes?" she said nervously as she sat in the green room, pretending to munch on a celery stick while Burke and Kelsey ate fresh veggie wraps. She hadn't meant to eat with them. But Kelsey had pretty much taken the choice out of her hands when she'd announced that she'd save the three of them the table by the window.

"I hope so," Burke was saying, looking far more approachable than a successful doctor ought to look as he took a large bite out of his wrap. Mayonnaise dotted his upper lip.

Kelsey shook her head. And reached over to get the food off her father's lip. "I was reading that you don't," she said. "Only the judges and Natasha. The rest goes to local homeless shelters."

Glancing at Mike, their biker dad, church-kitchen cook, Janie was glad to hear their entries were going to such good use.

At least her lack of a win wouldn't be a total loss.

Mike was sitting at a table for four with his stage-right kitchen mates.

The others had all pretty much paired up. Grandma and Mike had run into each other on layover in Nashville and traveled the rest of the way together. Janie had heard earlier that while she'd been on the phone dealing with Dillon late the night before, all of the out-of-towners had met up in the bar of their hotel. She'd rather have been having a glass of wine with them.

Janie supposed it was natural that, as the only locals, she and Burke would be outside the core group.

Truth be told, she was kind of relieved she wasn't going to have to socialize with a bunch of strangers as well as worry about winning. And being away from Dawson.

Still...

"Where's Dawson today?" Kelsey asked in between bites.

She told them about Corrine and Joe. Her childhood-best-friend lawyer, who was married to the greatest guy, who also happened to be a successful financial guru. Maybe she'd given them just a bit too much. So she didn't have to eat her celery stick. And perhaps... so they'd know that she had friends in their social class. People who valued her as family.

Who loved her and her son enough to give up their Saturdays so she could be on *Family Secrets*.

Not that either Kelsey or Burke had given her

any indication whatsoever they thought themselves better than her. Just that they thought the recipes they were using were better than hers.

"How's he doing today?" Kelsey asked while Janie's thoughts ran off with her brain.

"He was his usual happy self when I dropped him off," she said, wishing she'd hear from her friend. She didn't like to go for long without being in touch.

She'd texted Cor as soon as she'd come off stage. And was waiting for her and Joe to call. After therapy they'd been planning to take Dawson outside to play with the portable, pint-size basketball hoop they'd bought him for Christmas, and if he engaged, she hadn't wanted to interrupt. Shooting hoops would be a phenomenal hand-eye coordination exercise. As well as helping with the muscle tone in his arms.

Not to mention, it would be a normal little-guy pastime.

Dillon was right. She worried too much about Dawson. Let him consume her to the point of having no room for anything else in her life.

"I would have liked a taste of that pork dish," she said before Kelsey could ask her any more about her son. She'd managed a third bite of celery, too. She really should get herself something to eat. She just wasn't sure the butterflies in her stomach were leaving room for anything else and she didn't want to throw away a whole plate of food.

Kelsey glanced at her father and then down. And Janie remembered what Burke had told her about his daughter feeling bad that he was going to beat her.

He might. That day. But he wasn't going to win the competition. She had a little boy's future at stake. Especially now that she might need money to go back to court.

She had to talk to Corrine about that. Tell her about Dillon's call the night before. Find out her rights. And his. To hear what Cor thought her ex-husband was up to. Before this day was through.

The Carters continued to eat. She tried to think of something to fill the awkward silence. Wanted to ask about Kelsey's week. Burke had told her the other night that Kelsey danced in a junior company at a local studio. He'd also said that she hadn't recovered from her mother's death and wasn't participating like she used to. Janie didn't want to make the girl uncomfortable by subjecting her to an inquisition.

She'd hated that when she was a kid. Well-meaning adults asking her a bunch of questions because they felt sorry for her—the only child of a drunken drug addict.

Glancing away from the girl, she saw Burke studying her. He caught her eye. Smiled.

And the warmth that spread through her helped her relax enough to swallow another bite.

CHAPTER TEN

BURKE FELT his daughter's eyes like laser beams on him as he stood under the hot stage lights next to his deceased wife's pork dish. The bands around him—Lil, Kelsey's needs, his inability to meet their expectations, guilt, accountability, more inability—were strapping him in dead air until he thought he'd strangulate right there.

As he watched Showgirl cross the stage, with a perfectly sexy and confident look at the camera, carrying her dish to the judges, Burke had the thought that if he accidentally cashed it all in, suffocated right there on the stage, it would be a bit too much reality even for Natasha Stevens.

They had five judges to please. A local culinary expert. Someone flown in from LA. Another from New York. A person who was not a food expert and had nothing to do with food service, period. And, of all things, a child. He hadn't cooked to please a child's palate. He'd purposely told Kelsey that he wanted nothing to do with the judges prior to that moment. Didn't want to know how many or who they were. Didn't want them to distract him from his cooking.

Family Secrets was a show based on secret family recipes. It stood to reason that a recipe had to get by the kids to be a true family favorite.

And it wasn't like one vote was going to carry the day. Unless the other four split...

Sweat trickled down his back and he reminded himself, for about the millionth time, that nothing rested on that day. He had three more tries before Kelsey would know he'd let her down.

Three more weeks to get her interested in something else so she didn't fall off her emotional cliff when her mother's recipes didn't go on to become famous.

The remaining contestants who'd yet to present stood in their kitchens. Facing the judges. None of them looked at each other. Maybe later, when they were all more familiar with the process, they'd start to loosen up on stage.

And maybe not. Who knew what they all had resting on this contest.

He didn't want to know.

His focus was Kelsey's emotional health. Period. Giving her the strength to pick up her pieces and embrace life again. She thought she needed her mother's memory living on in the food that would be mass-produced and bear her name in order to make that happen. He kind of thought so, too. But hoped not.

He was the sixth contestant called. Only Janie and Mike were left.

All of the others were lined up on the side of the stage with a camera trained on them. Filming their reactions as they watched the judges' faces. For cameo shots in the final version.

Reminding himself that he cut into bodies and repaired bones for a living—successfully—Burke crossed the stage with his nine-by-thirteen glass pan resting against the pot-holder mitts covering his hands. Concentrating on getting it there without dropping it.

Not remembering, until too late, that Kelsey had asked him to turn toward the camera as he walked so they could be certain the front of his apron would be seen on national television. His walk before the judges was the only time they'd been guaranteed to be part of the chosen footage.

Well, and winning, of course. Each week's winner would get five minutes of camera time, reaction and interview, at the end of each show.

But according to his knowledgeable daughter, the shots could be from the waist up. Or head shots only. It was dawning on him that his kid watched too many cooking shows, or too much TV or something, as he set his pan down before the judges and served them each a sample of his pork on the clean plates they held out.

The stack of plates in front of them had dwindled from eight to two.

Had they already chosen their winner?

Burke felt the slipup before he saw or heard it. But comprehended it at once. The piece of pork slid off his metal serving spoon, bounced off the plate the boy judge was holding out to him and plopped onto the tabletop with enough of a splash to hit the kid's white shirt. Center stage. Of course.

He could hear Kelsey's groan. Whether she'd uttered it or not. Could hear her disappointment. And knew the tears she would shed that night when she was alone in her room.

His mind roiling, he did what any good contestant would. He calmly scooped up another spoonful of pork, placed it on the kid's plate. Gave a head bow. And turned a thumbs-up to the camera.

As though his cooking was so good, no one would notice that he was the only one who'd screwed up that day.

Ha!

Leaving his pan of pork with the show's assistant in charge of getting leftovers to the homeless shelters, he took his place in line next to Bountiful-Haired Phoenix Chef.

"Tough break," she whispered while still facing the camera.

He didn't let his grin slip at all. Luckily the camera couldn't see the sweat pouring down his back.

If he had to have a global fail, he'd rather it be under stage lights than the bright heat of an operating room.

So Lil was right after all. Fitting, that in this moment of crisis, he'd prove it to himself. She'd claimed that his patients meant more to him than his family did.

Little did she know how right she'd been.

No, wait. Lil was the only one, besides him, who did know. For sure.

She'd died proving her point.

SHE'D HAD A text from Cor telling her that Dawson loved basketball. And that they'd taken him for burgers.

Not surprised that Cor hadn't called—her friend was pretty general-like when it came to Janie taking time for herself—Janie stood on stage with her meatballs, thinking about missing Dawson's first basketball game, as the judges tasted the food she'd placed on their plates. She was the last contestant to be judged this week.

And was glad because it meant she didn't have to stand in line with the camera on her for so long. She wasn't sure she could smile that much. Not like Burke. Who was a natural charmer.

Something she needed to remember. He was charming to her because his daughter felt guilty. Because Janie was local. Because Burke was a natural at it.

Not because of her.

She had too much reality going on in her life to let herself be carried away by a fantasy. Of any kind.

So she watched the judges' faces instead. Was certain that at least some of them were pleasantly surprised by her somewhat ordinary dish. She homed in on the ten-year-old boy. He was the one she wanted most to please, figuring he'd be the hardest to convince.

He asked for seconds.

And she could feel the smile rising from within her.

She was going to do this. Her son would get the therapy he needed. She just had to have faith in herself.

THEY STOOD IN a straight line. All eyes were on Natasha as she named each contestant while the camera zeroed in. Reminded viewers what they'd prepared for this first episode of the current *Family Secrets* reality cooking show and then looked at her list.

"You've all scored well," she said. "Not one of you received an 'I didn't like it' from the judges."

Burke stood as directed, smiling with anticipation at the camera because if he didn't he'd hear about his lack of effort nonstop from Kelsey over the next week. And because he really did want to win for her and would do whatever he could to up his chances. Inside he was rehearsing the motivational speech he'd be giving his thirteen-year-old miracle all the way home. Reminding her that it was only week one. That meat dishes weren't her mother's specialty.

He didn't look at his fellow contestants. Probably wouldn't have been able to see them under the staggeringly bright lights anyway.

"The time has come to announce week one's winners!" Natasha sounded like she had Christmas presents for everyone. His gut tightened. He fine-tuned his Kelsey speech.

"First…"

He almost swore out loud. And hoped the

tension didn't show on his aching face. Just in case, he widened his smile with completely posed anticipation.

"Though they didn't win, the judges found a couple of your dishes impressive enough for a formal mention."

There. He'd take that. Lil's pork was definitely worth a mention. Even his rendition of it.

"Shondra Estes. Your bacon-wrapped smothered chicken…"

What? Bountiful Black Haired was a better cook than Lil? Not that hairstyle had a thing to do with cooking. It was just that he'd seen her kitchen. It looked like a tornado had hit it. How any flavors had managed to stay contained and not contaminate each other as they flew around her space, he'd never know.

"And…"

Okay. Here it came. His look of anticipation wasn't faked as he waited…

"Janie Young! Your meatballs received high praise from all five judges…"

Something inside him leaped. Janie! Good for her!

And…

There must be one more…

"That brings me to today's winner…"

He didn't even get an honorable mention… not an easy fit into his motivational speech.

"And that is Mike Wrenchfort! All five judges agreed your medallions were to die for!"

Mike stepped forward. The rest of them relaxed. They'd been told to maintain position for the next couple of minutes for a pan or two, but then all cameras would zero in on Natasha and the winner.

"I can only imagine how much the people your church feeds adore you." Natasha gushed well.

Burke couldn't fault her there.

Or anywhere else. He'd known he wasn't a winning cook.

Somehow he had to convince his daughter that her life was worth living happily without her mother's recipes going viral. He hoped that he'd find a way to be better at that task than he was at cooking.

"It's just the first week, Dad." Kelsey met Burke before he was even fully off stage and stayed glued to his side as they made their way to the green room and his locker to collect his keys. With Mike still on stage, the overall mood of the group appeared to be low-key. A couple of people were congratulating Shondra and Janie.

"I'm happy for Janie," Kelsey said, glancing over at her. "I really hate that she's not going to win and at least she'll know that her cooking's really good."

He got his keys and headed for the door in record time. He wasn't even sure why he was in such a rush. He just had to get his daughter out of there. Get back to the life they were slowly carving out with each other.

"It's not like she won't have other chances," Kelsey said as they turned out of the lot. "I mean, she's young. And alive."

Obviously. But he knew what his daughter meant. Lil's chances were dwindling while Janie had her whole life in front of her.

"I…" He didn't know what to say to her. Felt the failure of his ability to even get a mention as an almost unendurable weight. Like his life was spiraling out of his control.

Or Kelsey's was.

Same thing in his book.

Her hand touched his arm on the rest in between them. "It's okay, Daddy," she said, her voice softening. "It's just the first week. And meat was never Mom's specialty. We knew that going in. You still have three weeks to make it to the finals. Remember, next week is dessert and Mom's Buckle is the best there is. Hands down."

Her strawberry pie was pretty stellar, too.

So much so that the recipe was currently on the menu in the fine-dining restaurant of a five-star hotel.

He nodded. Glanced over at Kelsey as he waited for the bar to rise that would let them out of the gated lot. "You're a pretty smart kid," he told her.

"I know." She grinned. "And that's why when I say we're going to win this thing, I know we are!"

He wanted to believe her. To have that grin a regular occurrence on Kelsey's face, he'd move any mountains he could move.

But he wasn't Hercules.

He was the guy who'd ignored his wife's phone call when she'd needed him most.

CHAPTER ELEVEN

CORRINE OPENED the door to Janie before she'd raised her hand to knock. She'd called her friends to let them know she was on her way.

She hadn't told them she'd lost the day's competition. She hadn't needed to. They'd have known by her squeals that she'd won. Lack of squeals told its own story. Corrine glanced at her, nodded at Joe, who disappeared into the house, and then took her hand, pulling her into the little room filled with books and claw-footed furniture and a tea set in the middle of a coffee table. They settled in the cushioned bay window, looking out over the luscious green of a golf course and a lake in the distance. Closer to the house were Cor and Joe's fruit trees, a beautifully landscaped pool with a rock waterslide—and off to the side, Dawson's new half-size basketball hoop in its plastic stand.

The oversize window seat was Janie's "safe" place, she'd once confided to her friend. Back when she'd been pregnant, learning how to raise a child with Down syndrome and going through a divorce.

"It's only the first week, Janie." Cor's voice was firm.

She needn't have bothered.

"I know. And I got an honorable mention," she said, smiling. "Second only to the winner, actually! Over all those folks with professional cooking jobs and credentials! The meatballs are a snooze in terms of my abilities," she continued. "I really think I can do this, Cor. Or at least now I'm starting to believe that I really have a chance."

Corrine jumped up. Squealed. And hugged her. "Why didn't you say so? Your tone of voice when you called, you sounded so worried, I was sure that you lost and that I was going to have to force you to go back next week…"

"What's going on?" Joe came to a halt from a half run as he reached the doorway, frowning and smiling at the same time. "I thought…"

"She got honorable mention!" Corrine said. "Second out of eight!"

Joe insisted on popping the cork on the bottle of champagne they'd picked up that afternoon, just in case. "And when Dawson wakes up from his nap, he and I will go to Giorgio's for takeout," he continued, naming the same Italian restaurant Burke Carter had referred to the week before. Janie had an instant thought that maybe Burke and Kelsey would be having dinner there, too. Or maybe, with the loss, they'd be back in their kitchen, working on next week's recipe.

"No way you're slaving in the kitchen tonight after that hard work," Joe was saying, with Corrine nodding next to her.

She took the champagne. Laughed out loud when her friends continued to show their love. And agreed to stay to dinner, too.

Because she had to talk to Cor. The lawyer, not the best friend. She couldn't afford another sleepless night.

"WHAT AM I going to do?" Janie hated the helplessness she heard in her voice as she and Cor sat on the couch in Corrine's tea room while Joe and Dawson were getting dinner.

"You're going to let me talk to a friend of mine and not talk to Dillon again until I get back with you."

She nodded. But said, "If he wants to see his son, I can't deny him."

"No, probably not. Not without ample proof that Dawson would be in imminent danger with him and…"

"Dillon would never hurt Dawson," she

said. Knowing in her heart that the words, in and of themselves, were true. "Not in any way that the court would see as causing harm," she said. "Not without some long court case that would have to set precedent for a lack of therapies hurting a child, or some long-term proof of the effect of Dillon's general coldness where Dawson is concerned…"

She might not have a law degree, but she'd been Cor's friend for a long time. And done a lot of reading, too. She wasn't schooled, but she was smart.

"I know we can argue that he hasn't taken on visitation in four years' time…"

"But he's paid his child support."

"Once you beg for it."

"He'll be able to prove to the court that he's paid in full." Who was the lawyer here, her or Corrine?

Still, Janie's heart was warmed by her friend's avid defense.

"The truth is, Cor, Dillon's not a bad guy overall. For years he was a much-loved part of our foursome."

"Until he showed us what a creep he was…"

"In his defense, I did the changing, not him. I wanted a child. He still didn't."

"That may be, but you didn't get pregnant

on purpose. You didn't trap him, like he told Joe."

No. It had just happened.

She'd been asking him to consider having a child. To just think about it.

And when she'd turned up pregnant, in spite of them doing as they always had in the prevention department, she'd taken that as a sign that it was meant to be.

"He felt so trapped," she said now. Understanding Dillon's feelings even if she didn't like them.

"Again, not your fault. Or Dawson's."

No. But Dillon considered Dawson to be all her fault. The short arm and leg bones, Down syndrome indicators, had shown up on her first ultrasound. The doctor had given her the option to end the pregnancy. Given her and Dillon—the doctor had strongly urged his presence at the meeting—statistics of the numbers of Down syndrome pregnancies that were terminated in relation to the numbers that were not. She'd been staggered.

Dillon had been elated. Though, to give him a small measure of credit, he'd managed to show sympathy to her, too, as he knew how much she'd wanted a child.

The pregnancy, whether she'd continued it or not, had ended their marriage. He'd seen how badly she'd wanted a baby. They'd both known he wasn't going to willingly be a father.

But she hadn't been able to terminate the pregnancy. Medical recommendation or not. It wasn't about debated issues. Rights or wrongs or beliefs. It was just something she could not bring herself to do. Her heart cried out at the thought.

"Can you see our boy over at Dillon's?" she asked Corrine, feeling the threat of tears and forcing them back. "The noise in the garage will have him covering his ears and screaming, and you know as well as I do Dillon will never stand for that. He'll punish him, and Dawson won't understand and…"

She started to shake.

"I can't picture him doing any of Dawson's therapies, either. Not that a day or two off would hurt all that much."

"It will if Dawson's emotionally a wreck when he comes back. And it sounds like he could want to start enforcing the standard visitation order, which would mean one night a week and every other weekend."

She'd never spent a night away from her son. Not once in four years.

Not that that was any reason to hold Dawson back if the prospect in front of them would be good for him.

But she knew, deep down inside, that it wouldn't be.

"If Dillon wants to see Dawson, I have to let him," she said now. Something she'd known, in her heart, too, since the night before. "He's Dawson's father. He has legal rights."

But she'd needed to talk to Cor. First.

And she was getting through the muck in her mind to clarity. To know what she'd really needed from her friend.

"I have to know why he really wants to see him," she said, looking at Corrine. "He's still with Wendy. They're living together. As much as he abhors the idea of having a child, she'd also have to be someone who doesn't want children. He'd never be with her otherwise."

He hadn't asked Janie to marry him until he'd known for sure she didn't want children.

She'd been barely an adult. Having children was the last thing on her mind. Hadn't thought she'd be good at raising one. Most particularly if she'd been "blessed" with her mother's lack of mothering instincts.

Corrine put her glass of tea down on a painted wooden coaster. Focused on her.

Janie could tell the second when she made the switch from friend to shrewd lawyer.

"I was thinking this was just another one of his stunts to make you pay for ruining his life's plan."

She nodded. "I wanted to think so, too." He'd pulled some doozies over the four years since Dawson's birth. Including trying to use his power as Dawson's father to have his son institutionalized. He'd dropped the whole thing when he'd realized she could use the information he'd been collecting about Dawson's needs and cares to take him back to court for more child support...

"But it doesn't make sense. Dillon doesn't get satisfaction from anything that puts him out." And keeping Dawson would definitely cramp her ex-husband's style.

"What makes even less sense..." Corrine's face grew shadowed. Janie's stomach tightened. Their minds often traveled a silent, but similar, road.

"He's embarrassed by Dawson's 'differentness.'" Corrine said what Janie couldn't. "There's no way he'd have him around the people he hangs with unless he thought there was something big in it for him."

She'd been unable to completely land on

the theory herself. Though she recognized it, felt the familiarity of it, as Cor said the words.

"What does he stand to gain?"

And it hit her. "As stupid as this sounds... I'm on TV," she said. "He has no way of knowing how much money I could make. And if I hit it big..."

Dillon had always been about money. Working all hours of the night and day to make as much of it as he could. Telling her, again and again, that money would make them happy.

Their shared interest in making money had been the bonding factor between Joe and Dillon from the first time Corrine and Janie had introduced them to each other.

"If he takes enough of an interest in Dawson's life, he could petition for some kind of partial custody, and with you making enough to cover your expenses, he could try to petition to have your decree changed to get out of fourteen years of support," Corrine finished.

Janie wanted to leave it at that. It was bad enough. "This is Dillon we're talking about. His financial plans are always on a grand scale, if you recall. I could see him trying to get close to Dawson with the idea that at some point he'll sue for full custody—Dawson being a boy and all, and me busy with being so successful—and then sue me for support.

Maybe that's a bit out there, but I can't get over the sense that he wants to use Dawson to somehow get part of my supposed fortune…"

"He can't do that, honey." Corrine squeezed her hand. "The law doesn't work that way."

She knew Corrine was right. But right didn't stop her from being uneasy. Dillon felt robbed. Cheated. She'd forced him to be the one thing he'd never wanted to be—a father.

And then she'd rubbed salt all over his gaping wound by having a child that was less than perfect in his father's eyes.

"Maybe the law doesn't work that way, but since when has the obvious ever stopped Dillon. Tell me you can't see that as his motive."

Corrine started to speak. And stopped. Picked up her tea and took a sip. "You want me to have Joe try to talk to him?"

Of course she did. Who didn't want an army protecting their back? Even an army of one? When that one was Joe, it could have the same effect as a dozen.

"Not yet," she said. "Dillon will just lie to Joe—you know that. Like he did when he told him that I teased and lured him into a state the night Dawson was conceived. That I'd planned the whole thing."

"I was thinking more along the lines of Joe setting Dillon straight on a few things…"

Janie was already shaking her head. "That will only anger him more. You know that."

"I hate that he's such an idiot when it comes to trying to come up with ways to make a quick buck. Why didn't we see that about him before?"

Corrine had known Dillon as long as Janie had.

"We were young, his energy was compelling, and his belief that he could succeed was… sweet. I loved that he was always willing to try…"

She'd loved that he wasn't interested in partying, getting drunk, taking social drugs, like so many of the kids their age.

Unfortunately, they'd all grown up.

"If I win this thing, Dillon's going to see it like I'm robbing him of the fortune he'd have been a part of if he'd still been married to me."

Why hadn't she thought of this aspect before?

And if she had? Would it have stopped her? The answer to her silent question came in the form of a resounding no.

"If he'd still been married to you, you wouldn't have been desperate enough to force yourself to apply to the *Family Secrets* cooking show."

Corrine was right. She'd never have dared to take such a chance on herself. Not for herself.

Only for Dawson.

And now, somehow, she was going to find whatever strength it would take to deal with Dawson's father. Again.

For the very same reason.

For Dawson.

CHAPTER TWELVE

"JUST CALL HER, DAD. What would it hurt? If she's too busy, or doesn't want to, that's cool, but at least we tried."

Burke was thankful for the cover of darkness as he drove his daughter home from the dance studio Tuesday night. She'd been after him since Saturday to try to set up another get-together with the Youngs. She wanted to see Dawson again.

"I feel so bad for her," Kelsey was saying. "Living in that little house. Working so hard. If it wasn't for Mom, I'd want her to win. But this is Mom's only chance. So I was thinking… maybe I could offer to babysit for her for free or something sometimes. While she's doing the stuff she does at home. Maybe. Or something."

Kelsey was talking. Not sulking. And not putting the pressure on him by constantly discussing ingredients and practicing, either.

Problem was, she was a bit too hyped up for his liking. She'd always been a happy kid. With plenty of energy. But she hadn't been one for extremes. Either highs or lows. That was what they had to find. Happiness without the manic part.

"You're nervous, aren't you?" he asked as she fell silent. And was a little proud of himself for figuring *something* out. "And you don't want to make me screw up by putting pressure on me."

It shouldn't have taken him three days to figure it out.

Her eyes glinted with moisture as he glanced her way. They were stopped under a streetlight.

"We've only got three tries left, Dad. What if...?"

"You counting me out already?" he asked her as steel bands of disappointment closed in around him. Trying to save her in the moment while knowing he was setting her up for bigger disappointment.

What in the heck was he doing? Leading her on when he knew he wasn't going to win.

But when he'd seen the glow of life light her face for the first time in months, how could he not?

They still had time for a miracle. Like, maybe she'd enjoy being out and living life enough over these next weeks that she'd find a way to stay out.

And maybe, just maybe, he'd be good enough, long enough, to win this one for her.

The light changed and he pushed on the gas. Harder than necessary. Kelsey looked at him.

When had he started to hope? Did he really think he had a shot? Could he maybe provide what Kelsey needed?

"I'm not counting you out." She sounded like her mother. A Lil from the early years when he'd been flogging his way through medical school and some days her encouragement had been the only thing that had kept him going. "I'm just trying to think about other things so I don't make it harder on you."

"I like it when you're hard on me."

How was that for an admission?

"You do?"

"Mmm-hmm." He nodded, staring at the road in front of him as he spoke the complete truth. In spite of incredible discomfort. "Keeps me focused."

Lest he get so caught up in his career that he put his patients ahead of his family.

Her silence drew his attention. She was staring straight ahead, too. "It also lets me know that you care," he said softly.

She glanced at him. Smiled with trembling lips. And then said, "You aren't by any chance trying to work me over so that when you're telling me what to do I'm supposed to think it's because you care, are you?"

She almost confused him. Not quite, though. With all the time they'd been spending together lately, he was getting a tad better at keeping up with her. "I don't work you over, period. You know that."

"Sorry."

"And you already know that I tell you what to do because I care."

"Yeah."

Feeling like he'd won—but not sure what the victory really was—he sat back. Thought about a hot shower and a few minutes with a game on his tablet before bed. After dinner. And the trial run on Buckle that was scheduled for that evening.

"I can call her if you don't want to."

Oh, good Lord. That again. She wasn't giving up.

"I'll call her. But don't blame me if she says no."

"Tonight? Will you call her tonight?"

Reaching out to Janie Young was right up there on the list of things he most certainly did not want to do that evening. The woman…got him going. Like she was asking something of him that he didn't have to give.

Which was crazy because she was the most self-sufficient, independent individual he'd ever met. When she'd told them that day in her home about working two jobs—only because Kelsey had seen all the papers spread on her table—and then talked some about Dawson's schedule and tried to explain away the sheets sitting on the chair, he'd wanted to fix that, too.

He'd asked if there was anything they could do to help—not that he could think what it would be. He was just being polite. At least, that was how he explained to himself the odd need to reach out to her.

But her look of insulted shock, like he'd suggested they get naked and dance in the rain or something, had stuck with him.

He wondered what the phone version of that look would turn out to be.

FEELING LIKE SHE was walking a tightrope, Janie put Dillon off for a week. When she'd called him on Monday, as promised—because she'd known that if she didn't he'd not only call her, but be in a less amiable frame of mind—she'd given him the story she and Joe and Corrine had come up with late Saturday night.

That they'd already purchased tickets to a children's theater production that was in town only that Saturday. They'd all three been on the internet looking for some valid excuse, but it was Joe who'd found the show and bought the tickets.

Still, her heart jumped up and felt like it stuck in her throat when the phone rang just after nine Tuesday evening.

Dillon had actually been decent when she'd told him about Saturday's plans. He hadn't pushed for an evening visit. Had said he'd call her soon, to set up something.

She'd half expected him to call back with a changed mind.

The number on her caller ID wasn't her ex-husband's.

"Hello?"

"Janie? It's Burke. I hope this isn't a bad time…"

Her heart continued to pound. Just not in fear. Or dread.

She told her fellow contestant that the time was fine. Telling herself that he was absolutely *not* calling her for a date. Reminding herself she had no time in her life to date…

"Kelsey wanted me to call and see if we could, perhaps, have another meet-up this week. She's taken with your son and…"

Kelsey. Of course that was why he'd be calling.

"I think Dawson's been asking about her, actually," she told him.

"You think he has?"

"He's got a new sound. The word is one he uses often for a couple of things, but the sound that accompanies it, it's one I don't know. He's said it many times since you were here. And waits for a response every time." She sounded like an absolute idiot. At least to anyone who didn't live in her world.

"I imagine he hears and sees a lot of things that he tries to communicate." His voice was warm. Engaged.

Because he had good bedside manner? Or because... She didn't know what she wanted him to be.

"He says it every time he picks up that purple frog that he gave Kelsey to hold." Just because Dawson didn't communicate in plainly discernible English didn't mean they didn't have their own, understood, language. She'd been signing to him since he was born, but had tapered off a lot in an effort to get him to use his vocal muscles to communicate.

"He had fun with her." She paused, weighed how much she should say and then figured what the heck. "It's not often that he has people here to play with him."

"We're free Thursday night."

"I can make dinner. Something simple, not competition worthy."

"We had frozen pizza tonight."

"But you practiced for Saturday, didn't you?" He'd made mention of Kelsey's zealousness.

"Of course."

She wanted to know how it went. And didn't want to know because she needed it to have gone badly and didn't want to wish ill on him.

"I think we should set the ground rule that we don't mention cooking or the competition while you're here," she said, figuring again that she must sound completely inane to a distinguished doctor like him.

"You have no idea how glad I am that you said so. We're just two people with kids who want a playdate."

Playdate. She'd had a couple of mothers from preschool suggest playdates between their children. It was time to start branching out. She just didn't have the time or energy to pursue the idea yet. And figured Dawson got enough "other kid" stimulation at school.

But she'd just hinted to Burke that Dawson would like to have someone to play with at home. Something she hadn't yet admitted to herself. Partially because until she'd seen him with Kelsey, sharing his favorite toys with her, she hadn't known.

Janie shook her head. Overwhelmed. And yet…oddly energized, too.

Life was coming at her and Dawson—change—and she was going to have to engage with it.

They set a time. He didn't hang up.

She asked him how Kelsey was doing. General conversation. A parent asking about another parent's child. Not expecting, at all, the response she got.

"Truthfully, I'm worried sick about her."

She sat on the edge of the couch. "What's wrong? Is she sick?" He'd lost his wife. She didn't know the circumstances. Was there something genetically wrong? Something that was going to take Kelsey's life, too? Was that part of why she was having such a difficult time recovering from her mother's death?

Not that any child would have an easy time with something like that. Not even her. As horrible as life with her mother had been—she'd loved her.

"No…" His pause made her second-guess her immediately compassionate response. "I told you she's been struggling…"

"Yes." She didn't want to say the wrong thing. Too much or too little. And wondered at herself. She'd long since quit caring what people thought about her. It was how they treated Dawson that concerned her.

"She's bordering on clinical depression." His voice had dropped to a near whisper. "I'm sure she doesn't want me talking about this and, frankly, I'm not sure why I am. I've never been one to confide in people, but…"

Suddenly feeling as though she was in her own world, she said, "Anything you tell me is safe."

"She's become almost reclusive. You and Dawson are the only ones she's been normal around in months. She's like her old self when she's around you. And when we're home cooking," he added.

"What about at the dance studio?"

"She has friends, but last week she turned down a solo that I know she wanted. And she's still spending way too much time staring vacantly at the television or in bed. She's already asleep now. It's an obvious escape mechanism."

"I'm guessing you've taken her to see someone…" He was a doctor. He'd know what to do.

"Of course. They're recommending medicating her. She's refusing. And, frankly, I don't want to start down that path, either, unless it's absolutely necessary. There are side effects and, while I know the risk is minimal, I just…"

He was a doctor. He'd know more than most that the one in a million did happen.

"Nothing is without its price," she agreed, thinking of the number of times she'd had to make tough choices in Dawson's care. From surgeries and preventative measures to school integration and therapy theories.

"I just… Her mother always handled the emotional, girlie things," he said. "I'm out of my depth here, but I'm all she's got."

"I get that," she told him, pulling her knees up to her chest. "You love them so much. More than life. More than you ever thought possible to love anyone. Far more than you love yourself. You'd die for them, but if you did, they'd be all alone. You give them everything you have. Gladly. Spend all of your days doing all you can. And you feel like no matter what you do, it won't ever be enough. You won't be enough…" She heard herself and stopped. What was she saying? This wasn't about her…

"Wow." The one word spoke millions. And warmed her in a way she wasn't sure she'd ever been warm. "You sound as though you've spent a week in my skin."

Chuckling, trying to lighten the moment, she said, "Try four years in mine."

Burke asked what time he and Kelsey should be at her place for dinner. They discussed schedules. Homework and Dawson's bedtime. She asked if Kelsey liked boxed macaroni and cheese. It was Dawson's favorite, though he was a pretty good eater overall.

He offered to pick up some barbecue from a family-owned carryout that had expanded into catering due to its success.

She told herself they were just two parents talking about their kids. A thing normal parents did.

Told herself he wasn't a man to her. Just a parent.

That he wasn't someone who occupied her thoughts for any reason other than her son liked his daughter and his daughter liked her son. That the sound of his voice only resonated within her because she didn't have a lot of interaction with other parents.

And tried, constantly, to forget that Burke Carter was her opponent in the biggest stakes she'd ever faced in her life.

CHAPTER THIRTEEN

BURKE COULDN'T DENY that he was looking forward to Thursday's dinner. At work he was completely focused, his mind consumed by the people who trusted him to make and keep their bodies well. Wednesday was generally reserved for surgery and he had two back-to-back knee replacements followed by a torn ACL to repair.

Working gave him peace. He was good at what he did. Knew he did it well. He didn't feel, when he was at work, that he wasn't enough.

There were times, like Thursday morning, when medicine wasn't enough. When there was no cure. When he looked at a report expecting one thing only to find another, much worse scenario. His job then was to give hope. To look at best case while delineating worst case, as well. And to give a referral for further testing and treatment he was not equipped to provide.

He knew he'd done all he could, but still

felt saddened as he saw the young patient out. And, in an attempt to clear his mind, and his heart, to find his upbeat bedside manner before seeing his next patient, he thought of... dinner that evening.

More particularly the woman who'd be providing that dinner. Who'd invited Kelsey and him to share it with her and her son.

Janie Young had already, albeit reluctantly, had his attention. After Tuesday night's conversation...she was on his mind constantly. He was attracted to her, certainly. That was an easy admission. He found a lot of women attractive.

But it wasn't her body that was consuming his thoughts. That he could have shrugged off as normal. He was a guy. Guys noticed beautiful women. Most particularly when they remained beautiful even after all the paint and primping came undone.

It wasn't Janie's body that warmed him the most, though. It wasn't really her mind, either, though he was intrigued by how intuitive and quick she was no matter what topic he raised. How even when she didn't know a lot about something, she showed an interest, a willingness to listen and an ability to understand that seemed genuine. Like when, before they'd hung up the other night, he'd discussed that morning's young patient with her.

In vague terms only. More accurately, he'd discussed a condition, testing and the hoped-for diagnosis, when she'd asked him if he could come for an early dinner, and he'd found himself giving her an overview of his case-load for the day.

Much like he'd done with Lil. Until his wife had let him know that the details weren't important. She only needed to know when he'd be unavailable and when he'd be free. And where he'd be—at the hospital doing surgery or across the street at the clinic that housed his practice.

Burke didn't dwell on any of that as he took five in his office, with the door shut, to recover from the news he'd had to deliver to a teenage boy and his parents. If the basketball player was lucky, he was only going to lose his foot…

Burke's gut feeling was that they'd caught the problem in time. But he hadn't been able to give definitive answers. Or make any promises.

He felt as Janie had described. Like he gave his all. Did all he could. And sometimes things were completely out of his control.

He wanted to talk to her more about that

particular circumstance. To hear how she dealt with life when things happened she couldn't control. That was what attracted him to her most. Her ability to see the heart of things.

And, maybe, a small secret part of him wanted to know if there'd ever been a time when she could have made a difference—and hadn't.

But that night, after dinner, when Dawson took Kelsey's hand and dragged her down the short hallway to his room, Burke didn't ask Janie the questions he wanted to ask as he helped her clear the table and dried the dishes as she washed them.

In jeans and an old black sweatshirt, with her hair falling out of her ponytail and minimal makeup, she looked—great to him. A woman he'd look forward to coming home to. Beautiful and real at the same time.

He thought she should have a dishwasher. But saw no place in the small kitchen where one would fit.

And then thought about the fact that Janie had to cook every meal in that home alone. Wash and dry all of the dishes. And his need to know why finally won out over his warning to himself not to get too close.

"Clearly you're single, but what about Dawson's father? Isn't he in the picture?"

Her hands froze in a pot of soapy water. The macaroni pan. She'd had it soaking. Saved it to last.

Burke had nothing else to dry until she washed that pan. Standing there, damp towel in hand, he looked at her bent head and wished like heck he'd kept his mouth shut.

THE WARM WATER calmed Janie. She told herself it did. And willed her heart rate to slow down.

Burke Carter was not taking a personal interest in her, despite the intimacy of the situation. The two of them standing together in her small kitchen, her washing while he dried, asking personal questions as though they had every right to do so...

Not that his question was really all that personal, given the situation. Or at least, it wasn't at all unusual. Personal to her—normal coming at her. Burke wasn't the first person who'd asked. He probably wasn't even the hundredth.

She'd been dealing with that exact question, regularly, for four years and six months. Had a rote answer that stopped the questioning every time. *He's unable to be present in Dawson's life.*

Could be in prison. Could be dead. Or could just be a man who was emotionally unable to deal with having a son who had Down syndrome. She didn't say. Not one person had ever asked…

"Funny you should ask," she found herself saying. He'd confided in her when, clearly, he wasn't used to confiding in anyone.

She told herself that was why, after too long a pause, her tongue didn't follow through with *He's unable to be present in Dawson's life.* Not sure how to proceed, she scrubbed the pan. Rinsed it.

And when she reached to put it in the drain board for him to pick up, he cut her off. Taking it from her. Holding her hand where it held the pan, until she looked up at him.

In a polo shirt and dress pants, he looked ready to go golfing or something. Except that his gaze was completely serious. And intent on her.

"Why is my asking funny?" He wasn't smiling at all. His brown eyes compelled her to talk to him. Maybe more so because that thick blond hair was such a contrast to them. She liked that he kept his hair a little longer than might be the current style. Thought about how it might feel if she ran her fingers through it, lifting it off his forehead…

And knew too many seconds had passed. Pulling away from him, Janie passed to his other side and reached for the plates he'd stacked. "Because for the first time since he heard I was pregnant, he's expressing a desire to see our son."

She could feel his gaze on her. Feel heat creep up her skin, as well. She put away the plates. Reached for the cups—plastic because of Dawson—and put them away, too.

"I have questions."

She nodded.

"I don't know what to ask first."

Was he asking permission? She didn't give it. But she didn't deny it, either.

Silverware belonged in the appropriate slots in the drawer.

"Dawson's father has never seen him?"

"That's right." Three knives. In the knife slot.

"You weren't…together…with him?"

In today's world, people had sex on first dates. Not her. But enough that Burke wouldn't be remiss in wondering.

"We'd been married a little over seven years when I found out I was pregnant." Four spoons in the spoon slot.

She wanted him to know. And had no explanation for that.

"Dawson's four."

Natasha had said as much, as had her bio

in the contestant packet they'd all received the previous Saturday.

Forks done, she shut the drawer. "Right."

"You got married twelve years ago."

"Yep." Without meeting his gaze, Janie took the pan from him—careful to avoid his hand as she did so—and, bending down, put it in the drawer under the stove with the other pans.

"You must have been a young bride."

"Six months out of high school."

Drawer shut, she rinsed out the sink. Wiped the counters. And couldn't think of anything else to do.

Burke was standing, feet crossed at the ankles, leaning against her counter. His musky scent sabotaged her attempt to keep him just a parent. She could not see him as a man. For so many, many reasons.

Marrying Dillon had been self-destructive. No more chasing dreams or believing in fantasies for her. She couldn't afford the distraction.

More important, Dawson couldn't afford for her to be distracted. His chances of leading an active, productive, fully functioning life depended largely on her. She had a selfish mother. She would not be one...

She was not going to follow her mother's

example. She was going to put her child first. Period.

Dawson made her happier than she'd ever been in her life and—

Burke leaned toward her. His lips touched hers. Briefly. Lightly. And were gone.

"What was that for?" She stared up at him. Not sure she hadn't imagined the contact.

"To get your attention," he told her, but she had a feeling that wasn't the complete truth. He looked a little surprised himself. "You'd drifted away, and by the expression on your face, you'd gone to an unhappy place."

The man was…

She didn't know what. But she didn't want to turn away from him.

"Dillon didn't want children."

"Dillon. Dawson's father?"

She nodded. Holding Burke's gaze now. She told him about thinking, before she got married, that she'd never want children, either— though she didn't go into the whys of that one. She told him how, over the years, her feelings on the matter started to change. But Dillon's hadn't.

"He didn't want a well child," she said softly. They could hear Dawson and Kelsey down the hall. And the sounds of a video game. But still, she was careful. What child should know, ever, that his own parent had rejected him?

"When the doctor told us, during the first trimester, that Dawson had Down syndrome…"

"You had an amnio?" She remembered she was talking to a doctor.

One who'd just kissed her. Sort of.

She nodded, slowly, trying to keep a hold on her bearings. "The ultrasound showed short arm and leg bones…"

His nod told her he understood. She told him about the horrible meeting with her obstetrician. And the ultimate outcome.

"He left you. Right then and there. Three months pregnant with his child."

"It was better than staying and filling our home with the silent anger that had been slowly growing inside him. Dillon was completely up-front with me about not wanting to be a father. He knew he wouldn't be a good one. I was the one who changed."

"Sometimes you don't get to choose what happens to you in life," Burke said, close enough to touch her. Close enough that she could feel his warmth. "Sometimes you have to stand up and face what you're given and do your best."

She wanted him to kiss her again. For real.

And gave herself a mental shake. No, she

really didn't. She honestly and truly did not want that complication.

She had a shot here to give Dawson the future he deserved. Not just the resources for extra therapies, but the time and the ability to take him to the sessions, to be available to participate in them as necessary.

She was going to ask Burke if he wanted to sit down. To join her in the living room. Suddenly that seemed too comfortable. Too much like he was a closer friend than she could have him be.

They were opponents—both determined to win—and her son's future rested on the outcome.

And they were parents whose kids had wanted to see each other. He'd be leaving momentarily. It was almost time for Dawson's bath.

Dinner was what they'd arranged.

And dinner was over.

CHAPTER FOURTEEN

BURKE KNEW IT was time to go. But he wasn't ready. Standing in Janie's kitchen, he glanced at the clock on her stove. Fifteen minutes yet until Dawson's bath time.

And she wasn't kicking him out.

"So, about Dawson's father... Now that Dawson's a little older, this... Dillon...wants to get to know him," Burke said. "Do you think time has matured him?"

He couldn't let it drop. Couldn't just go home to his life and leave Janie to hers.

Guys deserved second chances—though this guy was debatable in Burke's book. Burke might have screwed up when it came to supporting his wife through her pregnancy, but he'd never, ever, turn his back on his child.

"No. But he's Dawson's father. He pays his child support. And he has rights." Janie's voice had changed. Her whole demeanor had changed. Grown more distant.

Because of feelings dredged up by memories of the past?

Or because he'd kissed her?

It had been a stupid thing to do. Beyond stupid. If he'd thought about it, he never would have done it. Problem was, for the first time in a very long time, he'd acted without thinking.

"So you're going to let him see him?" He didn't like the idea. At all. He didn't know Dawson well, but it was clear the little boy needed to be cared for with kid gloves.

She shrugged. "I don't think I have a choice."

"I'd think you'd have the right to make certain that he's prepared to care for a special-needs child."

"He's only asking for him for an afternoon at this point. Dawson might not like going, we might have some emotional backtracking to do when he gets back, which will affect therapies, but it's not like one afternoon's going to ruin his life, either."

"So you're okay with him going, then?"

"Absolutely not." The unequivocal response did something to Burke. Filled him with some kind of protective need he was sure he shouldn't be feeling.

"What about your parents? What do they say? I assume they know him."

When she shook her head again, that sensation inside him strengthened. "My father left before I was old enough to remember him. And I haven't seen or heard from my mother in years."

He was out of his league here. Dealing with a walk of life he'd never taken. "You don't speak to your mother?"

"I don't even know if she's still alive." How such painful words could be said with so little emotion told a story Burke had not been prepared to hear.

"She left you, too?"

Janie shrugged, crossing her arms over her chest as she leaned back against the cupboard opposite him. "In a fashion," she said. "She's a drug addict. Heroin when I was younger. Later it was meth. The last time I saw her, she was being led off in handcuffs and so high she didn't seem to realize what was happening. She's been in and out of jail since I was in high school. Over the years, we lost touch. I can't really say either of us left the other. There just became a time when staying away from each other was a mutual choice. I had a good, clean, decent life. And she was never going to stay away from the drugs."

"What about your friends?" he asked next. "That couple who kept Dawson last week. You said they were his godparents, so I'm assuming they knew your ex-husband, too. What do they think of this?" He'd overstepped his bounds too far to go back. Even before the kiss that shouldn't have happened.

"They don't like it any better than I do. Corrine's been in touch with a lawyer friend of hers. I can refuse to let Dillon see Dawson and then he can take me to court for not abiding by the standard order. At which time I'd explain that Dillon has never even seen his son and he'd be required to explain to the court why he's had this sudden change of heart before I'm forced to abide by the standing order…all of which will cost me money and time I don't have.

"There could be a friend of the court assigned to Dawson, whose job it would be to visit my home and Dillon's, to interview both of us, but because, other than not seeing his son, Dillon's not a bad guy, he'll probably be granted the right to rectify his wrong."

"When does he want Dawson?" He was fact gathering now. As though he could have some effect on the outcome. Him, a stranger to this family.

"Saturday."

"While you're at the competition?"

"Yes."

It was as though she was trying to become a stranger to him again, and he didn't like it. At all. Mention of the competition only intensified the feeling.

He remembered, too late, that they'd agreed not to mention it. But… "Don't you think that will affect your ability to do your best?"

Which could help his own chances, but that did not make him feel any better about the idea.

He had to beat her if he could. Kelsey needed the win too badly for him not to win if it was at all possible.

But he didn't want to beat Janie when she was down. Or because she was down. He just wanted the judges to like Lil's recipes better than they liked Janie's.

He could see why she needed the win… It would ensure Dawson's best chance at reaching his full potential.

But money from another source could do that, as well. And he had a bit to spare—

"I've already told Dillon he can't have him this Saturday."

Janie's words broke into his racing thoughts. She'd started with something like "not this week."

"Oh. Okay. Good." His relief was genuine. He'd analyze it later. And then, "How did he take it?"

"Fine." Arms crossed, she still wasn't meeting his gaze as she told him about Joe buying tickets to the children's theater.

And he instantly thought of the little boy on camera during the Thanksgiving *Family Secrets* show. Of the woman who'd had eyes only for that little boy. Even when she'd been on stage getting her award. It had been all about Dawson.

When he started to envy the boy, he pulled himself upright. "They're taking him to the theater?" he asked, glad to hear Dawson could enjoy such an event.

Janie's shake of the head could have surprised him, but it didn't.

"None of us even considered doing it," she told him. And then continued, almost as though issuing him a warning. "Chances of Dawson sitting still in a seat for an hour and a half are minimal. Add to that the fact that he'd be in the dark in a strange place in close proximity to a lot of people he doesn't know, and then add in the concert-level volume, and you have a sure recipe for disaster."

Her life wasn't easy. He got that.

But did he get that being a part of even a minute of her life meant taking on Dawson's challenges, too?

Because, other than when absolutely necessary, she went nowhere without him?

He asked the questions of himself. But felt as though they were coming through her to him.

He'd kissed her. Did he want to be her friend?

And was he willing to take on Dawson, too?

She hadn't asked. He didn't answer. Didn't know the answer. But suspected neither of them would like it. He was drawn to Dawson. But he couldn't be sure he could meet his own daughter's needs. How could he possibly take on another child's?

As a man who'd failed his family—and inadvertently caused his wife's death—he'd already put his soul in debt. And couldn't afford another bill in that department.

"He's got tubes in his ears and is very sensitive to sound," she was saying as though purposely adding bricks to the wall between them. "When his ears start to hurt, he covers them and screams the same word over and over. But even if that didn't happen, he doesn't understand that he has to sit quietly.

At the very least, Joe and Cor would be pretty much guaranteed the shame of disrupting a nice afternoon for whoever was unlucky enough to be seated around them. And anyone they had to pass by in order to make their premature exit. It's not fair to do that to people who've paid good money for a fun afternoon with their kids."

HE WANTED TO be appalled enough to grab Kelsey and run. He wasn't appalled. He was just…sorry. So sorry.

For so many things. For things that were in his control and those not on him at all.

"So Dawson just misses out on even having a chance," he said, commiserating with her. Trying to imagine the heartbreak of knowing that your child didn't get the same opportunities as other children.

Heck, he'd been upset last year when the dance solo Kelsey had wanted had been given to someone else.

"Oh, we take him to things," Janie said, surprising him again. "Joe and Cor are taking him to the theater on Saturday. Before the show starts. Some of the characters are going to be out front welcoming the kids. If Dawson wants to get close, he'll have that chance. And they'll walk him around a bit, let him experience as much of the theater as he wants to. We're acclimating him—a kind of therapy, I guess—in the hope that someday he'll actually get to stay and watch the performance."

Burke thought again of the Thanksgiving *Family Secrets* show. And how Janie had been so distracted when her name was called. She hadn't heard because she'd been so busy helping her son maintain his equilibrium through the experience.

"I had to get up and take him out three times during the forty-eight minutes of taping for the Thanksgiving show," she said, as though she could read his thoughts.

At that point he wasn't even surprised they were traveling on the same wavelength.

"But I'd already alerted Natasha to my situation and they were prepared to redo some taping if need be."

"They didn't have to?"

"Nope." She sounded proud. And he smiled. Thinking how naive Kelsey and he must have seemed to her, suggesting that Kelsey could watch Dawson during the current competition. "But he's always much better when he's with me. He's secure, and that helps a lot when he's being attacked by sensory unknowns."

She looked Burke in the eye and a spark ignited within him. Something new. Unfamiliar.

It was time to go.

CHAPTER FIFTEEN

ON SATURDAY MORNING Janie's life unraveled once again. Dawson was up, fed, dressed and his teeth were brushed. She'd showered, dressed in her leggings and long, thigh-length, off-white sweater with the thick leather belt at the waist. And was zipping up the black leather boots Cor had insisted she borrow. She just had to do her hair—Cor thought she should pull it up in a twist with a gold clip and then wear the big gold earrings Cor's mother had bought her for her eighteenth birthday— and her makeup and she'd be ready to go.

With an hour to spare.

She was dropping Dawson off earlier this week—wanting more time at the studio to get her mind fully in the game. Last week's loss—but honorable mention—had been a start. She had three weeks left to solidify her spot in the final round—to guarantee her at least a chance to compete for the winner's circle.

Her dessert was scary in its simplicity. And

yet it was her most requested dish. She'd made it up in high school and had won the Best Recipe of the Year award in her home-economics class. The prize had been a ten-dollar fast-food gift certificate. With pineapple, strawberries and bananas, cream cheese, sugar and whipped cream and her homemade graham-cracker crust and topped with chocolate shavings, she'd simply made what she'd wanted to eat one day. And because she'd spent so many of her days home alone by then, she'd had no one to sway her from her less-than-stellar diet...

Dawson ran in carrying her phone and handed it to her. She hadn't heard it ring, but he always did. And knew right where in her purse she kept it.

It was Cor. Janie smiled. Her friend was making darn sure she didn't feel like she was doing any of this alone.

"Janie?" The second she heard her friend's tearful voice, Janie knew life had just changed again.

"What happened, Cor? Is it Joe?" He was young. In great shape. But things happened and...

"It's Beanie." When Cor started to sob, tears sprang to Janie's eyes. "What happened? Where is she?" Corrine's second-youngest sister was most like Cor—and was one of the little ones she and Cor had helped raise during high school. Beanie was the only one of Cor's eight siblings who'd ever stayed with her and Joe.

"Janie?" Joe was on the line.

"Sorry, hon," he continued. "We're heading to the airport. We're on our way to Chicago. Mom called half an hour ago. Beanie's been in a car accident and they aren't sure she's going to make it. We're on the first flight out…"

"Go," Janie said, sinking down onto the edge of the tub. Dawson was back in the living room. She could hear him losing another life on his video game.

"But Dawson…the show…"

"I'll take him with me," she said.

"I thought maybe, if you called Dillon… Or…if you wanted me to call him for you…?" Joe sounded sick to his stomach even as he made the suggestion.

"It's okay, Joe. We'll be fine."

Beanie was dying? Who cared about dessert? She'd have two more weeks to win. And if she lost…it wasn't the end of the world. Corrine losing a sibling was.

"Cor's worried about you. The show means everything to your future and she says she'd rather die than hurt your chances."

"You tell her that I'll be fine." She hadn't told Corrine and Joe about Burke. Or Kelsey. She wouldn't even let herself think about why that was. But she did tell Joe there was someone at the studio she could ask to help her with Dawson.

Someone Dawson had met.

It was a testament to how worried and frazzled her friend was that he accepted her answer without a single question. She'd probably have to answer to Corrine later.

But at the moment, later didn't matter.

"Tell her I love her, Joe," she said, crying now. "And let me know as soon as you find out anything. Text me as soon as you're with Beanie."

"We will."

"And, Joe?"

"Yeah?"

"Hold her tight, okay? Corrine's tough, but this will do her in."

"I'm holding on as tight as I can," he promised her. And rang off.

Sitting in her bathroom with the silent phone in her hand, Janie shook. Hardly believing what she'd just heard. Beanie dying? She should be flying to Chicago with Cor and Joe.

But Dawson couldn't fly. The cabin pressure was excruciating to his ears.

And Cor was counting on her to continue with the show. Her friend would blame herself if Janie didn't go. Even without Joe's comments to that effect, Janie knew her best friend well enough to realize how much the mother hen prided herself on watching out for her flock—giving to them, not taking from them.

And knew that the only way she could realistically give to Corrine right then was to go to the *Family Secrets* taping and make the best darn dessert she'd ever made.

She just hoped Dawson would be able to cooperate enough to let that happen.

With her precious boy, one just never knew.

To say that Kelsey was excited when Janie called to ask if she'd be willing to keep Dawson company during the taping would be an understatement. He worried about her being manic again. The depression and then an almost giddy high.

Don't borrow trouble, Dr. Dad, he admonished himself.

The girl was dancing around the kitchen just like she had before her mother's second pregnancy.

Why that particular memory rose to haunt him, Burke didn't know.

But because he was carrying around so much mental baggage, he tried to let the memory go. And when he couldn't, he dealt with it.

"You were excited to have a new baby brother on the way, weren't you?" he asked on the way to the taping that morning. If ever there was a day his daughter was in a good frame of mind for a difficult subject, it was then.

"Yes." She nodded. That was all. He'd expected more. Needed more.

"Because I was thinking about it this morning and for some reason it occurred to me that you kind of grew up that day we told you about him. You got a bit quieter." He was talking to her like she was an adult.

In some ways, she'd been made to take on adult problems. And he had only another couple of weeks to either win a cooking show or get close enough to the root of her depression to have a hope of them dealing with it without the need for medication.

"Or maybe I'm imagining it."

She didn't say anything. Not about his observation. But she wasn't chattering about Dawson Young, either.

Or Lil's Buckle. Which he'd made again the night before to her approval.

"You aren't imagining it, Daddy." He'd driven a mile in silence before her words set his mind reeling again.

They were to meet Janie at the studio half an hour before the contestants were required to arrive. Hoping to get Dawson settled in with Kelsey in the mostly empty audience.

In addition to his usual traveling things, she was going to include extra toys and a tablet with video games as well as boxed fruit drinks and snacks that Dawson liked.

Kelsey had also collected a bag from home of things she thought they might do. He'd gotten a little emotional with pride in his daughter when she'd included a flashlight in case Dawson got scared of the dark and some cotton for his ears if the sound got to be too much.

Dawson didn't like things on his ears, she'd told him. As she'd discovered when she'd tried to help him put on some headphones sitting with the music player in his room.

You aren't imagining it, Daddy.

He waited for more, but didn't push her about her comment. And pulled into the parking lot of the studio with a five-minute silence between them.

"I was jealous." Her words were so softly uttered, he had a hard time deciphering them. By the time he had, she had tears in her eyes. "I'm so sorry, Daddy."

"Sorry for being jealous?" He wanted to take her in his arms, but wasn't sure she was open to the coddling. Most days she'd give him a quick hug goodbye in the morning and that was it. "It's an expected reaction," he said. "I'd say a kid who didn't feel some moments of doubt, when they were being told they had to share the two people who were their whole world, is a not normal kid."

He thought they'd talked to her about that. About how the new baby belonged to all three of them. How her place in their hearts would always be her place. Only her place. Lil had told him that she'd had a long talk with Kelsey and that they were all good.

She shook her head. "I'm not sorry about being jealous," she said. "I'm sorry because I wasn't as sorry as I should have been when he died with Mom."

Just…*hell*. He was in hell. He'd had no idea.

But recognized the guilt. And wanted to take her on his lap and keep her safe from life's turmoil and confusions and hurts.

Making a mental note to talk to Kelsey's counselor, he said, "You have nothing to be sorry for, sweetie." He was the one who'd failed. And he prayed she never found that out.

He was living a lie. And yet...if she knew, she'd never be able to let herself love him. She'd never let him care for her.

And he couldn't do that to her. She needed him.

Long term. But right this minute, too. Thoughts came to him. He didn't analyze, didn't have time. He just spoke. "You need to trust that your heart was guiding you then as you needed to be guided," he told her, with no idea where his words were coming from. "You were buried in grief for your mother," he reminded her. And cringed. He was supposed to be distracting her from that grief. "Your psyche, your heart, knew that you couldn't handle two losses. So it allowed you to be sorry for the one you knew best. It allowed you room to grieve for the person who'd always been by your side, every minute of your life. And let you off the hook for the one you'd have loved but didn't yet know."

Tears were dripping down her cheeks. But she was holding his gaze.

"You really think so?"

"I do."

She nodded. But didn't unbuckle her belt.

So, though he could feel time ticking—and had already seen Janie's car in the lot—he sat there, too. If Kelsey needed to leave, they would.

A minute passed. And then five. She wasn't crying. He'd brushed her hair from her forehead a time or two. She'd grabbed his hand and was holding on.

"Daddy?" she asked after several more minutes passed.

"Yeah, baby?"

"You think Mom can see me taking care of Dawson?" Her eyes were wide as she stared at him. "I mean, like really, not all that woo-woo pretend stuff that people tell you."

She wanted to know if he believed in angels? That they all *became* angels when they died? Or if souls could look down in the afterlife and see those they'd left behind?

He had no idea.

"Maybe not as you and I would see it," he told her. "But, yes, I believe she knows."

She nodded. "So if she knows I didn't love her baby as much as she did, if she knows that I wasn't sad that she took him with her, me caring for Dawson, it will show her that I'm still a good person? Someone she could love and be proud of?"

Holy, holy. He'd had no idea. And some things were suddenly so clear.

"I think she already understood," he said now. "But, yes, I think she likes knowing that you're helping Dawson."

"Because he needs me, Daddy. He doesn't have a lot of friends and he likes playing with me. Every kid needs someone they like to play with. You know?"

She had it all figured out. And it was working for her. "I do," he told her. He'd just had confirmation it was as Kelsey's counselor had said. Her self-concept was all wrapped up in her mother's opinion of her, and with Lil dying so unexpectedly at such a critical time between Kelsey's childhood and growing into womanhood, his daughter was stuck in a no-where land. Trying to find herself through the eyes of a woman who was no longer alive.

"And when Janie loses, at least she'll have some new friends in town and we can help her with Dawson and make her life a little easier, too."

He thought of the kiss he'd given the woman Thursday night. Had thought of it far too often in the thirty-six hours since. He'd thought of her responsibilities, too. The way her life was all wrapped around that boy of hers. A boy who'd already had one man reject him. Thought of the way he'd failed his own family. And the risks he could not take.

But it had always come back to that kiss. Something was telling him that he and Janie weren't going to be able to be just friends.

And anything more was out of the question. For both of them.

Burke wondered, as he and Kelsey finally got out of the car, where this was all going to end up.

Most particularly if he didn't win.

As he walked beside his daughter, a young woman he would give his life for without hesitation, a cloud of dread hung over him.

CHAPTER SIXTEEN

"KEE! KEE! KEE!" Dawson's husky grunts alerted Janie to the fact that she and her son were no longer alone in the green room. She'd shown Dawson around the studio, audience portion and backstage, explaining what ropes and cameras were for, pointing out stage lights not yet illuminated. She'd told him how they had to be so bright so when they went home and watched on TV they could see everyone on the stage.

She didn't know how much he understood—probably not as much as a typical four-year-old—but she knew, in his own way, he took in what she was saying. And made his own sense out of it, too.

She'd introduced him to the techies milling around, getting everything in order. Had hoped to reintroduce him to Natasha, but the show host hadn't yet arrived at the studio.

"Kee! Kee!" Dawson said again, pulling at her hand. They'd just been getting ready to sit at the table by their locker, where they were going to roll a couple of his cars back and forth to each other.

Kelsey and Burke were walking toward them.

Letting go of Dawson, she watched as he ran toward his new friend and hugged her around her thighs. "Kee."

"That's the sound I told you about. When I thought he was asking for her," Janie said to Burke, hoping she was doing a successful job of covering the awkwardness she felt at being so happy to see him. She would not look at his mouth.

And was afraid to meet his gaze, too. Afraid that she'd start to cry.

They were on set. Opponents.

And even if they weren't, she needed to stand on her own. Because she didn't have time to invest in anyone new in her life.

"I'm so sorry to hear about your friend. Have you heard anything more?" He didn't seem to get the unspoken message about them being just opponents. And parents.

She shook her head. "Just a text that Cor and Joe are on the plane and will let me know when they land. I just got off the phone with Cor's mom a few minutes ago. She called me from the hospital. They don't know anything more yet. They haven't even seen her as the doctors are still working on her. But initial assessment is that it doesn't look good."

With a finger under her chin, he lifted her face until she couldn't help but see the compassion shining from his gaze. "If they're still working on her, there's still hope," he said. It wasn't until that second that she remembered he was a doctor. And would know what he was talking about. His professional life was so far removed from the man she knew, and the venues in which she knew him, that doctor was just way down on the list for her.

"Thank you." She tried to smile.

"You going to be okay today?"

She got absolutely no sense that he was asking as anything other than a friend. She needed a friend.

She nodded. Breaking contact with his finger. And missing it.

BURKE'S BUCKLE WENT together quickly. Basic homemade cake batter, a layer of fresh blueberries, cinnamon and butter mixture on top of that. He had to get it together quickly because he needed forty minutes for baking. There were no breaks for oven time in that week's competition as there had been for the meat segment. Toward the end of that time he'd make the icing and then had to get it swirled with ten minutes to set before he could cut and serve. Making the icing too soon would cause it to harden. Cutting the Buckle before it set would cause the dessert to ooze and judges would have to scrape their plates to get the full effect. They might or might not do so.

Whether Lil knew these things or not, Burke did. Because he and Kelsey had discovered them together as they'd worked on the dish that week. The three nights they'd cooked, Kelsey made lists on note cards and she'd tested him on them each morning on the way to school. And again this morning over breakfast.

Until the phone had rung and sent her running off to her room to pack up things for her time with Dawson.

The camera wasn't going to be zoning in on him standing in his kitchen while his dessert baked, so as soon as he was finished, he quickly exited the stage through the tunnel between two set walls, as they'd been shown to do, and made his way to the green room.

Janie hadn't asked him to check on their kids. Most particularly Dawson. Once they'd taken their places on stage they hadn't even looked at each other. As had been the case the previous times they'd appeared on camera as contestants.

It was like they were trying to pretend they weren't opponents.

He looked through the window at the top of the door before entering. Wanting to observe without being seen. One end of the room had a couple of couches and some chairs in a conversation area centered around two mounted television monitors. Several guests of other contestants were sitting there, some conversing, some not.

And at the other end of the room, still by their locker, his daughter was lying on the ground with Dawson Young sitting on her stomach. Kelsey's head was propped up with what looked like a cushion from one of the couches. Both of them were watching the television monitor.

His chin tightened as emotion welled within him. Two very special kids. Both with needs that a win on *Family Secrets* could assuage. Both of whom deserved that win.

And only one of them could possibly get it.

Turning around, he went back to the set.

JANIE WHIPPED AND FOLDED. She rinsed and dotted. Sliced and diced.

She was doing the best that she could. Her

little "sister" could be dying. Janie's Delight—as everyone had affectionately termed her dessert all those years ago—just didn't speak to her as it always did.

And she couldn't see Dawson.

She'd been assured by everyone from adult guests in the green room to stagehands that she'd be notified if there was a problem with her son. She'd agreed to disqualify herself from the day's competition if the problem prohibited her from finishing her dessert preparation on time—a legal requirement—and even Natasha had said she'd be glad to help if she could. The nation had fallen in love with her son.

Her nose was clogged from holding back tears and she couldn't smell. Were there too many strawberries compared to bananas? She couldn't tell.

She'd explained to everyone that Dawson was not good around a lot of people he didn't know. And that once upset, total chaos could break loose. People knew not to crowd him. And she knew that many willing and responsible adults were keeping an eye out.

She had no reason to worry. Her son was with the "playmate" he adored. She just wished she could check in. Today's experience was new to Dawson.

She melted and she mixed and crushed. Pressing her version of a graham-cracker crust into the chilled, square, glass dish, she cooked to find calm, to slow her heart rate, not to compete. It wasn't that she was conceding defeat. She wasn't at all.

Cor and Joe should have landed. No phones were allowed on the set. And it wasn't like she could do anything from Palm Desert anyway. Or like Cor was going to need her immediately no matter what she found. With seven siblings and her parents there—as well as Joe—her friend would be well held within the loving arms of her family.

Cream cheese spread expertly on top of the crust. Fruit looked perfect. And the whipped-cream topping lay beautifully beneath the chocolate shavings. Janie slid the dish into the freezer for the fifteen or so minutes before serving time. A trick she'd learned years ago when she didn't want to wait for the dessert to fully set in the refrigerator.

Purposely avoiding eye contact with any of the other kitchens or their occupants, she hurried through the tunnel to the hallway off the studio. Keeping her pace less than a run, she made her way to the green room. She wasn't going to go in. She couldn't chance upsetting

Dawson by leaving again so soon. But she had to see her son.

To know that he was safe and happy.

He and Kelsey were sitting at the table eating the graham crackers with peanut butter she'd packed for him. Drinking from identical juice boxes.

"How are they doing?"

Jumping, as though guilty of some wrongdoing when she heard Burke's voice behind her, Janie turned slowly. "Seems just fine." She looked him straight in the eye. "I can't thank you enough, Burke."

He shook his head. "And I can't thank you enough, either. You have no idea how being with Dawson is helping Kelsey…"

He could just be saying the words to be polite. She didn't get the feeling he was just being polite.

"This is my third time back to check on them," he added. And told her about seeing the two of them watching the show from the monitor, with Dawson sitting on Kelsey's stomach.

"I hope he didn't hurt her!"

Burke glanced in the window over her shoulder. "I didn't realize she remembered it, but I used to watch television with her that way. Usually if Lil was out for the evening and I was babysitting. I'd try to get her to lie down with me, but she couldn't see the television. I was afraid I'd fall asleep and she'd wander off, so I'd settle her on my stomach, where I'd feel her move if she tried to leave. Turns out having her there kept me awake."

She glanced at him. And knew without him saying any more that he was struggling, too. More so this day than usual, if she wasn't mistaken.

"You want to talk about it?" she asked.

He glanced at his watch. "We have to be back on set in five."

How could she have forgotten, even for a second, where they were? Who they were?

She nodded. Turned to head back. He grabbed her by the elbow. "But, yes, I'd like to talk about it. Can I call you tonight?"

Her heart pounded. And not because they were about to meet the judges. Meeting his gaze, she let herself stay there a second. Connecting with another soul. With him.

She nodded.

And hurried back to her kitchen.

FOR A MAN who'd always been pretty calm and collected, who'd won an award for the steadiest hands in medical school, Burke was decidedly not calm as he waited for the judges' results.

Kelsey had handled his loss fairly well the previous week. But she'd been in bed early every night since, other than the night they'd been at Janie's. And, clearly, she had an avalanche of conflicted and confusing emotions inside her.

She was getting professional help. But counseling could only do so much. And her psychologist had determined that they'd reached a need for chemical intervention.

The cooking show was having an effect on her. Bringing serotonin back to her system naturally. And maybe some oxytocin, too. If he could just get a win…keep the hope going…they could relax for a few weeks, let the good chemmies flow and maybe build up enough of a positive flow inside her that they could cope with an eventual loss.

Thinking about brain chemicals while the judges huddled and then gave their final decision to Natasha, Burke found a measure of calm. Lobbing himself back to medical realm toned down the dopamine surging from his brain. He had enough anticipation running through his system to last him pretty much forever.

And it wasn't all about the judges, either.

He'd made a date with Janie. To talk about things that really mattered. To share intimacies far more private than the physical kind.

The thought made him nervous as a schoolboy. He wasn't an intimate kind of guy, which was partially why he was struggling so much to understand his daughter. It wasn't that he didn't have heart. He did. As much or more than the next guy. He could do compassion. It was just the whole "talking about feelings" thing...

Analyzing was more his style.

It was time to announce the day's winner.

At Natasha's urging, Kelsey had walked Dawson into the auditorium. The show's producer wanted him there enough to have gathered everyone's agreement for a re-taping of the final segment of the day's shoot if something went wrong with the boy that made the original unusable.

Burke understood it was at least partially about the ratings. Dawson had helped the Thanksgiving show a lot. And had probably added to viewership of this competition, as well. The camera had already panned over the kids once that he'd noticed.

He supposed it could be argued by some that Natasha might consider throwing the results and have Janie win just so that their viewers could get another chance to watch Dawson's glee when his mother was once again featured on stage.

Burke wouldn't join that camp. Not because he was becoming friends with Janie and her special young son. But because Natasha Stevens ran a tight ship. She didn't strike him as a producer who would risk the success of her show for one season's ratings. Not when it was already doing just fine on its own.

And since she wasn't network owned, she didn't feel as much pressure to play games. Ultimately she answered to no one but herself…

Second runner-up…

He wasn't really holding his breath. But he inhaled slowly, so as not to miss the name. If he could just get the honorable mention, he'd buy another week for his daughter to build up those good mood juices inside her brain…

Amber Kendrick—the Las Vegas showgirl— was named for her chocolate lava cake. He'd smelled it baking. Wasn't surprised.

She was, though, based on the tears in her eyes and the smile stretched across her perfectly made-up face.

Honorable mention with highest honors— almost a tie with the winner this week. He didn't really think it could be him—not almost tying with the winner—but he hoped...

"'Janie Young'!" Natasha read, grinning as she smiled at the line of contestants. "All of the judges agreed, Janie's Delight was superb."

Burke broke out into applause. And when he remembered where he was, why he absolutely should not have done that, he just kept clapping. Acting like he knew full well what he was doing and meant to do so.

If the cameras had panned to Dawson, they quickly moved back to the set as the other contestants in line joined in his absurdity and started clapping, as well. Everyone laughed. Spoke to their neighbors.

His faux pas had released a load of tension.

Natasha was smiling.

He couldn't see Dawson and Kelsey because of the bright lights straight above them, but he didn't hear any adverse human noises, so he assumed all was fine.

Chuckling, Natasha's announcement of the winner was almost anticlimactic. And quick. No drama. No buildup.

Just, "The winner of today's dessert contest is Burke Carter."

He nodded. Was kind of sorry he'd stolen the winner's thunder. And then realized what

Natasha had said about the same time he heard Kelsey's extremely loud, extremely high-pitched "Woo-hoo!" coming out of the darkness.

He couldn't believe it.

His prayers had been answered.

He'd won.

CHAPTER SEVENTEEN

WITH JANIE AND BURKE both in the winner's circle, Natasha wanted footage with Dawson and Kelsey. Kelsey led the little boy up the steps, but then he let go of her hand and ran to… Burke. Hugging his knees. While Janie watched, completely nonplussed, and maybe somewhat pleased, too, Burke swung the boy up and onto his hip. For the footage.

It was over in seconds. Dawson reached for Janie almost the second after Burke had picked him up. And Natasha called "cut."

Still, Janie had a feeling the moment would be ingrained on her heart forever.

Kelsey wanted Dawson and Janie to go out to dinner with her and her dad to celebrate Burke's win.

Janie just couldn't do it. Not because she was sorry he'd won. Not because she begrudged him the win.

But because she was worried sick about Beanie and because Dawson had already been out all day, was tired and starting to unravel.

It might not have appeared that way. But in her heart she knew, as she drove her and her son home midafternoon, that the reasons she'd given the Carter duo had been the full and complete truth.

She wasn't sorry Burke had won.

Every time she relived the second when Natasha Stevens had called his name, she smiled. It was pretty much the highlight of her day.

Her second-in-a-row, almost-win honorable mention came in closely behind. If nothing else, she now knew that even without schooling or credentials, her recipes, and preparation, were worthy of professional praise.

Maybe, if the worst happened and she didn't make it to the finals, and then win, she could at least use the honorable mentions to get her recipes out there. And then who knew what could happen?

Realistically, not much, she conceded to herself as she pulled into her drive and glanced in the back at her sleeping son. She'd have to wake him.

Hopefully he'd go right back to sleep and finish his nap. If not, their afternoon did not bode well.

The internet was filled with superb recipes that were completely free. Where once she could have hoped for a cookbook sale to a major publisher to make her a lot of money, that avenue was pretty much less a possibility than a win on *Family Secrets*.

She'd had a text from Cor. And one from Joe, too. They were at the hospital in Chicago. No one knew anything. Beanie had been taken into surgery to relieve pressure on her brain. Other injuries were not even being tended to unless she made it through the first procedure. Then they'd reevaluate.

No one in the family had seen her.

It was going to be a long night.

For all of them.

BURKE DEBATED WHETHER or not to call Janie for about five seconds after Kelsey was in her room for the night.

He didn't want to rub in his win. Most particularly when he'd pretty much figured how much winning the final competition on *Family Secrets* would ease the burdens in her life. Next to a cure for Down syndrome, he figured she probably didn't think anything could help more.

She didn't know about his ideas, though. They ranged from finding a way for Kelsey to donate some time to her and Dawson, to setting up some kind of fund for her—one that he financed but she wouldn't know that.

He might not be able to fix Kelsey's problems with his money, but he could fix the ones Janie was obviously trying to obliterate with the win on *Family Secrets*.

His ideas were not why he called her. He called because, quite simply, he couldn't sit in his home, thinking of her in her home— alone—with no one who even knew what she was going through. No one who understood how badly she was hurting and how hard it was for her not to be with her "family" during their time of crisis.

He also couldn't quit thinking about how cranky Dawson had been as she'd put him in his car seat in the studio parking lot. He'd fought her on fastening the belt. And had been hollering something at her as she'd shut the door.

He couldn't imagine living that way. And hated that she had to do it all alone.

All afternoon and evening he'd been thinking about that. Thinking about what kind of person could handle what she'd been given. He admired the heck out of her.

Not because she wanted to tend to her son. He'd want to, as well. Would do everything in his power to do everything he could. He just didn't see himself being successful at it. He'd reached his limit and he'd checked out.

Lil's death had taught him that.

Which was why he was so…frantic…to help Kels. He'd rather die than check out on her. Every day he promised himself that he would be enough—be what she needed. Somehow he was going to help her. Be there for her. Do the right and best thing.

Tonight, though, while Kelsey slept, he could call Janie.

HER PHONE WAS by her shoulder, right where she could grab it, when it rang. Lying back in her bathtub, soaking in a hot pool of lavender-scented bubbles, with a glass of iced water and a couple of pieces of cheap milk chocolate beside her, Janie closed her eyes.

Her hands, on the sides of the tub, were dry. Ready to grab the phone when Cor called. The doctors had given the family a three-hour window in which they expected Beanie to be out of surgery. That window had opened twenty minutes before.

Within ten, her stomach was in knots.

And because she'd determined that as Dawson's sole caregiver that night she was not going to consume alcohol, she couldn't sip on the glass of wine she might have used to calm her down and instead opted for the tub.

Hot water and lavender had become her crutches over the past almost five years. She admitted her addiction to them openly to herself.

And she sent up heartfelt requests to the great unknown that had seemingly left her high and dry for pretty much her entire life. Other than giving her Cor and Joe, Cor's family, and Dawson, of course.

So maybe she was the one who'd left her high and dry. She'd chosen to marry Dillon after knowing him only six months. She'd sworn off having children before giving herself a chance to grow up and find out if she wanted them.

If anyone was listening in the great unknown, she begged them to watch over Beanie. And all of Cor's family. And sent a request for Kelsey Carter's care, too. The girl had been a godsend to Janie that day. She'd never known anyone, other than Cor and Joe, who seemed to get Dawson so well. Or to honestly care about him so much.

She tried to ask for other things, but, as usual, her mind wandered. Back to the time when Beanie had been expelled from her high school typing class and, while admitting wrong and apologizing, had refused to go back to class until the teacher had apologized to her, as well.

Cor and Janie had both been appalled. Beanie had received her apology before class the next day.

And she remembered a night when she'd been staying over with Cor and Beanie had crawled into bed with them. Beanie had been about six at the time and had had a bad dream. She'd said that only Corrine and Janie were scary enough to make the monsters go away and had snuggled down between them.

She and Cor had lain awake worrying about being scary. And had finally decided that they were scary to Beanie because they made her mind. And figured that was a good thing.

The fact that the little girl had been sleeping soundly between them had helped ease their hurt feelings a bit, as well.

Her heart leaped when the phone rang and she sprang up—grabbing it before it pealed a second time.

It wasn't Cor. Or Joe.

"Hello?" She answered it anyway. She'd been playing mind games with herself on and off all evening. Would he call? Or would his win distract him from whatever he'd needed to talk to her about?

They were at different levels now. She could be out after the next two weeks. He was going to the final round. With Mike.

But then, they'd always been at different levels. She lived at a near poverty level. He was upper class.

She'd still wanted him to call.

"Are you free to talk?"

Every time fear for Beanie, worry or despair, came over her that afternoon and evening, she'd told herself he'd call. And had felt better.

"Yes." Climbing out of the tub, she wrapped herself in her thick, toweling robe, pulled the clip out of her hair and let it fall around her shoulders and down her back. "I'm just sitting here waiting to hear from Chicago."

He asked her how that was going. She told him what she knew about the surgery.

"It's delicate," he told her. "Usually a last resort. But not hopeless. Most particularly since she's so young. And I'm assuming in overall good health."

"Yeah."

He didn't sugarcoat things for her. Didn't really tell her anything she didn't already know—though he expounded on the medical details she had. And…some of her tension eased. As though Beanie was now in his hands, too.

"I'm sorry you didn't win today."

Letting the water out of the tub, Janie made her way to her kitchen. To put on a kettle for tea. And took a deep breath, too. She hated it when people felt sorry for her. How much did she have to do to prove that she didn't need pity?

That she wasn't pathetic. Or pitiful.

"I'm glad you did," she told him. Meaning it. His win would be good for Kelsey. Hopefully good enough to sustain her when her father didn't win the final round of the competition.

"You got another honorable mention," he pointed out. She had a feeling he'd rehearsed what he was going to say. Like he had to build her up.

Building her up was not his job. Nor did she want it to be.

"Yep." Truthfully, she was fine with the day's events. The fact that she could be as out of it as she'd been that morning, as distracted and worried, and still get second best was a huge compliment to her recipes. She'd left the studio with more hope than ever that she was going to win this thing.

"You're the only competitor to be in the top three both weeks."

She'd noticed. "Yeah."

Water on, she reached for her favorite cup—because of the brightly colored flowers on the front—and placed a tea bag inside. Normally she used the bargain stuff she could get at a dollar store. But Cor had put a box of wonderful English tea bags in her stocking and she still had a few left.

"How's Kelsey tonight?" she asked him. She didn't want his pity. But she didn't want him to hang up, either.

"For the first time since her mother died, she suggested that we rearrange the family room, putting Lil's rocking chair off to the side rather than in front of the television where it's been. Every night it sits there empty. Now it's empty at the side of the room."

"Wow. That sounds major."

"Not as major as another trip she suggested we make. To take the boxes I'd filled with Lil's clothes and things to a donation center."

"All today?"

"I could be wrong here, but I think it's been building in her, this need to clean out and start over, but she's been unable to let go. The show's giving her a way to honor her mother, to hold on to what Lil cared about most, to help Lil's dream come to life, and by doing so, she can finally let go of the things that are gone."

"Like her mom ever sitting in her chair again or wearing her clothes." Janie sat at the table, in the chair closest to the stove. Waiting for the whistle that would soon be coming.

She could use the portable microwave on her counter to make tea. She preferred it the old-fashioned way.

And she wondered if Kelsey would regret that trip to the donation center if Burke didn't win the final round. Hopefully, *when* he didn't win it. Because Janie had to.

"How are you with all of that?" she asked.

"Fine." He sounded like it. "I'd have done it eighteen months ago."

She wasn't sorry to hear he'd moved from grief to living again. For his sake, she hoped. Not her own.

"That didn't sound right," he said next. And she wondered where he was. If he was sitting in the dark. In his living room or somewhere else. If he was watching the television or computer screen while he talked to her.

Dillon had always had something else going, no matter whom he was talking to. Always watching stocks. Trading. All over the world.

Which meant there was something to watch all day every day.

If they'd had the money, Dillon would have gone to college, gotten a degree in finance, just like Joe. He probably would have made a mint.

Instead he'd taken over his father's garage. And had grown it to two times what it had been.

"It's not that I want Lil out of the house or out of our lives. It's just…our marriage… It wasn't what… Lil had become something of a hypochondriac, always thinking something was wrong with her. And yet she'd never take so much as an aspirin for a headache. She didn't like me to touch her anymore. At all. Said she was always afraid I was going to find something wrong with her. The night she got pregnant, it was our anniversary."

Wow.

The kettle's whistle was sounding, had been, and she hadn't noticed. Janie got up to tend to it.

And longed to have the right to Burke Carter's touch.

She shook her head. No. Poured her tea. She'd crossed a line and was crossing back.

There were some things you just didn't think about.

CHAPTER EIGHTEEN

"Do you?" Only because she was sitting in the near dark all alone at the end of a hard day did Janie allow herself to ask the question teasing her mind in the seconds since Burke had told her of his wife's aversion to a physical relationship with him.

It was out of line. It was late. She'd been so worried for so long. And thinking about him brought her a curious kind of joy. Even if she could only visit it from afar.

"Do I what?"

"Notice...you know, doctor things...when you're with a woman."

"I've only ever been with Lil since before medical school, and no, I can't say that I brought my work home to that extent."

"To that extent? You bring thoughts of your patients home with you, then? Or did you mean literally? As in paperwork?"

She was babbling like an uneducated idiot. Face flaming, she took a sip of her too hot tea. Making matters worse.

"I don't think I did either. Other than what's normal for anyone. You have passing thoughts. Maybe try to figure out this or that. The best way to face a particular challenge. But Lil… She said I put my work before my family."

"Do you think you did?"

"I didn't think so back then."

"But you do now?"

"I don't do it now." She was asking what he thought. Looking back. But she guessed he knew that. That he was deliberately avoiding her question.

And being her, she let it go. Because while Janie stood up for Dawson, she didn't have as much umph when it came to standing up for herself. Dillon had told her so often enough. She just stood in the middle of the road and let people run all over her. Let people ignore her. She didn't push for what she wanted or needed.

What he hadn't said, but what she'd figured out, was that she didn't push because when she needed something, she knew it was up to her to provide it for herself.

"I need to talk to you about something else." Burke's words brought her back to the present. To her bare feet on a cold, scarred linoleum floor. Bare wood underneath her as she sat at her table. The beautifully colored flowers on her teacup.

"What?" she asked, afraid she wasn't going to like whatever he had to say.

"Kelsey. And Dawson."

She knew what was coming. His daughter was tired of her son. Didn't want Janie to ask her to watch Dawson again. Was retracting her sweet offer.

Janie wouldn't bear her any hard feelings. Kelsey was still a child herself. One with burdens of her own...

"She told me something today and it hit me hard. Because I had no idea..."

Afraid now, ready to defend her son, Janie asked, "What did she tell you?"

"That she didn't want the baby."

"The one Lil was carrying?" She switched gears slowly. Sat straighter.

"Yeah. I should have known...but I didn't."

"How could you have? If she didn't tell you."

"I'm sure there were signs. A lack of excitement, maybe. Lil said the two of them talked and Kels was great with it all."

"There you go. It's natural for a daughter to go to her mother and for the mother to relay things to the father."

At least that was how it went at Cor's house

when female issues arose. A lot of times the issues never even made it as far as the father. They were just dealt with and gone.

"It's also natural, considering that she'd been an only child for eleven years and we had given no indication that we were trying for a second child, which we clearly were not, for her to have feelings of anxiety. To wonder how it was going to affect her daily life. To feel like she was being replaced."

She felt as though he'd just flipped over the Doctor Is In sign.

"Like you just said, you aren't a doctor at home. You can't be. You're too close to view things impartially."

"She asked me if she thought her mother could see her playing with Dawson. If, by stepping forward to help you, she can somehow redeem herself in her mother's eyes."

Janie stared at the dark liquid in her cup. Wishing she could see something other than tea there. For once, just once, she'd like to know why the mysterious universe seemed to mess everyone up so much.

"What did you tell her?"

"I don't remember for sure. Something about her feelings being natural. About her having nothing to feel guilty about. And about her mother already being proud of her."

"Is she ready to be done with Dawson, then?" Were they back to the beginning? To what he'd had to tell her? That Kelsey didn't want to be responsible for Dawson again.

She'd had no indication that that was the case. But she'd had enough adverse reaction to her son that she was always prepared for the worst. Ready to handle it and move on. Because if she didn't, Dawson wouldn't learn to.

"Heck, no! She had a blast today. Anytime she stopped jabbering about the show, she was going on about your son. Do you know that he knows when his pants are wet and how to change them himself?"

"Yes." She just hadn't realized that Dawson had done so during the hour he'd been with Kelsey.

"Kelsey was quite impressed."

"Did he go to the bathroom to do it?" she asked, dreading the answer. He hadn't at school one day. And had almost lost his right to be in the integrated classroom.

"She said she saw him pulling at his waistband and she asked him if he had to go. He nodded. So she took him."

Breathing a sigh of relief on that one, Janie couldn't help wondering what the two of them thought about Dawson not being potty trained. Felt the usual defensiveness creep up.

Dillon was going to hit the roof when he found out that his four-year-old son still wet his pants. If it got as far as Dawson visiting him.

"Hopefully it won't be much longer before he can control his muscles enough and be able to associate the feeling of needing to go with the rest of it," Burke said as though they were discussing cupcakes. "He'll like that a lot better."

Once again Burke surprised her. "That's what Joe says, too," she told him.

"I'd like to meet Corrine and Joe some-time."

She froze. She didn't bring strangers into their little family. And wanted Joe and Burke to meet so badly she almost started to cry at the thought.

"Will they be at any of the tapings?"

"I don't think so." Not unless she made it to the finals. "And now…with Beanie…" For a few moments there she'd forgotten.

She felt horrible.

And yet strengthened, too.

HE'D MEANT TO talk to her about the show. Most particularly about how important it was to his daughter's mental health that he win the grand prize. Because while he still wasn't convinced he could do it, the day's win had gone a long way in building his confidence.

He'd promised Kelsey he was going to give it his absolute best shot. And he would.

Honor was pushing him to make that point very clear to Janie. They couldn't both win. And if he had a chance to take the win from her, if they both made it to the final round and it came down to him or her, he was going to do everything he could to beat her.

Yeah, in one sense, it was just cooking.

But it was more, too. It was about energy. About projection. About wanting and believing and pushing as hard as you could. And it appeared to him that every bit of push Janie had went to her daily care of Dawson.

She didn't project herself to be a winner.

Which let people like him come in and run over her.

He hated that.

But fully intended to do it.

In one sense, he owed her nothing. They'd met as contestants. Had known from the beginning that their goals were pitted against each other.

But they hadn't known the motivation behind each other's goals. They did now.

He hadn't expected to like her so much.

To have her occupying his thoughts when he lay in bed at night.

Or to want to turn to her when something was bothering him.

He'd never, ever, expected to find a woman whose thoughts put his own at ease.

He called her on Sunday morning before making rounds at the hospital—it was his weekend rotation and he'd already had to trade the day before due to the taping—just to find out what she'd heard from her friends the night before.

She'd said that if anything critical happened, if anything major changed, she'd call him. No matter what time it was.

He hadn't fully believed she'd do so.

Beanie had made it through the surgery. The family was feeling more hopeful. If the swelling in her brain was able to go down, she might make a full recovery. Her other injuries were extensive, but all bone-related, no internal punctures or bleeding.

Or she could live and be permanently brain damaged. Janie didn't say so. Neither did Burke. But he knew.

He called on Monday, too, on his way to get Kelsey from dance. Just to check on Beanie. The young woman was holding her own. And was showing signs of waking, so they'd had to medically induce a coma to keep her inactive for another day or two. He asked if she'd heard any more from her ex-husband. She had not. They'd talked another ten minutes after that. About the twenty flower deliveries she'd made. Dawson's improved score on a motor-skill activity at school. About nothing. And yet…it felt like one of the most important conversations he'd had all day.

Still, he didn't talk about what was most on his mind. The fact that he was going to use the advantage of his push-ahead confidence to win the competition. He told himself the next time he called her that week—on Tuesday— that he'd warn her about the confidence that seemed to have given him an advantage all of his life. Warn her that he was going to use every emotional strength he had to win the final round, but ultimately refrained from saying anything because it wasn't necessary yet.

If she didn't win at least one of the next two cook-offs, she wasn't going to be a contender in the final round. He didn't have to beat her over the next two weeks. He was already in.

He saw the holes in his reasoning. He was still going to try to win the next two competitions. The more wins he got, the fewer people he'd have to beat in the final round.

On Tuesday, when he called her on his way to get Kelsey, Janie told him that Cor and Joe were heading home in the morning. Beanie had regained consciousness. She could talk—though not a lot. Could move her feet and her fingers. Both knees were crushed. Her forearm had compound fractures. She'd be in traction for a while. But she was out of immediate danger.

Janie didn't mention her ex-husband. He didn't ask about him.

She asked about Kelsey. He asked about Dawson. He had no idea how she did all she did for her son. Every meal. Every movement, it seemed, was designed to exercise something. Hand-eye coordination, swallowing, talking. Over the past couple of days, he'd asked. He had this need to be in her life—over the phone only, of course.

Just hearing about the rigor of her days made him uneasy. "I don't know how you do it," he told her. Knowing that if something happened to Kelsey and she required such care, he'd find a way to be there for her. But doubting that he'd be anywhere near as good at it as Janie was. Or as diligent. He'd do the exercises, of course. But he'd take days off, too.

"I don't know how I'd ever take up a knife

and cut into someone's skin," she said. "You do what you were meant to do."

She was feeding Dawson while they spoke and he could tell when she was going too slowly. The boy let out a very distinctive "Mo!"

You do what you have to do.

"We're all different," she went on, sounding like she was doing nothing more exhausting than lying on the beach. "Take writing, for instance. Writing five hundred words is like a death sentence to me. It takes weeks. Cor could write five thousand in a couple of days. We both got straight As in high school. She excelled in English and history. I whizzed through math."

Stopped in traffic, he smiled. Liked listening to her talk. And hoped she was right. If he was meant to raise a child like Kelsey, then he must have what it took to not let her down. Whereas Janie was meant to raise a child like Dawson. She was the type of person who could meet Dawson's needs. Who wouldn't let him down. Burke wasn't meant to be *that* person.

Made sense. Fit in all the right mental compartments.

And what about Lil? Had he been the wrong husband for her? Had he just not done his best? Or were some people put on earth to fail? Was it meant to be that his wife had died because of him?

The thought left him more than a little sad.

CHAPTER NINETEEN

ON WEDNESDAY, WHILE observing Dawson's speech-therapy session, Janie caught herself wondering if Burke would call that night. She caught herself again after dropping her son off at preschool, caught herself wanting Burke to call. If she wasn't careful, she was going to create problems she could ill afford.

Parked in the lot of the flower shop, waiting for an order that was late for delivery, she took out her phone and campaign binder and started making calls—getting her mind on other things. Things that helped her sustain life for her and Dawson.

And as she drove the flowers across town, she forced herself to stay focused on those things that were going to better her life.

The coming week's competition dish had to include pasta. She had pasta recipes for every occasion, many of them born out of trying to come up with new ways to eat the cheap individually bagged noodles her mother used to buy by the case and consider the cupboards stocked. She'd had them with butter and cinnamon for breakfast. With a peanut butter and honey mixture for lunch. With peas and lunch meat for dinner. She had some fancy pasta recipes, too, including a white cream sauce with ham, onion and saffron. Because she truly loved to cook and creating intricate dishes was a panacea for her.

They'd had to submit their recipes the week before so all ingredients would be purchased and in their kitchens, waiting for them. She'd vacillated between feeling confident she'd chosen the dish that would put her best foot forward and fearing that, considering the competition, she should have chosen differently. Winning wasn't just about how good she cooked or how great her dishes tasted. It was about her dishes tasting better than her professional opponents' dishes.

And she was getting down to the wire. Two more chances and she was out.

She couldn't let that happen.

Or allow herself any more distractions. Life provided enough of them without her making things worse.

In between flower deliveries, she stopped by Joe and Cor's. She'd needed to see them. And felt much calmed after doing so. They needed a dose of Dawson's naive happiness and said they couldn't wait until Saturday. She agreed to bring her son by for dinner that night.

And to bring dinner, too. She'd made Janie's Luscious Noodles the night before—with a secret cream cheese, green onion, butter, sour cream and cottage-cheese mixture layered throughout—to time herself, and the three-quart casserole sitting in her refrigerator had to be eaten.

She went early. So that she'd be too occupied for a lengthy conversation with Burke *if* he called on his way home. He'd said Wednesday was going to be a long day due to backed-up surgeries.

She went early because she'd had a letter in the mail that afternoon with the return address of Dillon's lawyer.

With shaking fingers, she handed the letter to Cor as soon as Joe had taken Dawson off to play basketball.

"I need to know if I have to comply with this," she said a lot more calmly than she felt.

Due to Dawson's special needs, Dillon's attorney had requested a formal meeting between clients and counsel, to discuss the boy's care in reference to establishing a regular visitation schedule for Dillon. She'd spend a week's worth of groceries and gas to pay for an attorney to represent her for the suggested hour-long meeting.

"You don't have to, no," Corrine said, frowning. They were in Cor's kitchen while Janie warmed up the pasta casserole and tossed a salad from fixings she'd also brought with her. It wasn't as though her friends had had time to shop that afternoon.

"But I should."

"He's going about this so un-Dillon-like," Cor said. "We need to see what Joe thinks, but this is not Dillon's usual pushy, strong-armed way. He's actually taking time to work through the process."

That was what she'd thought. And was scared to death. She wanted Burke to read the letter. To tell her what he thought. Which made no sense at all. He wasn't a lawyer. Had never been divorced. Probably knew next to nothing about California's visitation laws.

"He could be going for open visitation, which would mean there's no set schedule and you two work it out between you. But the court usually only approves that kind of order if the parents get along well and don't disagree when it comes to the child. But with you having sole physical and legal custody..."

Which didn't mean, as she'd first thought, that she could refuse Dillon's rights to see his son. It meant only that she was responsible for making any and every decision pertaining to her son—including health and education choices—and that he would live with her.

"It's more likely the court would only approve a pre-agreed-upon visitation. It sounds like that's what Dillon is trying to work out here."

"Eee!" Dawson came out to the kitchen, putting his fingers to his mouth again and again in rapid order. His version of the sign for eat.

Joe, taking the letter from Corrine, read while Cor helped Dawson into his booster seat at the table. "I Kee!" Dawson said, smiling before leaning forward to put a wet kiss on Cor's face.

"You can have ice cream after dinner," she answered, kissing him back.

"If I look at this from the perspective of one who knows, fairly well, how Dillon's mind works, I'd say he's stalling," Joe said, dropping the letter. "If you lose *Family Secrets*, he'll probably drop the whole thing."

"I can't lose, Joe." He and Cor knew, down to the penny, how much she needed the win. Not just financially, but emotionally, as well. If she was ever going to fully recover from Dillon's ability to make her feel bad about herself, she had to be able to provide for herself and her son.

She had to live down the legacy her mother had left her.

And...

"You need to go to this first meeting or you're going to open up a bigger can of worms," Cor said while reaching to hold Dawson's hand to stop him from banging his plastic knife up and down on the table.

The boy was not patient when it came to his eating.

"There's always a chance that Dillon has had a change of heart. That he's sincerely looking for a way to be a contributing part of his son's life. And if that happened...if he could help with therapies and exercises, with exposing Dawson to different aspects of life as Dawson is capable of taking them on... then that would be a help to you."

Logically it made sense. Her heart wasn't buying it.

But then, her heart had led her wrong before. Like when it had led her to Dillon in the first place.

"Do you really think he's had a change of heart?" she asked with no defensiveness. She needed to know. Respected Corrine's opinion. Trusted it.

"Considering the hard time he just gave you over the added money for therapy? No. I don't. But looking cooperative is in your best interest."

The foreboding in Cor's voice gave her pause as she put pasta on her son's plastic plate and then placed it in front of him. Joe, behind Dawson now, tied his bib while Cor filled his sippy cup with milk.

Picking up his fork, Dawson jammed it down onto the plate, raised it to his mouth empty, jammed again, and then a third time, quite patiently, before holding the fork midair and picking up a fist full of pasta with his free hand and shoving it into his mouth.

His tongue pushed against his teeth in a really good attempt to do its job as he chewed, but some of the food fell out anyway. Dawson caught it with his hand on his chin and shoved the half-processed bit back into his mouth.

Joe and Corrine, plates filled, were taking their seats across from him, completely unaffected. Janie tried to imagine Dillon sitting there with them. And could only picture him taking his plate into the other room with disgust.

Even if her ex-husband meant well, he had no real idea what he was getting into. Which made her wonder why he was putting out the money to pay a lawyer this early in the game. She'd led him to believe that he could see Dawson. Just not the previous Saturday.

He hadn't asked for the upcoming one. He'd just said that he'd be in touch soon to work something out.

She'd been waiting to hear from him again. Dreading his call. And thinking luck was finally going her way when the only personal calls she'd received from a man that week were from Burke.

The last thing she'd expected was an official letter from Dillon's attorney.

"I'll represent you for this first meeting," Cor said. It was set for the upcoming Monday. Four days before the last regular competition— her last chance to final, if her pasta didn't win. "It's basically just mediation."

Janie hated using her friend like that, but she nodded. Because she saw no other choice.

And vowed to herself that she was going to win *Family Secrets* one way or another. She couldn't take much more of feeling like she felt—trashy and hopeless, too—every single time she was forced to take another handout.

Not that she didn't appreciate the help— she did—but she also loved Corrine and Joe enough to care that she was a burden to them. That felt rotten, too.

All because she'd rushed into marriage with the wrong man. She'd made a bad choice. Somehow she had to find a way to pay for it herself.

WAITING FOR HIS last patient to wake fully from the anesthetic, Burke sat on a padded bench in a deserted hallway down from the room in which he'd just performed his third major joint surgery that day. He rubbed his face. He'd had to call Barbara, Kelsey's ex–best friend's mother whom he'd dated once, to pick his daughter up from dance and take her home.

Kelsey was not going to be happy with him. But she'd be safe. Next to Lil, Barbara knew Kelsey better than any other woman on earth. And loved her, too. In spite of their daughters' apparent parting of the ways.

For all he knew, the girls could be best friends again by then. Based on past experiences, fights between Carlie and Kelsey had a tendency to resolve themselves.

Of course, he could just be wishful thinking. Out of guilt over the fact that he hadn't finished in time to get her himself. They were supposed to be making Lil's spaghetti sauce that night in preparation for Saturday. But Burke had found a lot more damage than he'd expected when he'd opened up the college ball player's knee that afternoon. He'd done what he could. There was still a chance, depending on the amount of work the kid was willing to do, the limits of pain and therapy he could endure, that he'd play again.

And an hour-long surgery had turned into almost four.

While he felt great for the young man whose knee he was pretty sure he'd saved, he struggled with guilt about not being there for his daughter.

Other doctors worked the hours he did. Many worked more. It came with the territory. They just weren't the single father of an emotionally struggling thirteen-year-old.

He'd missed his late-afternoon chat with Janie. Wondered if her friends had arrived home as expected. If she'd heard anything more from her ex-husband. And he thought again about setting up some kind of fund to help her. He'd made a few calls on his lunch hour. One to his attorney. One to his financial planner. And another to Missy Chamberlain, the wife of a friend of his from medical school. Missy was a grant writer and sat on the boards of many charities. He gave a significant amount of money to charities every year. Redistributing that into a charity of his own making, in a way that would still allow the tax write-off, was actually not that difficult.

Or all that unusual.

He could set up a privately funded grant. He'd just need to figure out how to tailor the qualifications in such a way that Janie would be a sure win. And then get her to write the darn thing. But that was a bridge he could cross later. Legal logistics first. Fine-tuning later.

He'd hoped to talk to Kelsey about the idea that night. Not that he had to answer to her about any of his financial investments, but thought she should know her father was funding a grant.

Or, maybe, he just wanted her to know so that she'd have a reason to be proud of him in case he lost *Family Secrets*.

And in case she ever found out that he was the reason her mother had died?

Or was he completely out of his head? What was he doing, considering donating his charitable funds to a woman he'd known only a few weeks?

More to the point, why was he so consumed with doing so?

CHAPTER TWENTY

KELSEY WASN'T UPSET that he hadn't picked her up. "You were saving a guy's whole future, Dad," she said in the car on the way home from Carlie's house. "It's not like you can walk out of an operating room when you get in there and find out that things are different than you expected."

True. "But a few weeks ago you were upset when I picked you up late."

"I was just in a mood then. And it wasn't like it was life or death or anything. It was just an office visit. And it was just Dan needing cortisone. Again. Like someone else couldn't give it to him. Or he couldn't just deal with the pain and play his game. Or sit out and let his knee heal if it hurts that badly…"

She was on a roll. Saying so much that he should probably be paying better attention. Her aversion to medication that was not absolutely essential was nothing new. But…

I was in a mood then.

Did that mean she was out of the mood just for now? Or forever?

Or did it mean that when she was *in a mood* he was free not to take her displeasure to heart because she'd get out of the mood?

"Did Janie's friends get back?" she asked before he could find out how it went with Carlie.

He'd been planning to go to the door to get her. To thank Barbara properly, if nothing else. His daughter had prevented that by zooming out the front door before he'd put the car in Park.

"I assume so," he told her. And wanted both of them to move on.

Kelsey looked at him. "You didn't call her today?"

Unease crept up his spine.

"I hope you aren't thinking what it sounds like you might be thinking…" Lord, he was starting to sound like her.

When she was at her most confusing…

"What?"

"That Janie and I… That there's something starting…"

"Oh. My. Gosh. No! Eww. Dad. We're *Family Secrets* friends. Why would you even say that?"

Well. For having just dodged a bullet, he'd

sure stepped in front of another one. Why had the idea ever jumped into his brain? He didn't want to analyze that one.

"Anyway, I was just thinking that we should call Janie and see if we can do dinner again tomorrow night. Like we did last week. I need to keep seeing Dawson so he doesn't forget me."

The topic seemed loaded. Should he broach the subject of her guilt over the baby brother they'd lost? Talk about the fact that with Janie's friends back in town it wasn't likely that Janie would be needing Kelsey's help this week?

He went with his third consideration. "What do you plan to do when the show is over?" It was the question that seemed least likely to upset her. And yet one she needed to consider. No matter how much she believed she was helping Janie because she was going to lose, or how much freer she felt working off her guilt over her baby brother—at the same time she was befriending a little boy who really liked her. Who was asking for her in her absence. And who could feasibly miss her when this short episode in their lives ended. She had to consider his feelings, as well.

"What do you mean? As far as the Lil label is concerned? Or the packaging for national distribution? I'm only thirteen, Dad. I don't think they'll let me help with any of that."

"I meant as far as Dawson is concerned. If he gets too attached to you, it will be mean to just dump him."

"I don't plan to dump him! I thought…you know… I could maybe babysit him sometimes. Or go over there and play with him while Janie takes care of things around the house. You know…if she likes me well enough and wants me to."

She'd clearly thought about it. More than once.

"Anyway, we should call and see if she wants to do dinner. Especially since I might not get to see Dawson on Saturday with her friends back and all."

He'd promised himself he was not going to call Janie Young tonight.

But he told Kelsey he would.

Because he'd do just about anything to get that look of approval shining at him from his daughter's eyes.

His call came as she was scrubbing the toilet. Dawson had filled it with his socks when she'd been making campaign calls earlier that evening, and since she'd been fishing them out, she'd decided to go ahead and clean the bathroom at the same time.

She'd been running behind with the calls because of having dinner with Joe and Cor and, out of desperation, had asked Dawson to put on his pajamas and get ready for bed. She'd never sent him off to do it on his own before and had given him fifteen minutes alone to see what would happen. She'd hoped for pajamas. Expected to find him playing with his cars.

Instead she'd found the toilet bowl stuffed with socks. No telling what he was trying to accomplish. There was always the possibility he was being a typical little kid acting upon curiosity. Perhaps he'd been meaning to flush when he was done.

If so, she was lucky she'd caught him before he'd emptied the entire drawer. The upside was he'd also put on his pajamas. With clean and dry Pull-Ups.

"I guess he only needed five minutes, not the fifteen I gave him," she told Burke.

"I guess it's better than sticking a peanut up his nose," he said with a chuckle. She didn't detect distaste. Or even pity. They were parents talking about their kids.

"Did Kelsey do that?"

"No, but I'm told I did."

She smiled then, too, sitting on the floor, against the bathroom counter, antibacterial-laced cloth in her hand.

She wondered about his parents. But didn't ask. Familial background was a no-trespassing zone as far as she was concerned. She'd said all she was going to about her own situation.

He asked about Corrine and Joe. She told him about dinner. And about Dillon. Again, because she could. He was easy to talk to.

Nothing more. They were just talking. On the phone. Not talking as in building something bigger.

She was going to ask about his surgeries that day—not that he could give her any identifying information—but stopped. Afraid the question was too personal.

"Kelsey wants to know if we can do dinner again tomorrow night."

She froze. Until the leap of her heart jump-started her system. And then she frowned. At herself, mostly.

"She knows Corrine and Joe are back in town and figures she's not going to get to see Dawson on Saturday. She's afraid if too much time passes between visits, he'll forget her."

"He won't." But she understood Kelsey might not believe that. Janie wanted to invite them for dinner. So badly that she was worried about it.

But if she mentioned her worries to him, told him that she was afraid they were getting too close, wouldn't that just shine a spotlight on the issue? And be hugely embarrassing if he didn't agree.

Humiliating.

To have him think she was thinking about them in terms of getting…personally…close.

How awkward would that be when they met on the set? Or in the green room?

It dawned on her that to refuse the invitation could have the same effect.

"We can meet you somewhere if you'd like," Burke said. He named a fun gourmet burger place that had games and a playroom for kids.

Dawson would go nuts there in about ten seconds flat. Unless, of course, it was deserted. Then he'd have a blast.

"My treat, of course, since you made dinner last time."

She couldn't believe how much she wanted to accept his invitation. She *had* made dinner the previous week, at her expense, so him paying wouldn't be any more than a return favor.

Not charity. And not a date.

"I wasn't going to call tonight," Burke inserted into the silence. "But Kelsey insisted.

She really wants to see him and so…" His voice trailed off.

He was putting pressure on her to accept. Because of Kelsey. He'd called because of Kelsey.

Janie breathed a little easier.

Dawson was medicine to Kelsey right now. While she worked through the guilt of not wanting the baby her mother had been carrying.

Janie made a mental and very deliberate turn away from the realization and attached hurt that Burke hadn't wanted to call. That he wasn't calling because he'd wanted to talk with her as badly as she did with him. She'd pull that one out later. When she could use it to remind herself not to even think about falling for him any more. Not even in her fantasies.

"Of course we can have dinner," she said before he mistook her silence for more than it was. Before awkwardness fell between them. "But if you don't mind, I'd rather do it here, again."

"Then can I at least bring dinner?" he asked. Her first thought was ease of swallowing so Dawson had a fairly clean meal.

And then she stopped herself. What did it matter what the Carters thought? Or if they were grossed out by half-chewed food drooling out of a mouth and down a chin? She was going to know them only another couple of weeks. It was time to keep that in mind.

And maybe, a tiny part of her managed to slide into her consciousness, *maybe you need to know if Burke will be grossed out.*

Was she testing him?

"That's fine," she said before she could answer her own question.

He asked what Dawson liked on his pizza. "Cheese," she told him.

"Same as Kelsey," he said. "I prefer ham and onion, but Lil liked supreme and I can eat that, too, if that's your favorite."

Her favorite was any kind that was not store bought from the freezer section. Pizza was a luxury she'd never been able to afford at home. She'd eaten it at Cor's growing up. But not at home. Not with her mom. And not in the years since Dillon, either.

"Ham and onion sounds wonderful," she told him. Thinking it did. And thinking of sharing with him, too.

It was only two more weeks. The show would end. And they'd all go on with their very separate lives.

Worrying about her growing attachment to him was moot. Irrelevant. Two weeks and he'd be gone and she and Dawson could look back at knowing him and Kelsey with fondness.

JANIE WAS JUST climbing into bed when her phone rang again. Feeling far too exposed in the panties and T-shirt she slept in, she grabbed up her phone before it rang a second time. As though the longer it rang, the more chance Burke would have of seeing her.

It wasn't Burke.

"Hey, Cor, what's up?" she asked, a thread of alarm shooting through her. She'd just seen her friend that evening. No need for her to call. Unless something had happened.

She steeled herself for bad news about Beanie.

"That's what I want to know," Cor said softly. In her 'I'm your best friend and you aren't getting away with this" tone.

"What are you talking about?" Even she could tell how fake that sounded.

"You were different tonight. You know you were and I know you were…"

"Did you ask Joe if I acted any differently?" she asked inanely. Buying herself time. She had to tell Cor something. Owed it to her. Best friends didn't keep secrets from each other. Not big ones.

But she couldn't let Cor make a big deal out of this thing with Burke. Couldn't let herself start to believe there could ever be more to it. That was the road to self-destruction.

"You know I did, and you always know what he says."

"He said he didn't notice anything different about me, right?"

"Of course."

"So, he's a smart man. Believe him."

"Why don't you want to tell me?" The slight hint of hurt trickled into her deepest heart.

Forcing her to be honest. "Because I don't want you to make something out of nothing."

"If it's nothing, you wouldn't care what I make out of it. You wouldn't be afraid of what I might make out of it. And now I know for sure something's going on."

She'd already known.

Dropping back against the pillows, Janie stared at the ceiling. She wasn't turning out the light. Wasn't going to talk about Burke in the dark.

She told Cor about Kelsey Carter. About her seeing the Thanksgiving show. About asking her father to compete, using her deceased mother's recipes. Even about Kelsey spending time with Dawson to ease the guilt over not wanting her baby brother. To redeem herself. How she thought by helping another little boy, she could show her mother in heaven that she was a good girl. A giving person.

"So that's who watched him for you last Saturday?" Cor asked.

"Yeah."

"We saw the show tonight. We'd taped it."

She hadn't figured they'd had the wherewithal. They'd left so quickly.

"Oh."

"So Dawson is friendly enough with Burke Carter to let him hold him," Cor said.

And Janie gave up. Just gave up. She'd known Corrine was not going to let that go. Another man, other than Joe, holding Dawson? It was a first.

Too significant for her not to have mentioned it to her friend.

"It's nothing, Cor."

"There might be nothing between you," Corrine said, "but he definitely means something to you."

Ready to argue, Janie was choosing the most powerful words when Cor said, "You didn't even turn when Burke picked him up, Janie. You didn't try to help. You weren't worried. You were completely comfortable."

"Well, there's nothing between us."

"Have you watched the show?"

"No. I told you I'm not watching any of them. It'd make me too nervous to see what I look like. I'm there to win. Not to be on television."

"At the beginning, when the theme song is playing, they showed snapshot cameos. Randomly. Like a little photo album of the show. There's one where you're walking out on stage. Several of the contestants are sitting in a row on stage…"

"That was the first day."

"You need to check out the look on Burke Carter's face when he sees you. They closed in on it."

No. "Don't do this, Cor. Don't give me hope."

"Why, Janie? Why shouldn't you have hope?"

"I've only known the man a few weeks."

"So?"

"Look how quickly I fell for Dillon. And that turned out to be a disaster."

"You were kids. And it only got bad after you two grew in different directions. You and Burke are adults."

"From completely different worlds."

"Opposites attract."

"I have no time to invest in a relationship right now."

Cor's silence saddened her. But calmed her, too.

"And Burke has his hands filled with Kelsey."

A different kind of special needs.

"And we're contestants," she said. "I know how badly Burke wants to win *Family Secrets*. I know why. And I also know that I have to beat him. This is *my* chance, Cor. Mine and Dawson's. We've done all we can do. And it's not enough. I have to win this thing. With packaging and distribution of one of my recipes, I'll be earning money without any huge draw on my time. I'll be able to tend to Dawson, to enroll him in every class and camp and opportunity that comes along. And I'll be able to buy enough cooking equipment to finally be able to take on some small catering jobs."

She could get a television spot on another food show, too. A whole new world would be opened to her. One to which she'd never before had legitimate admittance.

The world Cor had grown up in. The one Burke lived in.

She'd gone into her relationship with Dillon with nothing to offer but herself. He'd wanted his wife at his disposal and had insisted on providing their income. Their security. He was the one with a family business to fall back on.

She couldn't even think about entering another disproportionate relationship. She couldn't do that to herself.

Couldn't stand to feel like Cinderella ever again.

She'd found out the hard way that fairy tales weren't all they were cracked up to be.

CHAPTER TWENTY-ONE

BURKE COULDN'T HAVE Kelsey carrying around this burden of trying to buy redemption by being responsible for a four-year-old with Down syndrome. He'd had a sick feeling in his gut pretty much constantly since last Saturday when she'd told him about the guilt she felt about her baby brother.

The times he'd had any relief, he'd been consumed by other emotions that did not sit any better with him. Anticipation. Intense attraction that spanned so much more than the physical—though that was there, too. Moments of pure calm. The carefree happiness of a college boy. A feeling he wasn't sure he'd experienced even when he'd been a college boy. Those were the times he found himself thinking about his competitor—Janie Young.

And the times that he'd spoken with her.

Which was why he'd made his calls about the grant. Moved mountains to get something going. The meeting he'd had with his attorney that afternoon had fleshed out a detailed plan that could work.

Things would fall into place. Both Kelsey and Janie would be fine. And he could get back to concentrating on his work. Assuming he won the show and Kelsey really did find enough peace to move on with her life.

Not that he was planning to stop focusing on his daughter. Not at all. He was just planning on her growing more and more independent and not needing him in such an all-consuming way.

Being an orthopedic surgeon raised a full gamut of emotions within him. But ones he could control. And that was the way he liked it. That was his version of happiness. Had always been his version, as far as he could see.

"I want to talk to you about something," he told Kelsey as they waited for the pizzas he'd ordered for pickup. They were in the car, in the designated parking space. The prepaid pizzas would be brought out to them when they were ready.

"What?" Kelsey's eyes shadowed with alarm as she looked at him.

It could have been good news. She immediately assumed it was bad.

"I think I've found a way to help Janie with Dawson…if she loses."

"When she loses... Let's face it, Dad. You're meant to win this thing. We have Mom on our side."

The words running through his mind would not have admittance in heaven.

"So...what's your plan?"

Kelsey's question brought him out of the panic pit into which her induction of her mother had thrown him. Right. He had to focus on the here and now. The things he could control. And do his almighty best to win that show.

"I think you're aware that your mother and I donated quite a lot of money to charity every year."

"Of course." She named a couple of the recipients. "I helped Mom with delivering toys that one year, remember?"

He nodded. "So I want to take that amount of money and put it in a single charity."

She was watching him, obviously interested as she nodded. "We could name it after Mom," she said.

He hadn't thought as far as a name. But it would need one. So he nodded. And continued on his mission.

"I can design the charity so that the money is given to a needy candidate in the form of a grant."

She nodded again.

"You understand how that works?"

"You grant money. Sure. You decide who to grant it to and I bet you'll grant yours to Janie. I think it's a *great* idea, Daddy. I'm, like, so proud of you. Mom would be, too." Her smile was tinged with a hint of the adult woman she was soon to become. There was a glint of moisture in her eyes, too.

He reveled in her gentle nature for a moment.

"It doesn't quite work like that." He could have let it go. But…he couldn't. It wasn't just up to him and if something went wrong…

It wouldn't.

He'd found a pretty fail-safe way to make his plan work, through their delineation of specifications, but it was still possible there'd be another single mother of a Down syndrome child who lived in Palm Desert city limits, in a less-than-1,500-square-foot home, who worked at least two jobs and could prove a history of taking advantage of every therapy available for the development of her child into a self-sufficient productive adult. One who had a lawyer friend with incredible writing skills. Not that the lawyer-friend part was a requirement.

"People have to write in telling why they meet the qualifications for a grant. It all has to be specified, legally." And, therefore, qualify for a tax write-off.

"So Janie will have to write this paper and then you choose her."

He shook his head. "The choice has to be made by an unbiased person."

"She has to write a really good letter."

"Right. But you know Corrine and Joe that she talks about?"

"Yeah." Kelsey was hanging on his words like they were ice cream. He reveled in her attention some more.

"Corrine's a lawyer, which means she knows how to present a case, and she's also a great writer."

He told her that, for now, until the grant was established and he could find a way to introduce it to Janie without letting her know he was involved—because he didn't want to take a chance she'd be embarrassed and refuse to let him help her, or injure her pride—they had to keep it a secret between the two of them.

And hoped that Kelsey would now begin to relax about Janie and Dawson and the responsibilities she'd felt she had to take on her own shoulders.

Nodding, Kelsey smiled slowly—the expression spreading across her face until it was alight. "I think it will work," she said.

Something upon which they completely agreed.

The world was definitely looking brighter.

JANIE TOLD DAWSON that Kelsey was coming for dinner. That her dad was bringing pizza.

"Kee pee?" His husky little grunts as he signed "to eat'" made her smile.

"Yes," she told him as she took him into the bathroom to put on fresh Pull-Ups and wash his hands and face. He'd had a Popsicle for a snack when they'd come in that afternoon and was still wearing a little bit of orange on his chin. On his shirt, too, she noticed, so she helped him change that, as well.

He stood on her toes as she pulled off his shirt and then grabbed her around the neck, dragging her down so he could kiss her. Licking her cheek first.

And that was why she lived. Nothing felt better than Dawson's honest and open, unconditional love.

When the bell rang, Dawson ran for the door, trying to get enough of a grasp on the handle to open it. She helped and he pulled and then flung himself against Kelsey's legs before she was completely inside.

"Kee," he said. And then again. He stepped

back to look up at her and then, grabbing her hand, started to pull her toward his room.

Handing a pizza box to her dad, she grinned at Janie and allowed herself to be led away.

"He's really taken to her," Janie said as she found herself suddenly and unexpectedly alone with Burke. With Cor's conversation from the night before still fresh in her mind.

Did he know that she'd started to…like…him? In a way that wasn't really appropriate between two unmarried parents brought together only by their kids?

Because if he did, she'd die of humiliation.

"She's fond of him, too."

"As a means of proving something to herself," Janie said, leading him into the kitchen and arranging his pizza boxes on the counter.

"What do you mean? Proving something to herself?"

"That she's not a bad person for how she felt about her brother. She needs to know that she has what it takes to care deeply for a small boy."

"She wants to know her mother doesn't think ill of her. That Lil is proud of her."

"A girl's self-concept is all wrapped up in her mom," Janie said. "It gets kind of confused in there, one melding into the other. And I'm no psychiatrist, for sure. But just based on what I've learned about myself, I'm guessing that your daughter is struggling with her own self-worth. Have you talked to her counselor yet?"

"I called, but since it's not an emergency, the soonest appointment I could get is next week."

She got out paper plates and napkins. Reached for plastic cups, a carton of juice and some cold bottles of water. Made sure she stayed far enough away not to run into him. And didn't look directly at him, either.

The black polo shirt and blue jeans he was wearing were right off some bachelor set. Or something. She didn't know. Looking at him confused her.

"You struggled with your own self-worth because of your mom's addiction." She heard his guess, delivered more as a statement than a question.

And heard Dawson barreling down the hall, too. "Eee. Eee. Eee. Eee." The little guy came around the corner with two fingers pinched together, tapping them to his lips over and over.

And the moment for adult conversation had ended.

Thank God.

KELSEY WANTED A little more time with Dawson after dinner. After consulting with Janie, Burke gave his daughter half an hour.

"If you need us to leave earlier, we can give them another five and I can go get her," Burke told Janie as they cleared the table. He broke up the pizza boxes. And noticed the full trash in the plastic push-top can on the far side of the cupboard.

"She's fine," Janie said. "I'm cooking to-night and I can't do that until after he goes to bed anyway."

An indirect reference to the show. He was eager to tell her of his plan.

But needed to know that she'd be as open to it, hopefully as excited by it, as he was. Oftentimes the way people took things—in a positive manner or a negative one—boiled down to the delivery.

Pulling the trash bag out of the can, he held it open while she shoved in paper plates, nap-kins and the pizza boxes.

"Surely you cook when he's awake," he said, kind of pushing her to talk more about the competition. He shouldn't. They'd agreed— no talk of *Family Secrets* off set.

And yet…with only two competitions left and with his win—he felt compelled to get some things settled.

"I'm timing myself and I can't do that ac-curately when I'm also listening to and tend-ing to him."

He'd figured it was something like that. When he practiced, he had Kelsey there, timing him, taking notes, making suggestions, coaching him. Tasting.

Janie had to do it all on her own.

"Have you looked into getting a grant?" He tied the flaps of the bag together, reached for the new bag she'd just pulled off a roll and re-lined the trash can. It wasn't like him to tread such a thin line.

He wasn't sure why he was doing so now.

Janie shook her head. "Government grants are for particular projects." She was telling him what he already knew. What he'd just found out that week. "A child's life isn't a particular project. If I wanted to start up a therapy group, I could try to get a grant to fund that group. Not Dawson or me, but the group. And there's a lot of legal stuff involved. Not to mention the additional complication with taxes."

"But there are funds for children with special needs."

"He gets what government assistance he's eligible for," she told him. "It helps with some of the therapies and provides a full-time aide to be with him at all times when he's at school. It's part of the integrated classroom program he's in."

She opened the door off the kitchen and he followed her with the filled trash bag.

"What about private grants?"

"Those are charities," she said, nodding toward the city trash can out back. One with wheels to be rolled around to the front on pickup day. "They also are a onetime fix—not something you can count on receiving every year. It's like giving a man a fish rather than teaching him to fish. I have to make ends meet and provide for my son."

He dropped the bag into the nearly full can. The conversation wasn't going at all as he'd planned. She wasn't supposed to know about the existence of such grants. He'd been going to give her the great news that there were possible monies available to help her out.

Even though he couldn't yet reveal his "charity" as, officially, it didn't yet exist.

"When's trash day?" he asked, closing the lid on the large black can.

"Tomorrow."

"I'll wheel this out, then," he told her, expecting her to go back into the house.

She strolled beside him instead. Around the house, toward the drive. "I'll work my fingers to the bone to provide for my son," she said. "But I draw the line at taking charity. It makes me feel like trash." She knocked her knuckles against the side of the can he pulled as emphasis. "I know it shouldn't. I'm so glad the monies are out there and available to people who cannot provide for themselves. But I just can't go back to feeling the way I felt…"

Her words broke off. As if she'd just stopped herself.

He wanted more of the glimpse she was giving him. Needed to know how to help her feel good about taking the money he was setting aside for her. He thought she was referring to her ex-husband. And his disdain for their son.

"If anyone ever made you feel bad for needing assistance with Dawson…"

"It's not that," she said. "And not anything you'll probably ever understand."

"I'd like to." They'd reached the curb.

Looking sideways, he caught her eye as they started back up the drive. And had to resist taking her hand. Holding her hand as they made the short trek back.

After a brief few seconds she glanced away. Shook her head. "You wouldn't get it."

She was shutting him out. Understandable. They weren't… Well, he didn't know what they weren't. Or really, what they were. He just knew he didn't like her shutting him out.

"Sounds to me like you think I'm a snob

or something. Like you're passing judgment on me just because of what you think you know."

The words weren't fair. Most particularly considering that he was in the process of setting up a grant to fund her because…he could. Easily. Without any detriment to himself, his daughter, his lifestyle…

He worked hard. Did good work. Helped people. Because he enjoyed it. Felt good doing it. And because it provided a very comfortable living for his family.

She worked herself to near exhaustion doing things that bored her, making calls for causes she didn't necessarily believe in, just to make ends meet. Because she was determined to make ends meet.

His ends met without him even thinking about it. And he was accusing her of *thinking* he was a snob?

"When I was fourteen I'd haul my mostly comatose mom out to the car. I'd drive us the couple of blocks to the store. I'd go in and shop for groceries, leave the basket at the checkout, go out and get my mom, and have to practically hold her up while the clerk rang in the groceries, because Mom had to hand over the food stamps. I will never *ever* forget the looks on those clerks' faces. And I never *ever* want to feel that way again—"

She broke off. And Burke had the very distinct impression that she'd said far more than she'd meant to.

She'd said far more than he'd meant her to.

He wanted her to take the words back.

He had the money to support her—just in his yearly charity givings. But he couldn't afford to care the way he cared when he thought about what she'd just told him.

That caring…it was strong. Take-your-breath-away strong.

A brick-between-the-eyes strong.

He wanted it to be pity. Who wouldn't feel sorry for the kid she'd described?

It wasn't pity. And it was way more personal than friendship.

And it was way out of his league.

He didn't have what it would take. Was in no way good enough for her. Not with the death of his wife on his shoulders.

A secret shared with no one.

Burke followed her back to her door, unsure what to do or say. Unsure of so many things.

Like how he was going to make certain that he won his daughter's freedom from depression with her mother's recipes.

And how on earth he was going to convince Janie Young to get her friend to write a grant letter.

CHAPTER TWENTY-TWO

TO BE STRIPPED of all clothing and then to be left to shiver alone, exposed in the cold, was not a horror Janie had ever experienced.

But it was how she felt as she stood outside her kitchen door with Burke after dropping off her trash can.

Sixty degrees wasn't all that frigid. She felt cold in another way.

Made somehow worse by the fact that he'd asked about trash day. Been aware that it was a responsibility she bore and then had taken the initiative to take it out.

These things...they exposed her to feelings she couldn't unwrap.

"Thank you." She stumbled over the words. Standing in front of her door, closest to the door, but not opening it. She didn't want him back inside. In the closeness of her small home.

She didn't want to ever be without him.

Her life didn't include him.

"For the trash," she said. Looking down at her feet.

That finger under her chin was familiar. She didn't resist as he raised her face. Wearing her big-girl panties, she met his gaze.

"You aren't alone."

She was. She really was. In the end, she'd always been alone. It was all she knew. All she knew how to be.

The breakup of her marriage…it hadn't all been Dillon. On some level she'd expected it to happen someday.

It was just as if opening up to Burke had created this fissure within her. Thoughts escaped, hitting her all at once.

"My daughter has this idea that, after *Family Secrets*, she's going to continue coming over here. She wants to be a person in Dawson's life. To play with him, but also to help you. She figures she can spend time with him while you do whatever you need to do here at home."

She didn't know what to say. Didn't even understand the sensations bombarding her. Relief. Defensiveness. Warmth. Rejection.

Love?

"I just didn't want you to think that we're going to be here and gone," he continued. "Or that Kelsey is going to walk out on your son."

"She's welcome here as long as she needs us," Janie said. Kelsey was paying a penance. She was innocent of the atrocities for which she held herself accountable—but until she realized that, it was healthier for her to have a means of earning her way out.

Burke leaned closer, his lips slightly parted. "Dad? Janie?"

With a quickly indrawn breath, Janie jumped back. "Here!" she called, yanking open the door with more force than necessary.

"We're just taking out the trash," she said as she adjusted to the inside light she'd left blaring in the kitchen. "It's garbage day tomorrow and your dad was nice enough to wheel it out for me."

She was babbling. And had no reason to cover up what wasn't there.

"I just wanted to know if Dawson and I could spend our last ten minutes playing video games in the living room," she said, naming the character game Dawson was playing the first time they'd come over.

"Gah," Dawson said, holding on to Kelsey's hand.

"Of course." Janie smiled. "Dawson, show Kelsey how to turn on 'Cat's Playhouse.'"

With a hurried "Thanks" over her shoulder, Kelsey was gone.

"She never asks questions about him," Janie said softly, watching the children as they settled in the other part of the L-shaped room. "She just takes him as he is and acts like he's normal."

Hands in the pockets of his pants, Burke seemed to be focusing on the kids, too. "She's got a huge heart. And a way of seeing the world that is uniquely hers. She questions things I take for granted. And takes for granted things I would question." The video game came on—along with enough noise to mask their quiet conversation.

He sounded as much lost as filled with a curious kind of pride as he described Kelsey. Almost as though he couldn't take any credit at all for the daughter he'd helped create and was raising on his own.

"If there's anything she's doing wrong, anything she needs to know, I'm sure she'll be happy to learn…"

He was talking as though he was approving of Kelsey's idea to continue to see Dawson after the end of their time on *Family Secrets* together.

As in, they might see each other, from time to time at least, in the future.

"She's doing just great," she said now. There was too much coming at her at once. She couldn't figure out what was going on and if any of it was okay. "She pays attention to him, and other than things I do to supplement his therapies, Dawson can pretty much show you or tell you what he needs. As long as you listen."

Not listen with your ears, but with your heart. Until now she'd only ever known Joe and Cor, and a couple of his teachers, who had ever done that for her son.

And she knew one thing... Even if it meant her having to deal with some kind of unrequited affection for Burke Carter, as long as Kelsey wanted to be a part of Dawson's life, Janie would do what it took to give the girl the chance.

BURKE DIDN'T FIGHT with himself about calling Janie on Friday. Yeah, it was the day before the show. Yes, they both had to be focused. But there'd been a very deep, if imperceptible, change between them on her driveway the previous night.

He needed to call her. To stay in contact while he figured out everything else. He'd already called his lawyer. Given the go-ahead for machinations necessary to get his grant set up and put into motion.

Hoping that when she didn't win *Family Secrets*, she'd be open to letting him help her.

She answered on the first ring. Told him she was making macaroni and cheese for

Dawson's dinner. That they'd had a great therapy session that day. Her son squeezed his lips together on his own to sound an "oh."

She'd talked to Beanie, too, earlier that afternoon. She was sitting up in bed, with help, but the doctors were now acknowledging that with a lot of hard work and some luck thrown in, a full recovery was feasible.

In return, Burke told her about Kelsey's continued good mood. And that he didn't like it that she was still just engaging with talk about Dawson, with cooking. Not engaging with her friends or talking about kids at school. And that she'd gone to bed as soon as they'd completed their practice cooking session the night before. Her door was closed tight before nine with no light shining from beneath it.

And then their talk was done. Nothing was said about his day. Or hers. The night before, and anything they'd talked about, never came up. Still, he felt as he rang off as though he'd kissed her good-night. Just a peck. But it was good.

SATURDAY'S MANDATORY INGREDIENT was pasta. Any variety. Served as an appetizer, side dish or main dish.

At Kelsey's request, Burke had registered to

make Lil's favorite of all her recipes. Spaghetti sauce. Lil put things in spaghetti that didn't sound at all spaghetti-like. And yet everyone loved it. It wasn't hard to make—assuming you got the sauce right. Wasn't even all that fancy. The flavor was unmatched as far as he and Kelsey were concerned.

He worried when he smelled the stuffed shells coming from the kitchen next to him. But for only a moment. He was already in the final showdown.

The shells weren't Janie's. He wasn't sure what she was making but it involved the oven.

With Dawson at Corrine and Joe's, Kelsey spent the entire taping out in the audience. Burke focused on her. And felt Janie's presence on the stage with him in a way he hadn't before.

He didn't speak to her, though. Didn't get close enough to have a conversation. She'd already been on the set when he'd arrived. And hadn't left her kitchen since the taping began. She was determined to win. He knew that. He hoped she wasn't also trying to avoid him.

While he broke his spaghetti in half, as Lil had always done, before dropping it in boiling water with a hint of olive oil, he had this crazy idea that he'd love to take Janie out to dinner tonight. Just the two of them.

Like…a date.

He had a flash vision of her in the outfit she'd worn for one of the shows. The leggings, the sweater and makeup, the curls in her hair. And the smile she'd had on her face during the last moments of the Thanksgiving show. Only, the look in her eye would be different, one meant for a grown man, not a little boy. But it would be just as focused.

On him.

He dropped a handful of spaghetti, lifting it from the strainer to the serving plate. And was certain that the camera had caught his clumsiness. He could just hear the voice-over Natasha would record to go with it. "Dr. Carter looks nervous. Is he worried about who else might win? About the competition he'll face in the final round?"

He heard her voice. Calling his name.

For real.

He was up.

Burke won again. Janie could still hear Kelsey's squeal from the audience when her father's name was called.

Janie had already been standing with Luca Bartolo and Natasha in the winner's circle. The Manhattan Italian restaurant owner had come in second runner-up and Janie had been first with her noodle, cream-cheese mixture and meat layered casserole. She had been facing the front, instead of toward Natasha, as the remaining candidates had been doing, and had seen Kelsey jump right up out of her chair. She saw the girl wipe away tears, too.

And wasn't sad that Burke had won again. And she wasn't going to panic about her own status, either. She'd made herself enter in the first place. Had won a spot on the show. Managed to cook well enough for three runner-up mentions. She was not going to give up on herself now. To the contrary, she was going to take her unique designation of being the only cook on the stage to impress the judges with all three dishes, and she was going to win this thing.

No amount of critical self-talk was going to change her mind this time. She had as much right, as much of a chance, to be a winner as anyone else.

FLYING HIGH, LOOKING forward to a night of restful sleep, Burke tried to get to Janie before she made it out of the studio.

She was going to be fine. He needed so badly to tell her that. But until he figured out how to change her mind about grants, just knowing it himself felt good. She might be worried about losing, about what she'd do when she did, but one way or another, she'd have his yearly grant money to sustain her for the foreseeable future. Once she saw that it was in no way "trashy" for her to avail herself of what he wanted to be rightfully hers.

When she understood that it wasn't pity money, but money she'd earned simply by being herself. Hardworking. Loyal.

A woman who, even though she was at her wit's end, strapped for time, was willing to have Kelsey around as long as Kelsey needed to be around. No strings attached. Because she understood Kelsey and had such over-flowing compassion that there was plenty to spare for the daughter of someone she'd known only a few weeks.

And he'd won a second time! He couldn't help believing now that it was as his so-wise-for-her-age daughter had known from the beginning. Lil was taking care of this. For their daughter. In spite of everything, she was going to have his back again.

He'd give his all—and his all was going to be good enough. This time. Because of Lil.

"Call her," Kelsey said as she saw him watching Janie's old car pull out onto the road after he and Kelsey stepped outside the studio.

"She's bound to be upset. Maybe now would be a good time to tell her about Lil Cares."

He glanced down into the blue eyes gazing up at him. "Lil Cares?"

"The name for the charity. It's good, huh?" She was grinning. Had been since they'd met up at the door of the green room. She'd launched herself at him, and as he'd caught her, Janie had slipped past them.

Several of the other contestants had stopped to offer him what honestly felt like sincere congratulations and he'd missed his chance to see Janie.

"Yeah," he told her. "I like it." Just wasn't sure the name would help him convince Janie that the multiyear grant for which she could apply was *not* charity.

"You have to call her, Dad," Kelsey said as they walked to his car.

Because his daughter was giving him an excuse to do what he really wanted to do, Burke pulled out his phone.

He hit the speed dial for her number—programmed only for the duration of the show, he'd told himself at first. But now, with Kelsey planning to be a regular visitor in Janie's home, he'd probably keep the speed dial active.

"Hello?"

He was sure she had him on speakerphone

so she could talk hands-free. But the reception wasn't all that good. It wasn't as if Janie's car would be equipped with modern technology.

"Kelsey and I wanted to take you and Dawson out to dinner tonight." The offer was bold. Not quite the date he'd fantasized about, but this was real life. And he wasn't going to screw up this chance he had to get it right by letting himself lose focus.

"Oh, that's sweet, Burke, but not necessary. I'm fine, really. Like Natasha said, I'm the only one who's won the accolades of judges from all three weeks. I just have to make certain that next week I step it up a notch."

She sounded chipper enough. He was a bit taken aback. But…relieved, too.

"It wasn't a pity dinner, Janie. We just thought it would be nice to celebrate together."

"Oh." He waited through a pause. "Well, actually, it would be. But I'm on my way to Cor's."

"To pick up Dawson? We could meet somewhere close by. Where do they live?"

In a perfect world her response would be to give him her friend's address. To invite him to stop by and meet them. No, that was the fantasy world.

His current world was perfect. A glance at Kelsey's happy face was all he needed to convince him.

"No, to have dinner," she told him. "I just got off the phone with them. Joe has steaks on and they asked me to stay."

Steaks weren't something that you could stretch to feed more mouths. Not comfortably.

He started to look for a solution that would include him and Kelsey. But thought better of it. He didn't want anyone—Kelsey included—to get the wrong idea.

Wishing Janie a happy dinner, and giving in to the urge to tell her friends hi for him, he rang off. And put on his happiest face as he took his daughter on a date to celebrate their win.

Yep. It was a near perfect night.

CHAPTER TWENTY-THREE

CORRINE MET JANIE at the door with a hug. One that held on tight. For a while. Even after Dawson was there, his short, chubby arms wrapped as far around Janie's legs as he could get them.

"Ma. Ma. Ma," he grunted over and over. Like a chant.

And then he was gone, back to whatever he'd been doing, and Janie looked at Cor. "What's going on?" she asked, all best-friend tentacles fully extended. Cor hadn't been crying. Didn't look worried. Exactly.

Anxious, maybe.

"Is it Beanie?" She didn't think so. But after a day of taping and anticipation, a day of fighting her absurd attraction to something—and someone—she'd never have, she was tired. Beanie was the first thing that sprang to mind.

Cor shook her head. "I spoke with her a couple of hours ago. She's in a lot of pain, but ready to fight the fight. She plans to be well enough to come out this summer."

"Good. That's good." Cor stood in the foyer. Cor never stood in the foyer. If it was serious, they moved into the tea room. If it wasn't, they went for the kitchen.

"So what's going on?"

Cor grinned. Then started to cry. Still grinning. "I'm pregnant, Janie!"

Eyes wide, all sensation on hold, Janie asked, "Does Joe know?"

Cor nodded. "He was with me when I took the test…this afternoon…when Dawson was down for his nap. I was so nervous and wanted to do it when Dawson was here. He has a way of grounding you, you know? Of always making you feel like, no matter, everything will be okay in the end."

She nodded. And then nodded more profusely. Because Cor was right. Her son brought a very special sense to the world. One that she cherished. And needed.

Right then.

"So Joe's good with it?" Her words were almost a whisper. But she was frightened. Really frightened. For Cor. And Joe. For their marriage.

One of the things that had solidified the bond between Joe and Dillon was their adamant assertion that they did not want to father children. Ever.

But then Dawson had come along. And Cor had started to change, even though she'd been lying to herself about it. And her marriage had been in trouble.

Until Joe had come clean about the secret he'd been keeping. About the reason why he didn't want to have children. About not wanting to bring a child into the world who'd have to live with the shame of being the offspring of criminals jailed for life. Or, in this case, the grand-offspring.

"Joe's good with it." The voice was a lot deeper than Corrine's. Janie turned to look at the tall, handsome man who adored Cor as much as Janie could ever have hoped for her friend.

"You're sure?" Her look wasn't the least bit meek.

"I'm sure." His wasn't meek, either, as he looked her right in the eye.

"Because if you're not, we have to be open about it. Work on it. Deal with it…"

Corrine put an arm around her shoulders. Joe, standing on her other side, did, too. "We're going to do this together," Joe said. "Cor and I. And you and Dawson. Until Dawson grows up, I'm the man in this family and there's nothing I want to be more than that."

Janie laughed then. And cried some, too.

They toasted Cor's pregnancy and Janie's honorable mention with sparkling cider. It was a happy family dinner. A perfect dinner.

Janie was still smiling when she crawled into bed that night. Until she turned out the light.

Then, under the cover of darkness, and in total silence, the tears started to fall. There were no sobs. No big production. Just quietly falling drops of loneliness.

She knew, even if Cor and Joe didn't, that things were going to change. When the baby came, Joe and Cor weren't going to have as much time to help her with Dawson. And their financial resources were going to be less, too. Not significantly. But with a child of their own, their resources would have to go there first.

As they should.

As she honestly and truly wanted them to. Her happiness that evening had not been faked. Not even a little bit. She was thrilled for her friends.

Their news was just all the more reason why she had to win *Family Secrets*.

With Cor and Joe starting a family, she and

Dawson were truly out on their own. She'd known the time would come.

Had been preparing herself for years.

And didn't feel ready.

BURKE TOLD KELSEY they'd do whatever she wanted to do on Sunday. Her homework was done. She'd been giving her all at the dance studio. And he didn't want her to spend the day as she had for the past two years—on the couch in front of the television set, napping, or tagging along with whatever he'd made her do, not engaging.

She wanted to have Dawson over to play video games.

"He'd be great with Mario, Dad, but their system is, like, almost pre- even the first Mario."

Open mouth, insert size 11 shoe. And enjoy the spoils? An afternoon at home with Janie didn't sound horrible.

"I couldn't sleep last night, thinking that Janie was all alone and worried about not winning. She's going to be worrying about next week's show since it's her last chance. And when we win, she might not ever want to see us again."

"She's already said you can be friends with Dawson after the show," he inserted quickly.

"You talked about it?" Kelsey's eyes were

wide as she looked at him over her bowl of
bran flakes.

A good wide-eyed look or a bad one? Would
she be mad to find out that he'd been talking
to Janie about her behind her back? Or glad
to know that her continued relationship with
Dawson was all settled?

Didn't change his answer any. Truth was the
only way he went when it came to his daughter.

"Yes," he said. Gesturing with his piece
of toast, he added, "She didn't hesitate at all.
Said you're welcome for as long as you want
to be there."

Head tilted, she narrowed her eyes at him.
"You sure you didn't pressure her or anything?"

His kid was onto him. "I'm not saying I
wouldn't have," he told her, "but I didn't need
to. She's happy to have you there. So, since
you know your time with Dawson isn't limited, you want to go do something wild and
crazy today? Horseback riding? A hot-air-
balloon ride." He was winging it. Trying to
remember things she'd asked for in the past.

"I want to have Dawson over," she said in a
tone of voice that told him she wasn't budging.

A tone that kind of worried him.

"You have no penance to pay, Kels," he

said, his tone as serious as it had ever been. "If your mother is watching down on you, she already knows your heart. She knows that you're sorry for being afraid that your baby brother was going to change everything. And she knows that you truly care about Dawson Young."

He knew it now, too. Something Janie had said about Kelsey listening to Dawson—she couldn't have been speaking about verbal communication. Kelsey "got" Dawson. You couldn't do that with a selfish heart.

She ate a couple of bites of cereal.

"I just want to spend the day with Dawson, Dad," she said when he was beginning to think she'd shut down on him again. "It's not about Mom. Not completely, anyway. Being with him…it just makes me feel good."

He needed to point something else out to her.

"You do realize that every time you're with Dawson, it puts me alone with his mother?"

"I know." She frowned but then gave him a pleading look. "I get that you're doing a lot for me," she said. "And from now on, I'll go to his house, and you can just drop me off. It's just… I want him to see my stuffed animals. I figure, if he likes one, he can take it home with him and have a part of me with him when I'm not there. And… I really want him to try Mario…"

She didn't get it. At all.

Convincing himself that there was nothing to get, Burke gave up.

Made the call.

And wasn't sure if he was elated or worried when Janie accepted his invitation.

BURKE'S HOUSE WAS twice the size of Joe and Cor's. She could certainly see how Kelsey could feel lonely with so much space around her.

The teenager had her own private bathroom attached to her room. And a sitting area, too.

No wonder she spent so much time in there. It was lovely. Secure. A purple-and-off-white haven. Janie kind of wanted to curl up on the cushioned sofa with the purple-and-white heart blanket and…sleep.

First. Then read a book. Cuddle Dawson. Sleep some more…

Dawson had other ideas. Kelsey had turned on Mario the second they'd come into her room and he was hooked.

"We've got a current game console downstairs." Burke, who was wearing designer jeans and a black polo shirt, led Janie down the hallway to the stairs they'd climbed moments before. They passed a couple of other doors. Slightly ajar. She kept her gaze pointing straight ahead.

The less she knew, the less she'd have to fight the fairy-tale fantasies her mind would conjure up.

Or the longing to be part of them.

"I debated letting Kelsey take the old console up to her room, but she's never been one to lose herself in video games—said she wanted it just for when she had friends sleep over. So I gave in."

"Does she have friends sleep over often?" Janie had the impression Kelsey had isolated herself almost completely—other than dance.

"She used to. But not since Lil died."

The woman's touch was all over the house. In the silk flower arrangements. The intricately designed, beaded lamp shades and color choices. Unless...

"Did you have a designer decorate before you moved in?"

The look he gave her made her feel more uncomfortable than she already did. Thank goodness she'd given in to her ego and put on the expensive black leggings—not the cheap box-store ones she usually wore—and long cashmere, short-sleeved, belted sweater Cor had bought her for Christmas. Together with her good boots, they gave a badly needed boost to her self-esteem.

To her confidence.

"Lil did it all" was all he said.

She didn't belong there. And had no idea what she was going to do for the hour she'd said Dawson could play with Kelsey. She'd turned down the lunch and/or dinner invitation attached to the outing. Now she wished they had a meal to take up the time.

"I was talking to a friend of mine on Friday," Burke was saying as he led her downstairs and around the corner from where they'd come in.

They were in a library of sorts. A full wall of bookcases backed an enormous desk. Dark leather furniture sat some distance in front of the desk in a communication-pit style. The hardwood floor was mostly covered with a maroon-and-gold wool rug.

"He's a pediatric specialist at the hospital where I was doing rounds. We've golfed together a few times. Anyway, he gave me a book that he thought you might like."

He'd been talking about her to a friend of his? Her first thought, accompanied by a sudden leap of her heart, was that he was experiencing some of the same attractions to her that she was to him. That he'd had as frank a conversation with his friend as she'd had with Corrine.

That she wasn't losing her mind, here.

Then he gave her the book.

"It's called a communication book," he said.

She could see that. The name was on the front cover.

"I'm not sure if you already have one, but when he offered it, I figured it wouldn't hurt to have two…"

She was shaking her head, greedily turning pages. And couldn't say anything because of a very different kind of emotion clogging her throat.

The book was for Dawson, not her. It contained pages and pages of colorful pictures, widely spaced, easy to distinguish, organized by topics.

"The idea is he finds what he wants to say and pushes it," Burke was saying. "It says the word or words. You know what he's trying to say and then, when you can, you try to get him to say the words before you give him what he wants."

Janie nodded. She'd seen a similar book, not nearly as nice, in the waiting room at one of Dawson's speech-pathology sessions. A little girl, a couple of years older than Dawson, had been using it.

"There are different versions, many with non-talking pages," she finally managed to say, still looking through the book. "These, though…they're out of my budget. I was hoping maybe he'd be assigned one from pre-school when he gets moved into kindergarten next year."

When she had her emotions more in control, she glanced up at him. "Thank you. It was very kind of you to think of us."

Taking the book from her, Burke set it on the table. She expected him to give her space. Was relieved—and finding it sweet—that he seemed to know she needed a moment, when he stepped closer.

His arms were around her before she could form thought. Before she could think about resisting him. This man who'd just given her a sign of his support for her son.

She wanted to pull away—knew with all of her being that she needed to—but when she glanced up, to tell him so, her gaze got lost in his. He mesmerized her, and when his mouth started to lower, she could only watch.

His lips were soft, leathery velvet. If there was such a thing. But there wasn't. Couldn't be. Just like this kiss couldn't be happening.

Janie's lips were open. She knew how to kiss.

She knew how to say no, too. But she wasn't doing it. Her entire body felt weak and incredibly energized at the same time. She clung to him. Let him kiss her a second time. Kissed him back.

When the thump came from upstairs, at first she thought it was her heart pounding through her. Burke was apparently in much better control than her. He pulled back. Listened. The thump came again. And again.

"She's got him playing dance studio," he said.

She. Him. Their kids.

The reason they were together.

She nodded. Stepped away.

She couldn't take back what she'd done. But she could make certain it didn't happen again.

At least, she hoped she could do so.

Ignoring what had just happened, afraid that Burke would apologize, or that he'd try to do it again, Janie asked him about his landscaping.

Landscaping? How was that for a subtle escape cry?

He didn't call her on her lack of class. As though he kissed women in his den every day, he calmly invited her to follow him.

Outside was a covered room with wicker, padded seating. A television set. And several feet away, behind a six-foot-tall, wrought-iron fence, a pool with a rock waterfall. Bright red bougainvillea vines climbed the fence. The whole yard was a masterpiece in natural aesthetics and colors.

Corrine and Joe's place was lovely. And didn't hold a candle to Burke's. She had no idea how far out of her league she really was.

And yet, as she sat, she relaxed. Just for the moments she was there. For her son to have his time with his new friend.

She relaxed until Burke approached with two chilled bottles of water, took the cap off one, handed it to her and then, holding the other, sat. Right next to her.

With his thigh almost touching hers, he turned and looked at her, his expression serious.

"You don't have to always go it alone, Janie."

He was so close to reading her mind, the words almost angered her. She might be poor, but she didn't need pity.

But…he was being so incredibly sweet. And she knew he meant well.

"I don't," she told him, hoping her smile was warm in return.

"No, you don't." Her response seemed to

have energized him. "There are a lot of ways you can get help and—"

She was shaking her head. "I meant, I don't go it alone."

"Oh."

"I appreciate so much that you and Kelsey have taken an interest in Dawson," she told him. "I hope that Kelsey's time with Dawson is helping her in return. Other than that, you don't need to worry about us. We're fine."

She was falling for the guy. And he was offering handouts. Small ones. A book. But still…seeing her as someone in need of his charity. Not his love.

Or even an equal, give-and-take friendship.

That was the one thing about Corrine and Joe. They might buy more things for her and Dawson than she felt comfortable with, but they needed her, too. She catered business dinners. She was Cor's rock. They were family.

He nodded. Kept looking at her like a cat with a full bowl of cream. "I'm just saying… if you don't win *Family Secrets*…"

Shaking her head again, she silenced him. "We aren't talking about the show. And I'm fine," she insisted.

"But I asked around this week. Couldn't

you at least look at some of the various ways, things you can apply for…"

Guess she needn't have been worried about the two of them alone with the kids upstairs. Burke looked at her and saw poverty. Need.

Financial need.

Not anything more personal. Like her needing him to kiss her again. Just once. So she could feel nothing and get over this sudden fascination for him. Get over—again—wanting a man in her life.

"I'm the queen of ways to get money," she told him. "How do you think bills got paid until I was old enough to get a job and earn the money to pay them? There are programs for schoolbooks and clothes, if you know where to look. Programs for food during school. You can get assistance for utility bills. Food stamps. Free clinics and various other ways to supplement the welfare checks. More if your mom's in jail."

She'd escaped the child welfare system. But only because her mother had never done enough time to lose custody and she'd had Cor's mom and dad, who considered her part of the family.

"Was it always that way then?"

He didn't look appalled, exactly. He hadn't pulled away from her.

And since she'd started—telling him things she'd never even told Dillon—what did it matter if she continued?

"No." Sipping water, Janie let herself enjoy the rare moment of peace. Of not having to work or listen for Dawson. The gorgeous backyard was like a garden of...good feeling. "My grandmother, Mom's mom, lived with us until I was five. Mom was good then. She worked. Grandma took care of me and the house. We laughed a lot. Then Grandma died and Mom just kind of...lost it.

"I later found out that my grandmother moved in with us because Mom lost it for the first time when my father left her high and dry. She just didn't have what it took to believe she could take care of herself. To actually do it. And when there was not only no one left to take care of her, but someone for her to take care of, she couldn't handle it. She wanted to. She loved me to distraction. She just didn't have it in her."

"The winning recipe on the Thanksgiving show. That was your grandmother's..."

He sounded as though he was just remembering that. "Right," she said. "She used to have me help her in the kitchen. She'd sit me on the counter and make games out of everything. She loved to cook, and though I was young, my best memories are of being with her in the kitchen. I'm sure she's the one who gave me my love of cooking. And probably my talent for it, too…"

But they weren't going to talk about cooking.

He'd taken a drink of water. And, sitting back, put an arm along the top of the couch. Behind her shoulders.

Meant nothing. Probably didn't even realize he'd done it. Her blood was racing. Her heart pounding.

"So you see…" She spoke too loudly. Felt the heat rise to her face. "One of the things I learned growing up is that you can't rely on charity," she continued. Because she didn't know how to quit. Wouldn't quit. Couldn't quit. "Because it's a full-time job. You don't just find a program, get everything in place, and sit back and rely on the money. It can be taken from you at any moment. Programs change. They end. Different people get in power and everything changes. Or tax cuts happen. Or someone else comes along who writes a better letter. Or has a worse circumstance.

"Relying on the charity of others means that you don't ever have a sense of security. I'm already availing myself and Dawson of every program there is to assist with his therapies and needs. Other than that… I'm a single mother who has to work and whose son needs a lot more of my time than another child might. I'm good with that. Really."

She hadn't asked for pity. And absolutely did not want it.

In an effort to convince him, she touched his hand. "I'm happy, Burke," she said, looking him straight in the eye. "Dawson really and truly makes me happy."

Her life might be two-dimensional. She might be missing an important adult experience with her lack of an adult partner relationship. But she *was* happy.

And would be a lot more so if and when she won *Family Secrets*. Dillon thought she was too nice. And maybe she was.

But she was also the girl who didn't quit. Ever.

CHAPTER TWENTY-FOUR

BURKE WANTED TO kiss her again. To just put his lips on hers and make her words stop coming. Every single one that escaped from her mouth hit him in the heart.

He couldn't remember ever admiring anyone more. The class with which she defended her right to not be as rich and privileged as he was, while never once even hinting that she thought he was a snob. Or privileged.

No matter what happened with the show, or with the grant he was setting up, he was not going to forget her. Didn't even want to try.

What he wanted was…

"Go out with me."

Her chin dropped. Her mouth fell open. And he felt like a first-class idiot.

"What?"

Chuckling, he drew on his bedside manner. "I like you," he said. "When a man realizes that he likes one woman in particular, and wants to get to know her better, he asks her out on a date." Levity helped. In all kinds of situations.

"You like me." She licked her lips. Took a sip of water. Stared toward her knees. And then added, "We're opponents on—"

"I know. But this isn't about the show. C'mon. Go out with me." Was he really so close to begging?

"Because of Kelsey and Dawson."

If he wasn't mistaken, that pulse in her neck had just leaped. Her respiratory rate had increased.

"Because of you and me."

Her lips trembled this time when she smiled. "You like me."

"Yes." There just didn't seem to be much point denying the fact. And he had to say more. "I have to be honest with you. I don't know that I wouldn't let you down where Dawson is concerned, if we ever decided to do more than date. I'm pretty single-minded when it comes to my work and don't always even manage to get Kelsey from dance on time."

"I don't need help with Dawson's schedule." She didn't sound defensive. But he could feel space between them that hadn't been there a moment before. And realized, too late, how his need for self-confession would have sounded to a woman whose husband had left her because of her son.

"I like your son, Janie," he said. "I enjoy

him, actually. For however long we might be…
friends… I will do whatever I can to engage
in both of your lives. I'm just… Lil… I know
my shortcomings and thought it best—fair—
to lead with them."

He had in no way intended for the afternoon to take a route in any way related to this
one. Didn't know how to get off the path now
he'd started down it.

"I don't do much of anything without him.
Except when he's in school. Then I do everything I have to do that I can't do with him."

"Your friends watch him when we're taping." He was playing devil's advocate. Against
himself.

She nodded. Gave him a sideways glance.
"Cor would be only too happy to keep him for
me to go out with you," she said half under
her breath.

"You told them about me?"

"I haven't yet found the secret that I could
keep from Corrine. She's apparently got half
ownership of my brain."

He grinned. Probably bigger than the comment warranted. "And do you mess around
in hers, too?"

"Of course. Probably more than she does
in mine. Cor's the practical one. I was the

aware one." She made quote marks with her fingers as she said the word.

He liked her hands. They were slender, with fingers that looked like they could move mountains if they had to.

Lord, he was getting…too far gone.

"So…it's a date?" Why was he pushing so hard?

But he knew. Because if he didn't get her to do this before the show ended, there might not be another chance.

One of them was going to be a loser. And the stakes were so high…

"You haven't asked for a particular date yet."

Was she messing with him now?

"Wednesday night. Kelsey doesn't have dance and I could bring her over to stay with Dawson." He was winging this. And prayed that his daughter wouldn't slap one of her unpredictable mood changes on him and refuse to babysit.

He didn't think she would. Since he'd won twice, he pretty much walked on water with her at the moment.

Like he'd done back when she was his happy little girl. When life had been easy and he'd been so much more focused on himself than he ever should have been.

"Shouldn't we ask her first?"

"Let's go now..."

"No." She hesitated and he was afraid she was backing out already. "It's not fair to put her on the spot like that. With me and Dawson standing here. Wait until you're alone with her..."

She wasn't backing out!

"If she says yes, will you go out with me?"

"If she says yes, yes." Janie sounded like she didn't think his daughter would comply.

But smart beggars didn't look a gift horse in the mouth.

At least, that was the hogwash he was going with.

It fit right in with the rest of his mixed-up life.

JANIE FIGURED THE good thing about having her final chance to win a place in the championship round, her meeting with Dillon's attorney and a possible fling night out with Burke Carter all happening the same week was that she couldn't get overwrought about any of them. One distracted her from the other.

The meeting with Dillon was...amiable. He was rational. Agreeable. Even kind as he listened to her concerns about just turning over a special-needs child to a man who not only knew nothing about his needs and routines, but was a complete stranger to him. He asked all the right questions about Dawson. Questions she'd have given a kidney to have him ask anytime over the past four years.

Together, the four of them worked out a potential schedule for Dillon to be educated as to his son's needs, his therapies, home exercises, routines and Down syndrome in general. And for him to be slowly introduced into Dawson's life.

Janie wanted to believe he was being sincere. She wanted to hope that Dawson would have his father in his life. Teaching him. Loving him.

So badly, she wanted to be able to share the hopes and worries, the fears and joys, of parenting their very special boy.

But he'd played her so many times in the past. Played on her penchant for believing everything she was told.

Burke called half an hour after the meeting. She'd just said goodbye to Cor in the law-office parking lot. She had to get back to work and Janie had to make one more flower delivery before picking up Dawson and getting him to a swim class recommended to help build his arm and leg muscle tone.

This was going to be their first lesson and

she was nervous about how well it would go. Dawson loved playing in the water in the tub. But was afraid of Joe and Cor's pool. And the shower.

"How'd it go?" Burke asked as she started her car.

"Good." She gave him an abbreviated blow by blow.

He didn't interrupt. And when she'd finished, he said, "Did he seem sincere?"

"Yeah." She turned onto the main roadway that would take her back across town. She'd already picked up the flowers—several dozen cut carnations—from the shop. It was cool enough outside that they were fine wrapped, with their stems in water, and lying in her trunk.

"You sound hesitant." She felt hesitant.

"What did Corrine think?"

"That he's up to something."

She'd already told him that Cor and Joe had been best friends with her and Dillon when they'd been married. "Cor's a bit prejudiced where he and I are concerned."

"So you think this new tack he's taking could be a good thing?"

"It could be."

"What would be a possible reason for him

doing this if he didn't want to get to know his son?"

Burke was a good man. So much like Joe in some ways. Neither of them would turn their backs on their own flesh and blood. Whether they wanted to be dads or not. Or thought themselves father material or not.

"Cor thinks he's doing it to somehow get his hands on my money if I win *Family Secrets*."

"How would he do that? Your divorce settlement is done, right? Does he pay alimony? I suppose that could change. But he wouldn't need to see his son to make that happen."

"No, he doesn't. Just child support."

"So, what do you think?"

She thought she wanted to know what Kelsey had said about watching Dawson Wednesday night. If Burke had even asked.

If he'd come to his senses, he wouldn't have.

"Janie?"

"Yeah. I'm here." She drove the speed limit. Not one mile an hour faster. She couldn't afford a ticket. Or traffic school. "I think that Dillon is trying to soften me up."

"To what end?"

"He says I'm a pansy." It was the bald truth. "I'm too nice. And in the past several years—

since I got pregnant—he's seemed to take delight in taking advantage of what he deems are my most nauseating weaknesses."

"But why go this far?"

"I lay in bed thinking about that last night," she told him, changing lanes so a car could get by her. "The timing of this makes me suspicious. I hear from him after the first taping of *Family Secrets*. After he sees that I'm actually going to have a shot at the grand prize."

"You have a good point. What did Cor think of that?"

"She'd already thought of it, too. And I agree with her that he's after any money I might get if I win. I just think it's a little more clear-cut than she does. He thinks if he can convince me he wants to be a good dad, if he gives me what he thinks I want, I'll share my bounty with him."

"He thinks you'll get back with him."

She'd thought of that, too. In the middle of the previous night.

But this wasn't about him wanting Dawson or her. "He has a girlfriend," she said now. At least, Dillon said Wendy was still in the picture.

"How long have they been together?"

"Three months."

"You think that relationship would be worth losing all the money you'd make if you won?"

"No."

"So…say we're right. You win. He tries to get you back. How do you feel about that?"

She could put up with Dillon, to know that Dawson's future was secure and she could be free to tend to him full-time. A month ago she might actually have tried to convince herself that Dillon had really had a change of heart. Now she knew that even if he had, she didn't want him in her life. Not as anything other than Dawson's father. And only then if he'd had a full change of heart regarding their son. She still wasn't convinced he had.

"I feel used." And she didn't like it. "It makes me angry that he takes advantage of my need to be open and loving rather than defensive and mean. That he says I'm weak because I don't 'toughen up.'"

Wow. She hadn't actually realized that. Until just then.

"Anger's good."

"I saw a lot of kids growing up, ones I met in counseling whose parents were addicts… They got hard. Defensive. Mean. I didn't want to live my life that way. If that makes me weak, then so be it. I'm not going to let him make me like him. I'm not going to fight dirty."

"So what are you going to do?"

"Follow the agreed-upon plan. Hope for the best. And wait to see what happens."

"You want me to have a talk with him?"

She thought he was kidding. But couldn't be entirely sure. "Yeah, that would be great," she said and chuckled.

He chuckled, too. And then said, "I talked to Kelsey this morning..."

He didn't say anything more. But she knew what he meant. "And?" Was she really this het up by the idea of one night out with a handsome doctor?

Not just any doctor.

Burke.

"She figured that we were giving her a trial run for babysitting Dawson after the show is done. She was excited."

"She said yes?" Her heart was thumping.

"Yes."

He didn't say any more than that. Just yes. She felt like he'd kissed her. Long and hard.

"Um, Burke?"

"Yeah?" His voice had lost its note of teasing.

"We... I'll go...but...can we agree? Like before? No talk of the show? We're just friends on a..."

"Date." He filled in the word she'd struggled to get past the constriction in her throat.

"And, yes, we can agree on no talk of the show." His jovial mood had returned in record time.

Janie smiled in spite of herself.

He told her what time he'd pick her up on Wednesday. Told her to dress casually—as if she had any other way to dress. And then said he had to get back to work. He had one more minor surgery to do that afternoon.

Nothing else was said about Dillon.

She made her delivery—to a cemetery with a section filled with single-flower urns—and wondered if, had she taken Burke's question seriously, he'd really have confronted Dillon for her.

It was something she was never going to know.

But just thinking about it kind of made her smile.

CHAPTER TWENTY-FIVE

BURKE WASN'T SURE where to take Janie. He wanted the night to be perfect. Wanted her to know that, no matter what, she was special.

He wanted her to see him again after he won *Family Secrets*. But he couldn't tell her that. He'd promised.

Which meant he couldn't talk about Lil Cares, either. Because to do so meant talking about her losing the show.

His usual haunts were out. He didn't want to risk making Janie feel uncomfortable. Out of her league.

And he didn't want to risk running into anyone he knew, either. The thought had bothered him at first. Until he realized that it wasn't that he was ashamed or embarrassed by dating a woman who delivered flowers for a living. He was shying away from his world because he didn't want to face the barrage of questions with which he'd be hit. About her. About them.

Because he had no answers for them.

And he didn't like that.

In the end, he settled on a picnic on one of his favorite mountaintops. Taking an early afternoon, he prepared the feast himself, having it packed and in the back of his car before Kelsey came home from school.

Lil's mango-and-cucumber wraps would be the perfect beginning. Followed by her potato-and-bean salad. And finishing with homemade brownie bites prepared with cream cheese, cocoa and real butter. Everything, including bottled water to drink, fit into the insulated backpack he used to take with him on hikes.

Back when he'd left his family to do their own thing some Saturdays and gone mountain climbing to clear his head.

The most important part of the meal—the blanket they'd sit on—was already in the car.

All that was left was getting his daughter to Janie's house and Janie out of her house before something could go wrong to prevent the outing.

He felt like a kid waiting for Christmas, fearing the house would burn down and destroy all the presents before he could open them.

And knew he was in serious trouble.

WEARING BLACK LEGGINGS and flip-flops, with a thigh-length, long-sleeved, tie-dyed top she'd borrowed from Cor a few weeks back, Janie wasn't prepared to climb a mountain. As soon as Burke had told her about the picnic they were headed to, she'd started to worry.

He seemed so excited.

And she didn't want him to turn around and take her right back home.

She needn't have worried. Or, rather, she should have trusted him, she amended as they walked the paved path up to the mountain-top. It wasn't really a mountain. More like a hill surrounded by peaks. Not anything that would interest someone wanting the challenge of a mountain hike. And that evening, in the middle of a workweek, no one else seemed interested in climbing a hill, either.

With her insides humming, she walked beside him, thankful for the cool breeze, the perfectly blue sky, the sun that was slowly dipping down.

"We need to be careful we don't get caught by darkness," she said, imagining, just for a second, huddling with Burke in the dark of night, to ward off the cold.

"Sun sets at seven-eighteen tonight," he told her.

He'd checked. Janie smiled.

She should have trusted him.

THE LAST THING Burke wanted to do on that mountaintop with Janie Young was talk about Lil.

So why had he brought his wife's food on the date?

Janie had loved every bite. And wanted to talk about each dish in detail, too.

Of course she did. She was a chef. Cooking was her love.

He'd wanted to be the love of her night.

The thought came unbidden.

And he allowed it, with a very clear distinction—the love of her night. Not of her life.

And then amended, the love of some of her nights.

No...wait...

"This was nice."

The woman consuming most of his free thoughts these days, and most of his sleeping ones, too, stretched those long legs out in front of him. The way she was leaning back on her hands brought other parts of her to his attention, as well. Her face upturned to the setting sun, to the larger mountain peaks all around them, seemed almost angelic to him.

Who lusted after an angel?

"Yeah," he said. Wondering how on earth he was going to kiss her without making it seem like he'd brought her up a deserted mountain simply to have his way with her.

Truth was, where Janie was concerned, he had no idea what his way even was.

What it possibly could be.

Should be.

"I'm glad we did this," she was saying, an almost peaceful smile on her face. "Just what the doctor ordered."

The look she sent him was almost flirty.

Implying that, as the doctor, he ordered well? And was maybe free to order again?

His heart quickened.

"WE NEED TO do this again."

Janie's breath caught. They were almost down the mountain. And Burke had just taken her hand. Was holding on to it.

She'd thought, when he'd packed up and said it was time for them to go without even trying a repeat of the kiss they'd shared the other night, that he was making the right decision to keep their relationship platonic.

Just friends.

It was what she wanted.

The only real choice she had.

But she'd been disappointed, too.

What would a little kissing have hurt?

She wouldn't have been the first woman to have a fling.

It had been so long since she'd been held.

"Maybe a different mountaintop," he continued, swinging her hand with his. "Until we eat on every mountaintop surrounding Palm Desert."

Now he was being silly. She liked that about him—the way he lightened her dark moments.

"You doing all the cooking?" she asked. Because she didn't know what else to say. Of course they weren't going to eat on every mountaintop.

Or probably any other mountaintop.

Neither of their lives was unencumbered. They had kids. Responsibilities.

And lived in two different worlds.

She was going to win *Family Secrets* and his daughter would be devastated.

That writing was just on the wall.

"I'm serious," Burke said as they reached the car. He dropped the blanket under his arm and shrugged off the backpack, leaving both of them on the blacktop of the small, deserted parking lot. He didn't let go of her hand.

He pulled her to him instead. The sun had finally disappeared completely, leaving them in dusky shadows. Burke's body warmed her torso against the evening chill.

"I want to see you again," he said, his mouth just inches from hers.

She wanted to see him, too. In the worst way. But what she wanted and what was right for her, or good for her, weren't always the same thing. That was one lesson she'd learned in the most difficult way. Paid for with her most precious asset—her heart.

She'd wanted Dillon. Had wanted to be married to him.

She'd refused to look at the dangers, the pitfalls, to listen to the doubts.

"I…"

She'd opened her mouth to tell Burke she couldn't do it.

He'd taken her lips instead.

BURKE SAW JANIE when he arrived at the studio Saturday morning. They'd spoken Thursday and Friday. More of the same kind of general talks they'd been having.

And yet different, too.

He'd known, as soon as he'd mentioned seeing her again, that she'd been going to say no.

He hadn't been ready to hear it.

So he'd stopped her.

And hadn't brought the subject up since.

There was something between them.

He had no idea what to do with it.

About it.

No idea what he *could* do with it.

Janie liked him. Probably more than liked him. He knew that.

He liked her, too. Maybe even more than liked her.

And then he thought about the secret he kept. She wouldn't find him nearly as attractive if she knew that he'd let his wife down in her last, most urgent hour of need.

Which was why she wasn't ever going to find out.

And yet how was he any different than Dillon, if he took advantage of her willingness to believe a person was who he said he was, when, in reality, he was someone very different?

Bottom line, he couldn't offer Janie what she really needed—not in the relationship sense. No matter how badly he wanted to be her "relationship."

For a time.

Feeling trapped, he determined to at least keep himself on her "friends" list. Until he could figure out a better way.

He and Kelsey had already decided they were rooting for Janie that last day of competition. A win for Burke wasn't going to make much of a difference, except to knock another opponent out of the final round. Which would be good. But if Janie could at least have one win, along with her honorable mentions, she could get the attention of some other cooking shows, even when she lost the final round.

Approaching with a need just to connect, to tell her good luck, after he'd seen Kelsey to her seat out front, he was surprised when she stopped only long enough to tell him, friendship or no, she had to win and moved right on past.

She wasn't mean. Or in any way unkind.

And had he needed the win to make it to the finals, he might have felt a bit sorry for her. In this, Dillon was, unfortunately, right.

Janie didn't have enough killer in her to take down all opposing forces. She was more the "change course" type and you couldn't do that in competition.

A piece of information he'd use to his advantage if she did make it to the final round. Because he had to win.

And she didn't. One way or another, he'd see that she got what she needed in terms of long-term security and care for her and Dawson.

After *Family Secrets* was over and done.

CASSIE LEONARD, THE home-economics teacher with seven kids, was second runner-up in the last full-contestant competition. Where hearing her name called would have been an honor the first three weeks, that day, her face fell before she smiled and walked across the stage. Janie felt every ounce of her disappointment. Cassie was the first of them to know that she was not going to the final round.

She feared she was going to be the next. Their last competing dish had had to be a breakfast dish. And they'd had only half the preparation time as Natasha allotted extra time to spend with the contestants going to the final round. And interviews with those who were leaving the show that day.

A breakfast dish. With only half an hour from kitchen arrival until serving. Pancakes. Waffles. Eggs. Omelets. Not enough time for a good soufflé.

Natasha was congratulating Cassie. Taking a moment to do a brief interview with her. Bringing out the emotions that hooked viewers.

Janie had been first runner-up three weeks in a row. She seemed like a sure call for the fourth. It would be good for ratings. A novelty. Something to talk about. Something they'd say she could take home with her.

She'd learned a long time ago that second best wasn't good enough.

But her dish—a breakfast wrap—was ordinary at best. Corrine had talked her into entering it. Because she'd been unable to come up with anything else. She had a special sauce she used—a vinegar, mustard, mayonnaise and sugar combination with spices—that was more commonly used on salads and lunch wraps. And she cooked the filling, potatoes first and then onions, all in the same pan—putting the eggs in last. Because when she'd first started making it, she'd had only one pan. She'd done a lot with onions and potatoes and eggs back then. They'd been staples in the free food boxes that had been delivered to the house.

"And our first runner-up, with the top honorable mention, is awarded to…"

Janie's heart thrummed in her chest. This was it. If she was named, right where she'd been named each week, she was done.

"Jenny Mitchell!" The grandmother, wife of a retired farmer. Janie had barely passed a word with her in the weeks they'd been competing. They'd exchanged a smile or two. Nothing more.

And now Jenny was going home. Permanently.

She seemed happy, though, beamingly so, as she crossed the stage. Jenny hadn't needed to win. She'd just been thrilled to be on television. And to have her recipes acknowledged. Apparently, according to what she told Natasha, she was famous now in the little town she'd lived in her entire life. She was happy as a bee.

Her words.

Janie was happy for her. And sick to her stomach. Her wraps had been a bad idea. But she hadn't had a better one.

She'd done her best.

And she needed to get off the stage.

From then on, her sole focus was on keeping a smile on her face and holding herself upright, until they were dismissed. She was not going to humiliate herself on national television. She'd drive straight to Cor's. They were expecting her anyway. They had Dawson.

They wouldn't know the results yet. The show didn't air until that evening.

"Janie Young!" She started when her name was called, her pasted-on smile faltering. She felt herself start to lurch forward before she straightened. But it was Kelsey's squeal that brought her back to earth.

She'd heard Natasha talking. Had known the winner was being announced. And had been trying to brace herself.

She took a step. And then another. But she

turned back, once. To look at Burke. He stood a few down from her in line with Mike, who was going to the final round, and the others who were not. His smile wasn't for the camera. She could tell it was just for her.

She'd won.

CHAPTER TWENTY-SIX

STAKES WERE HIGH NOW. Janie had had three honorable mentions. He'd had none. He'd had two wins. She had one. She'd won accolades all four weeks. He'd won them only two.

But he had two wins.

And killer instinct.

He was going to take this. But he had to stay focused. In tune with Kelsey. With her angels. This was all about Kelsey. For Kelsey.

She wanted to spend Sunday with Janie and Dawson.

"The competition is about recipes, Dad. And Mom's are going to win. Janie and Dawson are people. I don't want him to forget me."

"He's not going to forget you, Kels," he assured her. Afraid that if he saw Janie, he'd get soft. Screw up. Not come through for his daughter.

Focus. His lack of proper focus had killed his wife.

He'd been focused on his patient. Not a life-and-death thing. Not even a big thing. A young athlete who'd needed immediate attention if he had a hope of competing in the last football game of his high school career. A scout from a Big Ten college was going to be there specifically to see him. And he'd turned his ankle running down a flight of stairs to his locker in between classes.

He'd been looking at a girl, he'd told Burke privately.

X-rays had shown Burke that there was no real damage to the ankle. He'd taped it. Wrapped it. And sent the kid off to his game.

To find out that for Lil it was game over.

"Please, Dad, it's important," Kelsey said as she carried a plate of loaded scrambled eggs to the table. "We need to make certain that we stay friends. That the competition doesn't get in the way. It's what Mom would do."

She was right, of course. And what Janie would do, too, he was guessing.

But it wasn't what a cutthroat winner would do.

It *was* what he really wanted to do. It *was* what a man falling in love who wanted to see his woman would do. And he couldn't be that man. Not until he had Kelsey's win.

Far more than she needed a day with Dawson, she needed Burke to win.

Because if he didn't, they'd have a whole new battle to fight. He was professional enough to know that.

For the first time in a long time, he told his daughter no.

JANIE SPENT A little time Sunday with Cor and Joe. Joe "worked out" with Dawson while she and Cor were in the kitchen, discussing recipes. She had to turn in her recipe by Monday morning for the upcoming final showdown. Burke had called that morning. She'd been afraid, when she'd answered, that he was going to suggest another get-together.

Afraid that she'd give in and squeeze out time to go.

He hadn't. He'd just called to congratulate her again—as he had the night before. She'd been at Cor and Joe's then, too. On Sunday she'd suggested they keep contact down to a minimum that week. Just until the competition was done. She had to stay focused.

His ready agreement hurt her feelings.

For the final competition they were allowed to prepare whatever they wanted. They just had to be ready to serve fifty minutes after they stepped into their kitchens. The show was being taped, but in front of a live audience. Dawson and Cor and Joe were going to be there.

She imagined they'd be sitting with Kelsey since the kids were likely going to want to be together. Each contestant was entitled to only one seat, but Joe and Cor had purchased tickets to the final show ahead of time. Either just in case or because they really had had that much faith in her.

It was also likely that Burke was going to meet Joe and Corrine. That Corrine was going to meet Burke.

Janie couldn't let thoughts of that eventuality distract her, either.

In her weak moments thoughts of their date the previous Wednesday crept up to taunt her. To nurture her.

Sometimes she let them.

He'd said he wanted to eat on every mountaintop with her. He'd kissed her.

And hadn't once brought up seeing her again since.

After much deliberation, she and Corrine had landed on her Italian Crescent Roll for her final dish, with a side of fruit gelato. With a crescent-roll exterior and a meaty Italian mixture with various cheeses and secret spices inside, the roll was unique. Something the judges had probably never encountered before, so they'd have nothing to compare it to. It was also delicious. Easy for her to fix. Smelled wonderful. And looked intriguing. It wasn't gourmet. But it was Janie full force. The gelato was so simple for her to prepare it was embarrassing. Except that it tasted so good, Corrine figured the simplicity would be a plus.

She made it for dinner at Corrine's, with Corrine timing her. Giving her camera op suggestions. Suggestions on how to hold her fruit as she sliced it, so the camera focused on her hands and the quick sure strokes she used—showing how she excelled in the kitchen.

She made it again on Monday night, after Dawson's therapies, phone calls, bath time, reading time, flower deliveries and a quick stop at the grocery store somewhere in between it all. After her son had gone to bed.

She didn't hear from Burke.

The mouthwatering scent followed her to sleep and she dreamed about the show all night long. Not about winning or losing. She spent the night trying to get things right. Timing. Stirring. Camera angles. Again and again.

Trying. Never failing or succeeding. Just always trying.

When her phone rang on Tuesday, about an hour before she was due to pick her son up from preschool, her heart leaped. Burke.

Stopped at a light, with flowers in the back, she scrambled for her phone.

Was he missing their conversations as much as she was?

Did it make her a bad mom that she wanted him to call her, in spite of the competition? Or a selfish friend?

Dawson and his future mattered most.

Her feelings for Burke weren't diminished by that fact.

Where was her phone? Third ring. *Don't hang up.*

Kelsey mattered, too.

But there were other ways to assuage her misplaced guilt where her mother and brother were concerned. Other ways to honor her mother.

If Janie won, she was hoping to start a small catering business. She could use Lil's recipes and name the catering business after her, too. Kelsey could have input…

The caller wasn't Burke.

"Dillon, what's up?" she said, trying to sound…friendly.

"According to the schedule, you don't pick him up for another hour."

Him. Not *Dawson.* Not *our son.* But *him.*

"That's right." And he better not be at the preschool or go there. He'd agreed to stay away from Dawson until he'd been fully trained on how to care for his son. And then to allow Janie to introduce them so that Dawson felt safe. That was to Dillon's benefit. There'd be more of a chance that Dawson would accept him, take to him, if Janie was there.

"I'm at the park," he said. He didn't name it. But she knew immediately what he meant. Their park. Around the corner from where they used to live. Where he still lived. They used to take walks there at night. No matter how late their days had ended, they'd walked hand in hand through the park. Talking.

And then they'd go home and…

"I'd like to talk," he said.

She was five minutes away. "I can give you ten minutes," she said, looking at the clock on the dash. "I'm not trying to be difficult. I just have one more delivery to make before I pick up Dawson."

"I'll take the ten minutes. Thank you."

If she'd had more time, if she hadn't known Corrine was in court all afternoon, Janie would have called her friend. Something was wrong with Dillon. He'd never been docile.

Worried, wondering what was up, she saw Dillon as soon as the park came into view. He was sitting on the bench where he'd proposed to her. In jeans and a garage work shirt. Must not be too bad if he was able to go to work. She pulled into the first parking spot she found. Refused to straighten her black sweater or to smooth her hands over jeans-clad hips as she walked with purpose toward the bench.

She was fine just as she was.

Fully aware, as she approached, that he was probably working her, Janie still looked for signs of distress on her ex-husband's features. Their park. Their bench. Him being so amiable.

He said hello. Thanked her for coming. She sat—as far away from him as the bench allowed. Put her hands on her lap and waited. He had only ten minutes.

"Here's how the future is going to go," he said calmly. Almost kindly. He looked her straight in the eye. "I'm going to pay only the basic child support required from me by the state—the monthly amount that comes out of my paycheck. The part of our agreement where I am responsible for overages, for therapies not covered by insurance, for co-pays or tuitions, surgeries, or anything else that comes along, all monies for which bills were sent to me, to be paid directly to you or to a facility, is, as of now, defunct."

He couldn't do that. Not even with shared parenting, were it ever to get that far. His words struck a match to the panic never far from her surface, but she knew better than to let it flame to life. He had to pay. She might have to spend money to take him to court to get him to do so, but he had to pay.

She held his gaze evenly. Because she wouldn't give him the satisfaction of fighting with him. Wouldn't give him more reason to put her down. Because she was afraid her voice would waver and let him hear her fear.

"In exchange for your silence on any monies that were paid by me to you, or to a facility that you visit, I will drop all action to see your son."

Oh. Oh, God. Oh. She was getting it now. He'd never meant to see Dawson. He'd meant to strike fear in her that he would. Meant to show her he could. Meant to let her sleep on it a week or two, knowing in her heart that he could get visitation and that Dawson would suffer for it.

Dillon could not stand to see the boy and admit to himself that he'd fathered a special-needs child. There was no way he'd really do Dawson's exercises at home. Or help with therapies. To the contrary, he'd sit him in front of a video game, anything to keep him quiet, and pretend he wasn't there.

Dillon could get shared parenting. Half of Dawson's life would be spent with his father. Half of his life he'd live without love.

Half of his life he'd be unproductive, which meant his chances of reaching his fullest potential would be lessened.

Dillon knew her.

And once again, he'd used her weakness against her.

Not only was she not gaining the support of a partner in Dawson's care, she was losing a chunk of the financial support Dillon had been paying for four years.

Dillon placed a hand on her knee. "We have an understanding, then?"

She nodded.

He stood and walked away, already on his cell phone. She'd bet her life Wendy was on the other end of the line.

Eager to share the good news.

He'd won.

CHAPTER TWENTY-SEVEN

BURKE CALLED ON WEDNESDAY. Janie told him about her meeting with Dillon. He wanted her to fight him. To tell the court that he was blackmailing her.

But she knew that, in the end, it wouldn't be in Dawson's best interests. Dillon would never outwardly abuse his son. Nor would he neglect him to the point of losing parental rights. He just wouldn't ever support his special needs. Or engage in the frequent exchange of love and hugs that were so important to her son. Dawson would get no therapeutic help while at his father's. The entire science of habilitating Down syndrome children was the consistency of repeated small movements that would assist in building up low muscle tone.

Dillon thought Dawson belonged in an institution. That their son had an existence, not a life.

She couldn't take a chance that, if she fought for the money he would owe her, he'd push for shared parenting and win. She didn't want the man in the same room with her son. Ever.

In the end, Burke did not disagree with her. Though he still wanted her to talk to Corrine.

She would. When she was ready. But Cor wasn't going to change her mind, either. Janie was fairly certain her friend wouldn't even try. She knew Dillon.

For now, Janie's full concentration was on winning *Family Secrets*. Which was why she'd taken Burke's call. She needed him to know why, now more than ever, she was going to do everything she could to take the win from him and Kelsey.

She had no choice. Dillon had just turned his back on them for the last time, cutting them out as much as he possibly could.

She'd thought maybe Burke was going to say something about seeing her again. About eating on mountaintops.

He didn't even wish her luck.

It was as she'd known.

Dawson had her. Only her.

So be it.

Somehow, she was going to be enough.

BURKE NEEDED TO see Janie. To take her in his arms and tell her that she was never going to be alone again. These days apart from her had shown him what he'd done his best to try to avoid seeing. He was in love with a woman he'd known only a few weeks.

He craved her voice. Felt her hurts. Needed her calm, never-quit attitude on his side. He dreamed about her at night. Wanted to call her the moment he got out of surgery—when it went well and when it didn't.

He'd always been logical, analytic. No one fell in love after only one date. And a few visits. In less than a month.

Didn't seem to matter what he knew.

Sometimes there was just no explanation for why things worked out as they did. Why a young girl would have disease in her bone. Why an athlete had the ability to throw farther, run faster or jump higher than anyone else.

Why some kids were born with special challenges.

Or why two people who were worlds apart would be drawn to each other.

Janie was struggling. He'd heard it in her voice. Felt her pain. A pain he knew he could ease. Knew it in his head. And in his heart.

But before he'd be free to tend to her, he had to take care of Kelsey.

He had to win *Family Secrets*.

And then he could think about catching Janie before she could fall.

This was *his* redemption. He couldn't promise to love and care for Janie, couldn't even think about taking on Dawson, until he'd helped Kelsey. He was all she had. Because of him. He couldn't do more until he'd made up for what he hadn't done.

He and Kelsey cooked every night that week. Took notes. Compared notes. He didn't just take orders—he made suggestions. He critiqued himself. He studied and he went back at it. Again and again. The recipe he was making—Lil's version of a traditional French scallop dish served in all of the finest French restaurants—required superb timing to bring out the perfect combination of texture and flavor. He had fifty minutes from the time he stepped into his kitchen until his dish had to be served.

His last attempt had been exactly that, fifty minutes. No wiggle room. And so he spent all day Friday testing heating times against flavors and consistency. Finding where he could turn up the heat just enough to save a few seconds. Where he could cook ingredients separately but at the same time, to prevent the flavors from mingling too soon. Friday night was for just him and Kelsey. From the minute she walked in the door after school they were a team.

Lil's team. When they sat to eat, just after seven, they tasted perfection. Worthy of the fifty-dollar price he'd pay to order the dish in a French restaurant. He'd done it all himself. In forty-three-and-a-half minutes.

"We've got this." Kelsey sat back, plate empty, and looked over the candlelit table straight into his eyes. "You're going to win."

He nodded. Not just to please her. Not just because he loved her so much he'd do everything he could to prove her right.

But because for the first time since Lil's death he truly believed he *was* a winner.

CORRINE DRESSED JANIE. Without warning, she showed up at Janie's house Saturday morning with a big shopping bag. Pulling out a pair of designer, silk-with-just-enough-Lycra, ankle-hugging black pants. Heels that were higher than she usually wore, but platforms so that they were easy to stand in. An off-white, silky, figure-hugging blouse with a black-and-white neckline that looked like a scarf. There were earrings. Fourteen-karat gold housing onyx and pearl.

She curled Janie's hair. Did her makeup.

"You're priceless, Janie, and today, you're

going to feel like it" was all she said before she began.

And during the entire session, with breaks to tend to Dawson, the two of them talked about cooking. About minutes and measurements. Janie could make Italian Crescent Roll in her sleep. But what happened if she got nervous and forgot something?

Corrine had made up mnemonics for every step of the process.

They laughed over a couple of them. Laughed hard.

And Janie was ready.

"I'M NERVOUS." KELSEY stood with Burke in the hallway, down from the green room. She looked so grown up in her blue dress pants and blue-and-white-striped tunic. She was wearing heels. They'd purchased the outfit together the previous Sunday.

He had on a new white shirt and blue-and-white-striped tie to go with his navy dress pants. He'd taken her for a pedicure and manicure that morning and had his hair cut next door while he'd waited.

"I'm nervous, too," he told her. More nervous than he could ever remember being.

"Did you see Janie in there?" Kelsey pointed to the green room. They'd walked through it because it was their entrance to the studio, but he wasn't using the space that day. Kelsey was keeping his keys and cell phone in her purse in the audience.

"Yes."

"She looks beautiful."

"Yes." He'd noticed. And looked away. Filed the vision away. For whatever night she'd agree to go out with him again.

Or that night, if she'd see him.

"It was nice of her friends to invite me to sit with them."

The invitation had come that morning. A phone call from Corrine, via Janie's cell.

"I thought so, too."

"I hope they're nice." She flattened the tip of his already flattened collar.

"They love Dawson and he loves them. And Corrine is Janie's best friend."

"You're right." She grinned and nodded. "They're nice."

A couple of techies were hovering in the hallway, speaking softly into headsets. It was almost time. They'd have received fifteen- and then five-minute warnings in the green room.

He hadn't wanted to be distracted by green-room tension. And wasn't going to give his remaining two opponents a chance to psych him out.

He'd played high school sports. He knew how to prepare for the big win.

Rule number one. No sex before a game. Which also meant no interaction with the woman you think you've fallen in love with.

Most particularly when you were about to take her life's dream away from her.

"Just remember to flow," Kelsey told him, straightening his tie. "Let Mom do her thing. Don't fight it."

He nodded. Translated. *Relax and cook.*

"Don't worry about the finish," she reminded him. Something he'd added to the list that week. One step at a time. He had fifty minutes before he had to serve. And doable tasks to accomplish for each minute.

Natasha's assistant was at the door of the green room. Call time.

"I love you, Daddy," Kelsey said, her eyes glistening with tears as she gave him one last look.

"I love you, too, squirt."

He hugged her. Tight. She hugged him back.

And he knew he had what it took to do this.

THE STAGE EMANATED scents of richly cooked food. The judges had all been served. Mike's Bourbon Pecan Chicken. Burke's Scallops over a Bed of Mushrooms. Janie's Italian Crescent Roll.

Gourmet. Gourmet. And her.

Today's show was different because they had a live audience. There was one set of kitchens, all facing the front, with cameras at different angles behind and beside them.

And for the final judging, instead of being in a line facing Natasha, they were sitting on high-backed pub stools facing the audience.

There would still be two runners-up. But they would remain seated. The second runner-up would be called first. And then the winner.

In a recap, the first runner-up would be officially named. Both of the runners-up had nice prize packages coming to them, as well. Nothing life-changing.

"But," Natasha said, smiling at her three finalists as she sat with them, legs crossed, the winners' cards facedown on her lap, "you each have gained incredible exposure here these past five weeks. With the professional judges who've been called in to taste your food. And from our television audience, as well."

Janie heard her. But the words didn't ease her tension. If she lost, she could still get an offer down the road. Dawson couldn't be raised on ifs. Or possibilities.

Her little guy might not have any idea what his mother was doing up on stage. Or what this day meant for his future. But he'd benefit, or suffer, just the same.

She'd barely looked at Burke. Hadn't been able to.

She had no business wanting him to have her back. He had his own backs to watch. She longed for him anyway.

And when they'd been directed to take their seats on stage, when she'd been told to take the middle seat—the woman between two men—she'd been glad. He was right there. Next to her. She could almost hear him breathe.

At least if she had a heart attack while sitting there waiting, she'd be close to medical assistance. There was no humor in the thought.

It was time for the second runner-up to be called. The for-sure loser. She gripped the edges of her seat, not caring how she looked on camera. Television truly didn't matter to her. Dawson did.

For Dawson. Please, for Dawson. The words chanted themselves in her mind. But she knew her chances of winning were minuscule. She'd taken a chance on being herself. Doing what she did best. Making food from the things that were normally in the house.

Not for professionals who were used to fine French dining.

"...is..." Natasha opened the envelope. "...Mike Wrenchfort."

Clapping from the audience drowned out whatever Mike might have said as he, per instruction, stayed in his seat and nodded toward Natasha. Burke leaned behind her, reaching a hand to Mike. Who leaned back to take it. Neither of them touched her.

She felt...protected. From being the next loser. From not having enough money to provide for her son. From the challenges life had handed her.

Just for that second, under hot lights, someone had her back.

BURKE WAS READY to run a four-minute mile. Lift twice his weight. Do a hundred push-ups. Swim laps. Anything but stay seated under hot lights with a smile on his face.

This was it. As soon as he'd found out the dishes he was up against, he'd known Mike was his competition. Had worried there for a bit that he could be edged out at the last minute.

He'd wanted to grab Kelsey and run. As far

and as fast as he could. To distract her from the pain long enough to figure out what to do next.

Instead there he sat. Soon to get what he'd most wanted. Because Kelsey needed it so badly.

But instead of the heady feeling of success, of having the heavy weight of guilt over Lil's death lightened somewhat, he felt...less than that.

Because when his name was called, when he got up to get his award, he'd be leaving the woman he loved sitting alone.

He couldn't do it. In those two or so minutes that Natasha spoke with Mike, talking about his plans, doing a pan of the audience to see his wife and sons, Burke made a decision. He wasn't going to get up when Natasha called his name. It wasn't like they were going to stop taping with a live audience right there.

He was going to stay seated. To take Janie's hand. To lean over to her and tell her the win was for both of them. And then, still seated, he'd answer whatever questions Natasha had to ask.

Janie was going to know, on national television, that she wasn't alone. That she didn't have to go it alone. That she could rely on someone to stick around. To help her provide the security she'd spent her entire life seeking. And trying to provide for herself.

"So, we're here once again…at the end of a great competition. It's time to announce this session's winner. The next name I call will not only win our cash prize…" Natasha named an impressive amount. Enough to make a mark in Burke's financial plan. "…but will also win a contract with a food manufacturer to have one of his or her recipes mass-produced and sold in national grocery-store chains."

That was the one. There were other prizes attached. Natasha continued to talk about them. But that mass-production thing…that was what Lil had always wanted. She'd actually submitted a recipe or two. Had written up a plan for her own line of frozen foods. Foods with taste and originality. She'd always said that busy people should not have to compromise on taste and quality just because they didn't have time to cook.

"This is it, guys." Natasha smiled at the three of them. "This session, all of the contestants were so…likable. It's been hard to see you go. And now this…my two locals… I wish you could both win…"

For a split second Burke wondered if that

were possible. Could there be a tie? Could the world really be that perfect?

"But I can't. Today's winner, and our next *Family Secrets* overall grand-prize winner, is..."

She pulled open her envelope. Burke took Janie's hand. Wanted to jump up and grab the card out of Natasha's hand. To stop her from delivering Janie any kind of a blow...

And thought of Kelsey...his innocent and struggling thirteen-year-old daughter, sitting just yards away, probably holding her breath.

He prayed, as Natasha pulled out the card, that Janie would understand that he'd had to do this. For Kelsey.

"Janie Young!"

Burke stared. He'd heard the announcement. But wasn't sure he wasn't just hearing what he wanted to hear. Natasha's lips were moving. So was her body as she stood and approached Janie.

He glanced over. Saw the shock on Janie's face. The tears streaming down it.

And for that split second, all he knew was complete joy.

Janie had finally won.

But that meant Kelsey had lost.

The truth hit him.

Hard.

CHAPTER TWENTY-EIGHT

JANIE COULDN'T REMEMBER a lot about the first few hours after her win. In the space of seconds her entire life had changed. She'd changed.

She was no longer the girl from the wrong side of the tracks. A part of that girl would always be with her.

But she'd proved something incredibly important to herself. That with an open heart, hard work and a refusal to quit, she had what it took to provide for herself. And for her son. No matter the obstacles.

She had what it took to compete with the best.

And that was what she had to give to Dawson. That was the part of her that was to be his legacy. He had some extra challenges to face ahead of him. But as long as he didn't quit, as long as he worked hard and kept his heart open, he would be okay. Whatever "okay" was for him.

For her, it was an ability to provide.

Who knew what it would be for her son?

But as she stood there on the stage, answering questions, accepting congratulations, smiling with flashes going off in her face, all she could think about was Dawson.

It wasn't until they invited him to join her on the stage that she realized her win meant that Burke had lost. That Kelsey had lost. She hadn't allowed herself to think of either of them while she'd cooked.

And had tried not to tune in to him while she'd been sitting next to him, preparing for her loss.

She'd expected him to win.

And he hadn't.

She looked around for him as the houselights came on and Corrine led Dawson up to the stage. Burke and Mike had both left the stage. She looked out to Joe, seeking Kelsey, and found only Joe.

Corrine held Dawson's hand while he climbed the stairs onto the stage. Opening her arms automatically, Janie caught her son when he flew across the stage toward her. He tripped. Fell. A collective gasp came from the audience. Dawson stood. Brushed his hands. Looked at her.

"Kay, Ma. Kay," he said and sped toward her once again.

She caught him in her arms. Against her heart.

And thanked fate for her blessings. Sending a

silent plea out for Kelsey. Wishing that it could have been different. That both kids could have won. But completely thankful that hers had.

HOURS HAD PASSED. The hoopla was done. There'd been the after-show taping, interviews. She'd been invited to a congratulatory dinner with the judges, but one look at Dawson's tired face and she'd declined the invitation.

Joe and Corrine could have taken him.

Janie didn't want to spend the evening— her greatest evening ever—without him.

Joe and Corrine had wanted to take her to dinner to celebrate. She'd wanted to go to their house, where Dawson could play...and go to bed...and she could just relax.

She'd tried Burke several times. To make sure Kelsey was okay. To tell them about her idea to open a catering business, with Lil's recipes, her name, and share the profits with them. He didn't pick up.

And though she left several messages, he didn't call back.

KELSEY WAS INCONSOLABLE. She was sobbing so badly he'd had to take her out of the studio. She'd begged him to take her home.

"I just want to go home, Daddy," she'd said. Over and over again. He'd contemplated taking her to urgent care, to get her something to help her calm down. In the end, he'd figured the fight that would ensue, trying to convince her to let medicine help her, would be worse for her than being hysterical.

For the next several hours she alternated between sitting silently, staring at nothing, and sobbing. She wanted to put on her favorite movie, *Mary Poppins*, and sit in the dark and watch it. He'd look over and see tears trickling slowly down her face.

He stayed by her side every second. Convinced her to eat some toast and peanut butter. To drink a glass of milk. But only because he'd used them as a bribe to sit in the dark and watch another one of her favorite movies, *Annie*.

Old classics that Lil had loved.

She fell asleep on the couch, sometime before eleven, her head on his shoulder. Fell asleep on *him*. The one who'd let her down again. Pulling a blanket over them, and sliding around until both of them were fully on the couch, he let her sleep. And stayed there until she awoke, sometime in the middle of the night, and said she was going to bed.

He walked upstairs with her. Waiting while she got herself ready for bed. And then, in spite of her closed door, went in and tucked her in.

"I'm sorry, Kels."

"Me, too," she said, lying on her back and looking up at him.

Sorry because he'd let her down?

"I love you."

"I love you, too, Daddy." With that, she turned on her side, snuggled up and closed her eyes.

Wanting to remain close, he stayed upstairs. In his room. With his door open.

Listening.

If she called out, he was going to hear.

HAVING TO GO on medication was not the only concern with severely depressed teenagers. Burke knew that, of course. He'd just never considered that those other aspects of depression were even close to entering his home.

He lay awake all night. Scared to death that his daughter might try something drastic.

And Sunday morning, when, listless and drawn, she dragged herself down to the couch to sit and stare at the television, he called her doctor.

Dr. Zimmers wanted to see Kelsey. As Burke had expected.

He took her in Sunday afternoon. The child

psychiatrist had an office at the local children's hospital and, when Burke called, offered to meet them there.

"I'm not suicidal, Dad," Kelsey said as they drove home late that afternoon.

Dr. Zimmers had just given him the same diagnosis. But had added a very key word. "Yet."

"I didn't say you were."

She lay with her head back against the seat, eyes closed. "And I'm not taking pills."

"I didn't say you were." In light of the things Kelsey had told Burke about her baby brother, the doctor had wanted a couple more sessions with the teenager before prescribing any kind of treatment.

"Can I ask one favor?" She opened her eyes as she rolled her head to the side to look at him.

"Of course." He'd give her the world if he could. She had to at least know that Dr. Zimmers seemed to think his love for his daughter would make a difference. That contrary to Burke's feelings of inadequacy, it was his love Kelsey was holding on to.

"Can you please call Janie and let her know that I won't be seeing Dawson anymore?"

What?

"You said that…"

Arms crossed over her chest, she faced forward, closing her eyes again. "He's going to have all the help and friends he needs now," she said. "His life is going to be different. He won't need me."

"Kels." He hadn't expected this. At all. To the contrary. He'd been counting the hours until Kelsey went to bed and he could call Janie. He needed to hear her voice. To know that he wasn't alone.

Crazy...but there it was.

He needed to share her happiness.

And to have her share his sorrow. His worry. His bone-deep fear where Kelsey was concerned.

He pulled into their garage and touched her arm when she bent forward to open her door.

"I don't understand," he said. "Dawson doesn't care about wins and the types of changes you're talking about. He won't even be aware of them. Of course he needs you..." If she thought she was somehow unworthy... that she wouldn't matter anymore...

Dr. Zimmers had said that Kelsey's biggest struggle seemed to stem from how she viewed herself...

A motherless child. A brother-less sister.

Kelsey looked at him, and her eyes seemed to be begging for something. He couldn't figure out what.

"I can't go back there. I can't be with either one of them. Ever. Again." She was gritting her teeth against tears.

"Why not?"

"Because she beat Mom. How would that look to Mom?"

"You thought Mom would be proud of you for befriending Dawson."

"Because his mom was going to lose. That made him a loser, too. But now I'd be disloyal—caring for the winner's son, when I didn't love my own mother's baby boy." Her voice rose to a squeak and she scrambled out of the car. Slammed the door behind her and ran inside.

Burke, not only the loser, but completely lost, just sat there in his fancy car.

Alone.

FOR AS MUCH as her life was completely changed, it was oddly completely the same for Janie on Sunday. While she had prize money coming, there was paperwork to fill out and then a check to be issued. Which meant that she still had to work so she could pay the week's bills. She had campaign calls to make. Laundry to do. Therapy to get through with Dawson. His tongue and throat muscles didn't care if she'd become a winner.

Her son needed to eat. To have his routine.

And Cor and Joe were attending an afternoon soiree at the home of one of Joe's more profitable clients. They'd be gone until evening.

She tried Burke again. Twice. Left one message. And then stopped.

He didn't want to speak with her.

Because she'd stolen Kelsey's chance to be happy.

She understood.

Understanding didn't help her get over him. Every time she thought about her win, her changed circumstances, the gleeful jump of her heart was quickly quashed with thoughts of Burke and Kelsey.

She'd known that it would come to this. That Burke was only in her life for a brief moment. She just hadn't realized how hard it was going to be to let the moment end.

How much it was going to hurt.

Late Sunday night, she started to worry. What if something had happened to them? What if they'd been in a car accident on the way home Saturday night?

No one would know to contact her. Why would anyone think it necessary to let her know?

First thing Monday morning, after dropping Dawson off at preschool, she called

Burke's office and asked to speak with him. Just to see if he was there.

He was with a patient.

Though it told her for certain he was purposely not contacting her, she was still glad to know that he was all right.

More than glad. She cried when she heard he was with a patient. Tears of relief.

And that evening, life was very different.

She picked Dawson up from preschool as usual. But instead of going home to feed him, she drove through a fast-food place for nuggets and fries. Dawson loved finger food. In the parking lot, she did tongue and swallowing exercises with him while he ate. She had two more flower deliveries to make and got them done while he continued to shove French fries into his mouth and watched the video she'd brought on the portable player Cor and Joe had bought him. Or her. She'd never been quite sure about that one.

She took him to the public library to change his Pull-Ups. Stopped off at the box store to pick up a couple of things they needed—on sale, with coupons.

And then, when she knew it was time for Kelsey to be out of dance and for the two of them to be home, she drove to Burke's house.

He lived in a gated community, but he'd

given her the access code the previous weekend. She used it shamelessly. Drove through the
quiet streets with acre lots and luxury homes
as though her old car fit right in.

Turned into his drive and panicked when
she saw lights on in the house.

Then reminded herself that there was no
point in her being there if he wasn't at home.

"Kee!"

Janie stopped the car halfway up the drive
and turned to look at her son. He could be
asking for ice cream. He often did after dinner. She gave it to him half the time.

But the sound was also what he uttered when
he was around Kelsey. Or wanted Kelsey.

Could he know, after only one visit, that
this was Kelsey's house?

Dare she hope?

Or, as Dillon often told her, was she just
kidding herself?

"Kee. Kee. Kee," Dawson said. When he
wanted to eat, or have ice cream with that
much vengeance, the word was accompanied
by the sign to eat. Or the sign for ice cream.
Janie glanced in her rearview mirror. Dawson
wasn't signing. He was looking at the house.

And trying to get out of his car seat.

Whether he was asking for Kelsey or not,
Janie believed he was. The belief gave her the

strength to continue up the drive. To get out of the car. Unstrap her son.

Dawson's hand in hers gave her the courage to head up the walk, in spite of the fact someone might be watching them.

In spite of the fact they were uninvited and were most certainly not wanted.

Because they were winners.

And it was possible, just that little bit possible, that they were needed.

CHAPTER TWENTY-NINE

BURKE WAS AT his desk when the bell rang. Kelsey had insisted that she was going to make dinner. On her own.

She was going to keep her mother alive.

And while he wasn't happy she was so lost in her personal nightmare, the fact that she was fighting to keep her mother's memory alive meant, according to Dr. Zimmers, that she was fighting to keep herself alive.

She had the will to live. To thrive.

She just had to find her way.

And until she did, he was all hers. What she needed mattered most.

Which was why, though he'd listened to all of Janie's messages—more times than was probably healthy—he was not returning her calls.

Kelsey had asked. He had to honor that request.

"Someone's at the door." Kelsey, in flannel pants and a T-shirt, stuck her head in his office. He went with her to see who was there.

In their gated community it could only

be a neighbor. Which, most probably, meant someone she went to school with. A would-be friend if Kelsey had been open to close friendships anymore. Most likely someone needing a homework assignment. Kelsey had her own phone. But only for emergencies. And calling Burke. She wasn't allowed to text with friends.

And wasn't all that great about checking her email.

He was right behind her when she pulled open the door. But had no idea which one of them was more surprised.

"Kee," Dawson said, standing there with his hand firmly clasped in his mother's. He tried to take a step forward. Janie clearly prohibited the action.

With one glance at him, telling him without words he better take care of the situation, Kelsey turned her back and walked away. He'd expected her to head to the kitchen. Instead he heard her steps on the stairs.

She was retreating.

The sound of a door closing told him she was shutting herself in her room.

"She asked me to call you," he blurted. Janie's eyes didn't give away any feelings, but he felt Kelsey's rejection as though he were her. "I told her I would, but then, tonight, when she asked if I had, I told her I hadn't done it yet..."

Like any of that made any difference to the woman standing on his doorstep, looking exactly like the person who'd been to his home once before.

And changed everything about it just by walking through that door.

"Kee," Dawson said in a tone that was more demand than question.

"Can we come in?"

She looked so good. It took a great deal of willpower to keep from hauling her into his arms.

There was so much he wanted to ask her. Filled with this insatiable need to know every detail of every minute since Natasha had called her name, he led her into his home office.

She took the very same seat on the couch she'd occupied when she was there before, settling Dawson beside her. Pulling a tablet out of her purse, she gave it to him. But didn't turn it on.

Dawson did. Punched, pushed, slid his finger across the screen. Mouth open, tongue out, he appeared to be engrossed.

"I'm sorry I didn't call." He needed her to know.

She nodded.

He glanced at the ceiling, toward his daughter's bedroom. "It's been rough."

Nodding again, Janie frowned. "I'm sorry."

"No. You have no reason to be sorry." The words were a precursor to letting her know that he and his daughter would not be seeing her and her son again.

He wanted to learn how she was. How things were changing. "I want to hear your plans."

He wanted to tell her how good she looked. To kiss her hello. And hello. And hello.

"Weird, because that's actually why I'm here," she told him. In jeans and a sweater, with little makeup and her hair in a ponytail, she didn't look as though she'd planned to do anything but go home after a long day of work. And caring for Dawson.

And she looked more beautiful than she had on stage on Saturday. Because this was Janie. A real woman, who didn't have the time or energy to put on airs. And yet who brightened the air around her just by being in it.

"I'm not exactly sure how to go about setting this in motion yet…but Joe knows. And Cor. They're working on getting the basics for me and then we'll be moving forward, but I want to take a good portion of the winning money and invest it in a catering business."

He kept his face steady, but inside he was

grinning. Laughing. Because something in life was working out as it should.

"I'm going to put most of the initial cash prize in a safe investment so Dawson and I will have it to fall back on. And draw from..."

Just as he'd have advised. But she had Joe. Who made his living in finance.

"But the advance I get for signing for the mass-produced recipe, I want to invest in the equipment I need to start out with small catering jobs."

She'd made a lot of plans in a short period of time. He was honestly happy for her. And sad that he'd missed out on sharing that planning with her.

"But the thing is, if I had a partner, I could actually get space and start this out in a way that could grow very quickly. Especially if I could have a diverse enough menu to cater to kids and church events, and to the more elite, higher-paying jobs, as well."

He sat next to Dawson. The boy leaned over and patted his cheek. He kissed Dawson's head. And then realizing what he'd done, he glanced at Janie, as though he'd taken a liberty not granted to him.

She had tears in her eyes.

And he took hope.

He was letting her down. He didn't have

her back. At all. Hadn't even returned her calls. Because he couldn't.

But there she was. Sitting in his home. Welcoming his interaction with her son in a way that seemed to say it mattered to her.

"So... I need an investor," she said. And he came back to real life.

"I'm assuming Joe has plans for that."

She shook her head. "Well...yes, he did. He and Cor wanted to be first in line. But I have another idea."

The look in her eye was doing unusual things to his heart rate.

"I want you to be the investor, Burke. I know it's presumptuous of me. I have no idea if you're property poor with this house here, or otherwise invested to the extent of your ability, but surely, if nothing else, you could borrow against this place..."

He had no idea, whatsoever, how to react. She was there to hit him up for money?

But Cor and Joe had already offered.

"I want Kelsey to name the business," she said. "Something after her mom. I actually was thinking Lil's Place, like on your apron, but I want the decision to be hers."

His heart did more odd things. As did his throat. He sat there. Staring at her.

"I know she's only thirteen, and too young

to be in business, but she has good ideas and I want her input."

He continued to stare.

"She coached you to the finals," Janie continued. "She obviously spent a lot of time in the kitchen with her mom. She's probably a natural. And… I want to use Lil's recipes. I've got the kid and church crowd. But I'm totally lost when it comes to the more sophisticated gatherings. I mean, I know I can prepare the dishes. And I could look up recipes. But… I want to use Lil's."

He was an orthopedic surgeon. With a mortgage and financial obligations he had to fulfill. He also loved his job. Recognized that it was his life's work.

He had some money. Investments. Not enough to open a business and hire someone to run it for him.

But if he had a partner…an award-winning chef who wanted him to be a silent partner… with his daughter as a very vocal partner…

He didn't know what to say. He was a giver. A doer.

He'd never learned how to be a taker.

BURKE WASN'T SAYING ANYTHING. He was just staring at her. He didn't like her idea.

Maybe she'd read too much into what he'd

said the day he'd talked about them eating on every mountaintop together.

Read way too much into a couple of casual kisses...

"Now's when it would be polite to say something."

He'd asked her out. She'd been unable to find words to reply. He'd introduced levity.

"I...don't...know what to say."

"The truth."

He looked at her. Looked at Dawson. Sat forward and, elbows on his knees, clasped his hands and bowed his head.

He could have been praying, but he didn't look like a man in prayer.

"The truth," he said. He released his hands and clasped them again. His eyes were open. He stared down.

"The truth is, this is all my fault. All of it. I find that, no matter how desperately I wish it, I can't go back and make it right. And I can't seem to take a step forward, either." He glanced at her and then down again. "I'm afraid to take another step. Afraid of hurting those I care about."

Those. Plural. Kelsey was only one.

She shook her head. Confused, and yet feeling as though she stood on a precipice and if she just dared glance at what was before her, she'd have all the understanding she needed.

"What's your fault?"

Burke stood. He turned. Faced her. And said, "I am responsible for the death of my wife."

She'd had no idea what he was going to say. Could have made a hundred guesses. And not gotten that one. Ever.

"I don't understand." Lil had died in childbirth. Surely… He was a doctor… There was no way he considered himself responsible for the death of his wife because he'd gotten her pregnant…

"Lil was many great things…"

He turned away. Walked to the window and, with the distance between them, turned back. "She was also a hypochondriac…"

He'd told her that his wife had feared his touch lest he find something wrong with her. She nodded.

"Her pregnancy…it was unplanned…"

He'd told her that, too. She nodded again.

"She was in her midthirties. Not too old to have a perfectly normal birth. Not by a long shot. But she was intensely paranoid. From the moment she knew she was pregnant, she insisted on having every test out there. She had me take her to the clinic and get my technician to do an ultrasound on her when she was only four weeks along. It never quit. She had her doctor run every test, do every scan. Look for anything. She was so afraid that something would go wrong…"

"She really wanted that baby," Janie said. Understanding completely. And yet feeling sorry for the other woman, too. That she hadn't been able to reel in the fears that beset a lot of women who hadn't known how badly they wanted the child they hadn't expected to conceive.

"It got to where she was calling me five and six times a day. It seemed like if she burped too loud she'd call, just to make sure it didn't indicate something I should be aware of."

Janie nodded. And started to get a bad feeling. A really bad feeling.

"One day, I was in with a high school kid…" He told her about a player who had twisted his ankle on the stairs on the way to his locker between classes. About the scout who was going to be at his last high school game that night. About waiting for the X-ray to find out if it would be safe to tape and wrap the ankle so the boy could play.

"Lil had called while I was on my way to look at the X-ray," he said. And she knew.

"I told my receptionist to tell her I'd call

her back. She'd already called my personal phone, which was in my office. I'd been in an examining room."

"And did you? Call her?"

Turning his back to her, he said, "The kid was going to be late for the game. I taped and wrapped the ankle. And then I called her." He hit the wall. And turned around. "I was too late. If I'd taken her call—" He shook his head. "My wife's death is my fault, Janie. She was in distress, labor, and I didn't take her call. If I had, she might have lived. Kelsey, the depression…it's all my fault… I can't move forward or think about…"

"It's not your fault, Daddy." The tiny voice was barely audible. But the girl standing in the doorway, with tears running down her face, was clear to see as she came fully into the room.

Dawson's tablet hit Janie in the head. He scrambled off the couch. "Kee. Me," he said. "Kee. Me." He reached Kelsey. Took her hand. "Kee. Me." His tone of voice had changed. Become more gleeful. "Kee. Me." He looked up at her, grinning like he'd just had ice cream.

"It's not your fault, Daddy. It's mine."

Janie wasn't sure if Kelsey knew she was clutching Dawson's hand. But Dawson didn't seem to mind.

"I had a fight with Mom. I told her that it was all her fault. That she'd messed up everything. I told her I didn't want the baby…"

"What are you talking about?"

As if in slow motion, Janie watched as Burke approached his daughter. "You were at school and then dance the day your mom died."

"I called her from dance. I'd been offered a solo part, but it would mean traveling to LA to learn the choreography during the summer. When the baby was due. Mom said we couldn't go. And… I was a selfish brat. I told her how I really felt about the baby. And that…I wished she'd never gotten pregnant…"

The girl took a step toward her father. Pulling Dawson along with her. She was crying.

"Kee. Me." Dawson grinned up at her.

"Then…the next thing I knew…you were picking me up from dance and Mom was gone and…"

Dawson tugged on Kelsey's hand. "Kee. Me."

She glanced down. As if only just realizing she was dragging the boy along. She looked at him for a long minute. Fell to her knees. Wrapped her arms around Dawson and started to sob.

"Kee. Me," Dawson said. With his free

hand, he patted Kelsey on the head. And, tongue sticking out of his mouth, grinned at Janie.

BURKE HAD NEVER had a more difficult, or a more important, day in his life. He was ill-equipped to handle the revelation his daughter had handed him. On so many levels.

Lil's death wasn't all his fault?

Or maybe it was.

But Kelsey thought it was hers?

Lil had fallen down the stairs, sending her into early labor the day she'd died. It must have been after Kelsey had called her. But before she'd called Burke?

He'd always assumed she'd called as soon as she'd fallen. Before she'd gone into labor and hemorrhaged. But what if she'd called him right after she'd talked to Kelsey? And had fallen down the stairs purely by accident? What if she'd been unable to call after she'd fallen because the damage had already been done? It made sense. Because if she'd been able to make calls, wouldn't she have called 911 after she couldn't reach him?

Dawson had hauled Kelsey upstairs.

He and his daughter had to talk. Nothing had been resolved.

But the little boy had been enough to stop Kelsey's sobs.

Janie had followed them.

He didn't blame her.

But he took the chance to get to his computer. To call up all of the phone bills he had on digital file in proper folders. He claimed home business calls on taxes. So files were kept.

He'd just never looked at them before.

The truth had been so obvious to him—and he'd felt such incredible self-loathing—he hadn't been able to make himself look.

Nor had he known there was any reason to.

But there it was. A call from the dance studio number to Lil's. And the very next minute, from Lil's number to his cell. And then to his cell again. And a few minutes later, to his office.

It was possible that in those few minutes between calls she'd fallen down the stairs. Possible that she'd been nearly comatose on the floor—as he'd always assumed—and failed to tell the nurse how urgent the phone call was.

It was also possible, and more plausible, that she'd simply, in her pregnant state, tripped, lost her balance and fallen.

After she'd called him.

Maybe she'd tripped because she was upset. Maybe she was mother enough, mature enough, to know that her daughter had spoken out of fear of being replaced, of having her entire life changed, of being passed over for a new baby who would take all of their parents' love.

"Since it's time for confession, I've realized something over the past couple of days." Janie was back. Standing in front of his desk.

Looking glorious. Beautiful. Perfect. And troubled.

"What's that?" he asked her. He wanted her to marry him. As soon as possible. To have her and Dawson move into his and Kelsey's home and make it right. Fill it with love. With home.

"Dillon was right."

He stood. "No, Janie," he said. Prepared to do battle with the demons in her mind, understanding just how devious they could be.

She was nodding. And put a hand on his chest, holding him off as he attempted to draw her into his arms.

"He claimed that the reason that I let everyone take advantage of me is because I don't love myself enough."

Recognizing a tone of voice that warned him to listen, Burke stood still in front of her. "I thought he was wrong. That it was because I did love myself that I never gave up.

But he was right. I never thought I was good enough because I wasn't lucky enough to be dealt a fair hand. My mom's addiction. My father leaving. My grandmother dying. That all happened to me because I was somehow second-rate."

He needed to hold her. To reassure her. And forced himself to stand there, not touching her at all. Forced himself to let her do for herself.

"When I found out, so soon after I knew I was pregnant, that my baby had Down syndrome, that was just more of me being second-rate. I didn't deserve a child who didn't have special needs. I knew, rationally, that it wasn't my fault. But emotionally, I took on accountability. Like I'd done something wrong. I'd caused it…"

He had so much to say. And said none of it.

"And now?" he asked.

"Winning *Family Secrets*…it showed me… I have as much chance as anyone. For the good or the bad."

"Eee. Eee."

Dawson was back. Janie turned.

"Eee. Eee." He was putting pinched fingers to his mouth.

"Hasn't he already had dinner?" Kelsey asked, coming in behind him. "You always feed him at the same time and it's way past that now."

"He ate," Janie said. "He wants ice cream."

With her brow raised, Kelsey asked, "Can I give him some?"

"Of course. One scoop only, though. He won't stop, no matter how much he has."

With her head bowed, Kelsey turned to go. And he couldn't let her.

"Kels?"

She turned back.

"Eee." Dawson pulled on Kelsey's hand.

"Janie wants us to go into business with her. She wants to open a catering business. She'll run it. But wants me to put up some of the money for a share of the profits."

Kelsey stared. Didn't say a word.

"She wants you to name the place. After your mother. And she wants to use your mother's recipes as well as her own."

Maybe he wasn't being fair to either of them. He didn't know. He wasn't analyzing. He was just living.

"I want your input on other things, too," Janie said. "Whenever you want to give it."

"Eee." Dawson tugged. "Eee." He put his fingers to his lips.

Kelsey nodded. And then looked at Burke. "It's kind of like Dawson, isn't it?"

He was totally lost. Again. Wanting so badly to get her. For her to know he did. To trust that he could.

"It's not right, how he was born. That he has to work so hard to do things we all just do. But it's what he's given. And look at him. He doesn't care. He wants ice cream."

Burke felt the emotion welling within him. Still didn't have a full connection.

"And that's how it is with all of us," Janie said, stepping up to Burke. Taking his hand. "We all have things happen. Your mom, she fell down the stairs. You didn't push her. She fell. Your dad didn't do it, either. She just fell. It's horrible. Tragic. You were being a normal kid. He was doing his job. Both doing your best. And me, too. It's not my fault that I had a child with Down syndrome. It just happened."

"I think the Dawson part is your blessing," Kelsey said. "But then, that's just me." Turning Dawson around, she led him out of the room.

"I'm not sure, but I think my daughter just gave us her seal of approval."

"I hope she's getting close to giving it to herself."

"I have a feeling you could help her with that," Burke said.

They had a lot to work out. Things to take slowly.

And there were some things that weren't going to wait.

"I'll do whatever I can," Janie told him, her chin tilted up as she looked him in the eye.

"For me, too?" he asked. "Kelsey and I, we come as a pair."

"Just like Dawson and me."

"I'm fully aware of that."

"And?"

"I'd walk through fire for either one of you."

"Does that mean it's not too late for me to accept your mountaintop invitation?"

He couldn't speak. But he could nod.

And he could kiss.

So he did.

* * * * *

LARGER-PRINT BOOKS!

GET 2 FREE LARGER-PRINT NOVELS PLUS 2 FREE MYSTERY GIFTS

Love Inspired®

Larger-print novels are now available...

WESTERN WP PROMISES

YES! Please send me **The Western Promises Collection** in Larger Print. This collection begins with 3 FREE books and 2 FREE gifts (gifts valued at approx. $14.00 retail) in the first shipment, along with the other first 4 books from the collection! If I do not cancel, I will receive 8 monthly shipments until I have the entire 51-book Western Promises collection. I will receive 2 or 3 FREE books in each shipment and I will pay just $4.99 US/ $5.89 CDN for each of the other four books in each shipment, plus $2.99 for shipping and handling per shipment. *If I decide to keep the entire collection, I'll have paid for only 32 books, because 19 books are FREE! I understand that accepting the 3 free books and gifts places me under no obligation to buy anything. I can always return a shipment and cancel at any time. My free books and gifts are mine to keep no matter what I decide.

272 HCN 3070 472 HCN 3070

Name	(PLEASE PRINT)	
Address		Apt. #
City	State/Prov.	Zip/Postal Code

Signature (if under 18, a parent or guardian must sign)

Mail to the **Reader Service**:
IN U.S.A.: P.O. Box 1867, Buffalo, NY 14240-1867
IN CANADA: P.O. Box 609, Fort Erie, Ontario L2A 5X3

LARGER-PRINT BOOKS!
GET 2 FREE LARGER-PRINT NOVELS PLUS
2 FREE GIFTS!

✦HARLEQUIN®
super romance®

More Story...More Romance

YES! Please send me 2 FREE LARGER-PRINT Harlequin® Superromance® novels and my 2 FREE gifts (gifts are worth about $10). After receiving them, if I don't wish to receive any more books, I can return the shipping statement marked "cancel." If I don't cancel, I will receive 4 brand-new novels every month and be billed just $5.94 per book in the U.S. or $6.24 per book in Canada. That's a savings of at least 12% off the cover price! It's quite a bargain! Shipping and handling is just 50¢ per book in the U.S. or 75¢ per book in Canada.* I understand that accepting the 2 free books and gifts places me under no obligation to buy anything. I can always return a shipment and cancel at any time. Even if I never buy another book, the two free books and gifts are mine to keep forever.

132/332 HDN GHVC

Name	(PLEASE PRINT)

Address	Apt. #

City	State/Prov.	Zip/Postal Code

Signature (if under 18, a parent or guardian must sign)

Mail to the **Reader Service:**
IN U.S.A.: P.O. Box 1867, Buffalo, NY 14240-1867
IN CANADA: P.O. Box 609, Fort Erie, Ontario L2A 5X3

Want to try two free books from another line?
Call 1-800-873-8635 today or visit www.ReaderService.com.

* Terms and prices subject to change without notice. Prices do not include applicable taxes. Sales tax applicable in N.Y. Canadian residents will be charged applicable taxes. Offer not valid in Quebec. This offer is limited to one order per household. Not valid for current subscribers to Harlequin Superromance Larger-Print books. All orders subject to credit approval. Credit or debit balances in a customer's account(s) may be offset by any other outstanding balance owed by or to the customer. Please allow 4 to 6 weeks for delivery. Offer available while quantities last.

Your Privacy—The Reader Service is committed to protecting your privacy. Our Privacy Policy is available online at www.ReaderService.com or upon request from the Reader Service.

We make a portion of our mailing list available to reputable third parties that offer products we believe may interest you. If you prefer that we not exchange your name with third parties, or if you wish to clarify or modify your communication preferences, please visit us at www.ReaderService.com/consumerchoice or write to us at Reader Service Preference Service, P.O. Box 9062, Buffalo, NY 14240-9062. Include your complete name and address.

HSRLP15

READERSERVICE.COM

Manage your account online!

- Review your order history
- Manage your payments
- Update your address

> *We've designed the*
> *Reader Service website*
> *just for you.*

Enjoy all the features!

- Discover new series available to you, and read excerpts from any series.
- Respond to mailings and special monthly offers.
- Connect with favorite authors at the blog.
- Browse the Bonus Bucks catalog and online-only exculsives.
- Share your feedback.

Visit us at:

ReaderService.com

RS15